Anonymous

The University Hymn Book

For Use in the Chapel of Harvard University

Anonymous

The University Hymn Book
For Use in the Chapel of Harvard University

ISBN/EAN: 9783744774246

Printed in Europe, USA, Canada, Australia, Japan

Cover: Foto ©Andreas Hilbeck / pixelio.de

More available books at **www.hansebooks.com**

THE

UNIVERSITY HYMN BOOK

FOR USE IN THE

CHAPEL OF HARVARD UNIVERSITY

CAMBRIDGE
Published by the University
1896

Second Edition.

University Press:
JOHN WILSON AND SON, CAMBRIDGE, U. S. A.

PREFACE.

THIS hymn-book is designed for the use of young men in a University under an undenominational religious system. Ministers of different Christian communions should, therefore, find in it hymns which all can use with satisfaction, and young men should find in it masculine piety and honest aspiration. Hymns of a character foreign to the natural sentiments of young men have been excluded. The book, being intended for daily use, contains an unusually large proportion of hymns for morning and evening worship.

In 1886 each of the preachers to the University for that year, —

> Rev. EDWARD EVERETT HALE, D.D.;
> Rev. PHILLIPS BROOKS, D.D.;
> Rev. ALEXANDER McKENZIE, D.D.;
> Rev. GEORGE A. GORDON, D.D., —

indicated the fifty hymns which in his judgment were most desirable for this purpose; and the collation of this material is the foundation of the book. Since that time the collection has been reviewed, and further suggestions have been made by, —

> Rev. LYMAN ABBOTT, D.D.;
> Rev. BROOKE HERFORD, D.D., —

preachers to the University in 1891; but the final responsibility for the selection of hymns rests with the Plummer Professor, and for the selection of tunes with the Organist and Choir-master of the University.

Preface.

Great pains have been taken to give each hymn in its original reading; so that the University may have no part in perpetuating the garbled forms which occur in many collections. In some instances stanzas have been omitted from necessity, and in others stanzas have been transposed for convenience; but in all instances the author's language has been scrupulously sought for and retained. A few hymns, which seem to be historically and inevitably composite, are so noted, and their sources are explained in the index of authors. In the musical settings similar pains have been taken to secure accurate and authorized readings, as appears in the index of composers.

The verification of authorities has been made by Rev. Charles F. Russell, with assistance at the British Museum and elsewhere in England. Mr. Russell has also prepared the biographical indexes.

HARVARD UNIVERSITY,
September, 1895.

TABLE OF SUBJECTS.

Table of Subjects.

INDEX OF FIRST LINES.

Index of First Lines.

Index of First Lines.

Index of First Lines.

Index of First Lines.

Index of First Lines.

Index of First Lines.

Index of First Lines.

Index of First Lines.

Index of First Lines.

INDEX OF TUNES.

Index of Tunes.

Index of Tunes.

Index of Tunes.

Index of Tunes.

Index of Tunes.

Index of Tunes.

TUNE.	NO. OF HYMN.	METRE.	COMPOSER OR SOURCE.
TALLIS'S CANON	264	L. M.	Thomas Tallis.
TALLIS'S ORDINAL	58, 166	C. M.	Thomas Tallis.
TEMPLE	258	8.4.8.4.8.8.8.4	Edward John Hopkins.
TRURO	208	L. M.	Charles Burney.
TRUST	141	8.7.8.7	Felix Mendelssohn-Bartholdy.
TWILIGHT	246	11.11.11.5	Joseph Barnby.
UNIVERSITY COLLEGE	73, 237	7.7.7.7	Henry John Gauntlett.
VENI EMMANUEL	92	8.8.8.8.8.9	French Missal.
VENTNOR	189, 235	11.10.11.10	Joseph Barnby.
VERITAS	152	10.10.10.10	Joseph Barnby.
VIENNA	170	7.7.7.7	Justin Heinrich Knecht.
VULPIUS	144, 202	C. M.	Melchior Vulpius.
WALTHAM	132	6.6.6.6.6.6	William Henry Monk.
WARD	69	L. M.	Lowell Mason.
WAREHAM	15, 42, 220	L. M.	William Knapp.
WEBB	214	7.6.7.6.7.6.7.6	George James Webb.
WEBER	113, 254	7.7.7.7	Carl Maria von Weber.
WESSEX	150	8.6.8.6.8.8	Edward John Hopkins.
WILTSHIRE	180	C. M.	George Thomas Smart.
WINCHESTER NEW	5, 234	L. M.	Hamburger Musikalisches Handbuch.
WINCHESTER OLD	20, 129	C. M.	Thomas Este's Psalter.
WORGAN	118	7.4.7.4.7.4.7.4	Lyra Davidica.

METRICAL INDEX.

Metrical Index.

Metrical Index.

Metrical Index.

HYMN I.

OLD HUNDREDTH. L. M.

LOUIS BOURGEOIS.
GENEVAN PSALTER, 1551.

A - MEN.

1.

BEFORE Jehovah's awful throne
  Ye nations bow with sacred joy ;
Know that the Lord is God alone,
  He can create, and he destroy.

2.

His sovereign power, without our aid,
  Made us of clay, and formed us men ;
And when like wandering sheep we strayed,
  He brought us to his fold again.

3.

We are his people, we his care,
  Our souls and all our mortal frame :
What lasting honors shall we rear,
  Almighty Maker, to thy name?

4.

We 'll crowd thy gates with thankful songs,
  High as the heavens our voices raise ;
And earth, with her ten thousand tongues,
  Shall fill thy courts with sounding praise.

5.

Wide as the world is thy command,
  Vast as eternity thy love,
Firm as a rock thy truth must stand
  When rolling years shall cease to move.

ISAAC WATTS, 1674-1748.
JOHN WESLEY, 1703-1791.

HYMN 2.

ST. GREGORY. 6. 6. 6. 6. 4. 4. 4. 4.   JOSEPH BARNBY, 1838-1896.

A · MEN.

2.

1.

YE holy angels bright,
  Which stand before God's throne
And dwell in glorious light,
  Praise ye the Lord, each one !
    You there so nigh
    Are much more meet
    Than we, the feet,
    For things so high.

2.

Let not his praises grow
  On prosperous heights alone,
But in the vales below
  Let his great love be known.
    Let no distress
    Curb and control
    My wingèd soul
    And praise suppress.

3.

Away distrustful care !
  I have thy promise, Lord,
To banish all despair,
  I have thy oath and word.
    And therefore I
    Shall see thy face,
    And there thy grace
    Shall magnify.

4.

With thy triumphant flock
  Then I shall numbered be ;
Built on th' eternal rock,
  His glory we shall see.
    The heavens so high
    With praise shall ring,
    And all shall sing
    In harmony.   RICHARD BAXTER, 1615-1691.

Hymn 3.

SAINTS OF GOD. 8.8.8.8.8.8.   ARTHUR SEYMOUR SULLIVAN, 1842— .

A - MEN.

1.

LO, God is here! Let us adore,
    And own how dreadful is this place;
Let all within us feel his power,
And silent bow before his face.
Who know his power, his grace who prove,
Serve him with awe, with reverence love.

2.

Lo, God is here! Him day and night
Th' united choirs of angels sing;
To him enthroned above all height
Heaven's hosts their noblest praises bring.
Disdain not, Lord, our meaner song,
Who praise thee with a stammering tongue.

3.

Being of beings, may our praise
Thy courts with grateful fragrance fill;
Still may we stand before thy face,
Still hear and do thy sovereign will;
To thee may all our thoughts arise,
Ceaseless accepted sacrifice.

GERHARD TERSTEEGEN, 1697-1769.
Tr. JOHN WESLEY, 1703-1791.

HYMN 4.

ST. OSWALD. 8. 7. 8. 7.   JOHN BACCHUS DYKES, 1823—1876.

A - MEN.

1.

ROUND the Lord in glory seated,
 Cherubim and seraphim
Filled his temple, and repeated
 Each to each the alternate hymn : —

2.

'Lord, thy glory fills the heaven,
 Earth is with its fulness stored ;
Unto thee be glory given,
 Holy, holy, holy Lord ! '

3.

Heaven is still with glory ringing,
 Earth takes up the angels' cry, —
'Holy, holy, holy,' singing,
 'Lord of hosts, the Lord most high.'

4.

With his seraph train before him,
 With his holy Church below,
Thus conspire we to adore him,
 Bid we thus our anthem flow : —

5.

'Lord, thy glory fills the heaven,
 Earth is with its fulness stored ;
Unto thee be glory given,
 Holy, holy, holy Lord ! '

RICHARD MANT, 1776-1848.

HYMN 5.

WINCHESTER NEW. L. M.   HAMBURGER MUSIKALISCHES HANDBUCH, 1690.

A - MEN.

1.

O LIFE that maketh all things new,—
 The blooming earth, the thoughts
  of men, —
Our pilgrim feet, wet with thy dew,
 In gladness hither turn again.

2.

From hand to hand the greeting flows,
 From eye to eye the signals run,
From heart to heart the bright hope glows.
 The seekers of the Light are one :

3.

One in the freedom of the truth,
 One in the joy of paths untrod,
One in the soul's perennial youth,
 One in the larger thought of God,

4.

The freer step, the fuller breath,
 The wide horizon's grander view,
The sense of life that knows no death,—
 The Life that maketh all things new.

SAMUEL LONGFELLOW, 1819-1892.

HYMN 6.

BELMONT. C. M.

A - MEN.

1.

WHEN all thy mercies, O my God,
  My rising soul surveys,
Transported with the view, I'm lost
  In wonder, love, and praise.

2.

Unnumbered comforts to my soul
  Thy tender care bestowed,
Before my infant heart conceived
  From whom those comforts flowed.

3.

When worn with sickness, oft hast thou
  With health renewed my face,
And, when in sins and sorrows sunk,
  Revived my soul with grace.

4.

Ten thousand, thousand precious gifts
  My daily thanks employ,
Nor is the least a cheerful heart
  That tastes those gifts with joy.

JOSEPH ADDISON, 1672-1719

HYMN 7.

HANOVER. 10. 10. 11. 11.   WILLIAM CROFT, 1678—1727.

A . MEN.

7.

1.

O WORSHIP the King all glorious above!
O gratefully sing his power and his love, —
Our Shield and Defender, the Ancient of days,
Pavilioned in splendor, and girded with praise.

2.

O tell of his might, O sing of his grace,
Whose robe is the light, whose canopy space;
His chariots of wrath the deep thunder-clouds form,
And dark is his path on the wings of the storm.

3.

Thy bountiful care what tongue can recite?
It breathes in the air, it shines in the light,
It streams from the hills, it descends to the plain,
And sweetly distils in the dew and the rain.

4.

Frail children of dust, and feeble as frail,
In thee do we trust, nor find thee to fail.
Thy mercies how tender, how firm to the end!
Our Maker, Defender, Redeemer, and Friend.

ROBERT GRANT, 1785-1838.

Hymn 8.

SWABIA. S. M.   JOHANN CRÜGER, 1598 — 1662.

A - MEN.

1.

O EVERLASTING Light,
   Giver of dawn and day,
Dispeller of the ancient night
   In which creation lay,

2.

O everlasting Health,
   From which all healing springs,
My bliss, my treasure, and my wealth,—
   To thee my spirit clings.

3.

O everlasting Strength,
   Uphold me in the way,
Bring me, in spite of foes, at length
   To joy and light and day.

4.

O everlasting Love,
   Well-spring of grace and peace,
Pour down thy fulness from above,
   Bid doubt and trouble cease.

HORATIUS BONAR, 1808-1889.

HYMN 9.

ST. MICHAEL. S. M.

LOUIS BOURGEOIS.
GENEVAN PSALTER, 1543.

A · MEN.

1.

STAND up and bless the Lord,
Ye people of his choice,
Stand up and bless the Lord your God
With heart, and soul, and voice.

2.

Though high above all praise,
Above all blessing high,
Who would not fear his holy name,
And laud and magnify?

3.

O for the living flame
From his own altar brought,
To touch our lips, our minds inspire,
And wing to heaven our thought !

4.

Stand up and bless the Lord,
The Lord your God adore,
Stand up and bless his glorious name
Henceforth for evermore.

JAMES MONTGOMERY, 1771-1854

Hymn 10.

PASTOR BONUS. 8. 7 8. 7.　　　　CHARLES STEGGALL, 1826—

A - MEN.

1.

GOD, my King, thy might confessing,
　Ever will I bless thy name;
Day by day thy throne addressing,
　Still will I thy praise proclaim.

2.

Honor great our God befitteth;
　Who his majesty can reach?
Age to age his works transmitteth,
　Age to age his power shall teach.

3.

They shall talk of all thy glory,
　On thy might and greatness dwell,
Speak of thy dread acts the story,
　And thy deeds of wonder tell.

4.

Nor shall fail from memory's treasure
　Works by love and mercy wrought,
Works of love surpassing measure,
　Works of mercy passing thought.

5.

Full of kindness and compassion,
　Slow to anger, vast in love,
God is good to all creation;
　All his works his goodness prove.

6.

All thy works, O Lord, shall bless thee,
　Thee shall all thy saints adore,
King supreme shall they confess thee,
　And proclaim thy sovereign power.

RICHARD MANT, 1776-1848.

HYMN II.

OLD HUNDREDTH. L. M.

LOUIS BOURGEOIS.
GENEVAN PSALTER, 1551.

A - MEN.

1.

ALL people that on earth do dwell,
 Sing to the Lord with cheerful voice,
Him serve with fear, his praise forth tell,
 Come ye before him and rejoice.

2.

The Lord ye know is God indeed ;
 Without our aid he did us make ;
We are his folk, he doth us feed,
 And for his sheep he doth us take.

3.

O enter then his gates with praise,
 Approach with joy his courts unto ;
Praise, laud, and bless his name always,
 For it is seemly so to do.

4.

For why, the Lord our God is good,
 His mercy is forever sure ;
His truth at all times firmly stood,
 And shall from age to age endure.

WILLIAM KETHE, *circa* 1562.

HYMN 12.

MELITA. 8. 8. 8. 8. 8. 8.

JOHN BACCHUS DYKES, 1823—1876.

A - MEN.

12.

1.

CREATOR Spirit, by whose aid
The world's foundations first were laid,
Come, visit every pious mind ;
Come, pour thy joys on human kind ;
From sin and sorrow set us free,
And make thy temples worthy thee.

2.

O source of uncreated light,
The Father's promised Paraclete,
Thrice holy fount, thrice holy fire,
Our hearts with heavenly love inspire ;
Come, and thy sacred unction bring
To sanctify us while we sing.

3.

Plenteous of grace, descend from high,
Rich in thy sevenfold energy ;
Thou strength of his almighty hand,
Whose power does heaven and earth command,
Proceeding Spirit, our defence,
Who dost the gift of tongues dispense,

4.

Refine and purge our earthy parts,
But O, inflame and fire our hearts,
Our frailties help, our vice control ;
Submit the senses to the soul,
And, when rebellious they are grown,
Then lay thy hand, and hold them down.

5.

Chase from our minds the infernal foe,
And peace, the fruit of love, bestow ;
And, lest our feet should step astray,
Protect and guide us in the way ;
Make us eternal truths receive
And practise all that we believe.
Tr. JOHN DRYDEN, 1631-1700.

HYMN 13.

DECIUS. 8. 7. 8. 7. 8. 8. 7.

NICOLAUS DECIUS, — 1541.

A - MEN.

13.

TO God on high be thanks and praise,
  Who deigns our bonds to sever;
His cares our drooping souls upraise,
  And harm shall reach us never.
On him we rest, with faith assured,
Of all that live the mighty Lord,
  Forever and forever.

Tr. WILLIAM BALL, 1784–1869

HYMN 14.

PRAISE, MY SOUL. 8. 7. 8. 7. 8. 7.

1ST STANZA. UNISON.

JOHN GOSS, 1800 — 1880.

Praise, my soul, the King of heav - en; To his feet thy tri - bute bring;

Ransomed, healed, re - stored, for - giv - en, Who like me his praise should sing?

Praise him! Praise him! Praise him! Praise him! Praise the ev - er - last - ing King!

2D Stanza. Harmony.

Praise him for his grace and fa - vor To our

fa - thers in dis - tress; Praise him, still the same for -

ev - er, Slow to chide, and swift to bless. Praise him!

Praise him! Praise him! Praise him! Glo - rious in his faith - ful - ness!

3D STANZA. UNISON.

Fa-ther - like he tends and spares us; Well our fee - ble frame he knows;

In his hands he gent - ly bears us, Res - cues us from all our foes.

Praise him! Praise him! Praise him! Praise him! Wide-ly as his mer - cy flows!

5TH STANZA. UNISON.

An-gels, help us to a - dore him! Ye be - hold him face to face;

Sun and moon, bow down be - fore him! Dwell - ers all in time and space,

Praise him! Praise him! Praise him! Praise him! Praise with us the God of grace! A - MEN.

HENRY FRANCIS LYTE, 1793 - 1847.

HYMN 15.

WAREHAM. L. M.　　　　　　　　　　　　WILLIAM KNAPP, 1698 — 1768.

1.

O GOD, whose presence glows in all,
　　Within, around us, and above,
Thy word we bless, thy name we call,
　　Whose word is truth, whose name is love.

2.

That truth be with the heart believed
　　Of all who seek this sacred place,
With power proclaimed, in peace received,
　　Our spirit's light, thy Spirit's grace.

3.

That love its holy influence pour,
　　To keep us meek and make us free,
And throw its binding blessing more
　　Round each with all, and all with thee.

4.

Send down its angel to our side,
　　Send in its calm upon the breast ;
For we would know no other guide,
　　And we can need no other rest.

NATHANIEL LANGDON FROTHINGHAM, 1793-1870.

Hymn 16.

EVER FAITHFUL, EVER SURE. 7. 7. 7. 7.

ARTHUR SEYMOUR SULLIVAN, 1842—

16.

1.

L ET us, with a gladsome mind,
　　Praise the Lord, for he is kind;
For his mercies aye endure,
Ever faithful, ever sure.

2.

Let us blaze his name abroad,
For of gods he is the God;
For his mercies aye endure,
Ever faithful, ever sure.

3.

His chosen people he did bless,
In the wasteful wilderness;
For his mercies aye endure,
Ever faithful, ever sure.

4.

Let us, therefore, warble forth
His mighty majesty and worth;
For his mercies aye endure,
Ever faithful, ever sure.

5.

Let us, with a gladsome mind,
Praise the Lord, for he is kind;
For his mercies aye endure,
Ever faithful, ever sure.

JOHN MILTON, 1608-1674.

HYMN 17.

FRANCONIA. S. M.   JOHANN SAMUEL MÜLLER'S CHORALBUCH, 1754.

A · MEN.

1.

G OD of the earnest heart,
  The trust assured and still,
Thou who our strength forever art,
  We come to do thy will.

2.

Upon that painful road
  By saints serenely trod,
Whereon their hallowing influence flowed,
  Would we go forth, O God,

3.

To draw thy blessing down,
  And bring the wronged redress,
And give this glorious world its crown,
  The spirit's godlikeness.

4.

No dreams from toil to charm,
  No trembling on the tongue,
Lord, in thy rest may we be calm,
  Through thy completeness strong.

SAMUEL JOHNSON, 1822–1882.

HYMN 18.

HUMILITY. L. M.   SAMUEL PARKMAN TUCKERMAN, 1819 — 1890.

A · MEN.

1.

Mysterious Presence, source of all, —
  The world without, the soul within, —
Fountain of life, O hear our call,
  And pour thy living waters in.

2.

Thou breathest in the rushing wind,
  Thy spirit stirs in leaf and flower ;
Nor wilt thou from the willing mind
  Withhold thy light, and love, and power.

3.

Thy hand unseen to accents clear
  Awoke the psalmist's trembling lyre,
And touched the lips of holy seer
  With flame from thine own altar fire.

4.

That touch divine still, Lord, impart,
  Still give the prophet's burning word ;
And, vocal in each waiting heart,
  Let living psalms of praise be heard.

SETH CURTIS BEACH, 1837-   .

Hymn 19.

SAMSON. L. M.   GEORG FRIEDRICH HÄNDEL, 1685—1759.

A-MEN.

1.

THOU Lord of hosts, whose guiding hand
  Has brought us here before thy face,
Our spirits wait for thy command,
  Our silent hearts implore thy peace.

2.

Those spirits lay their noblest powers
  As offerings on thy holy shrine ;
Thine was the strength that nourished ours,
  The soldiers of the cross are thine.

3.

Send us where'er thou wilt, O Lord,
  Through rugged toil and wearying fight ;
Thy conquering love shall be our sword,
  And faith in thee our truest might.

4.

Send down thy constant aid, we pray ;
  Be thy pure angels with us still ;
Thy truth, be that our firmest stay,
  Our only rest to do thy will.

OCTAVIUS BROOKS FROTHINGHAM, 1822–1895.

HYMN 20.

CHRISTOPHER TYE, 1508 — 1572.
THOMAS ESTE'S PSALTER, 1592.

WINCHESTER OLD. C. M.

A - MEN.

1.

OUR God, our God, thou shinest here,
 Thine own this latter day ;
To us thy radiant steps appear,
 Here goes thy glorious way.

2.

We shine not only with the light
 Thou sheddest down of yore ;
On us thou streamest strong and bright,
 Thy comings are not o'er.

3.

The fathers had not all of thee,
 New births are in thy grace ;
All open to our souls shall be
 Thy glory's hiding-place.

4.

On us thy spirit hast thou poured,
 To us thy word has come ;
We feel, we thank thy quickening, Lord,
 Thou shalt not find us dumb.

THOMAS HORNBLOWER GILL, 1819 –

HYMN 21.

PARKER. 10. 10. 10. 10.   HORATIO WILLIAM PARKER, 1863—

A - MEN.

1.

O THOU whose power o'er moving worlds presides,
    Whose voice created, and whose wisdom guides,
On darkling man in pure effulgence shine,
And cheer the clouded mind with light divine.

2.

'T is thine alone to calm the pious breast
With silent confidence and holy rest:
From thee, great God, we spring, to thee we tend, —
Path, Motive, Guide, Original, and End.

BOETHIUS, *circa* 475-525.
Tr. SAMUEL JOHNSON, 1709-1784.

HYMN 22.

MELCOMBE. L. M.   SAMUEL WEBBE, 1740—1816

A - MEN.

1.

O SPIRIT of the living God !
   In all thy plenitude of grace,
Where'er the foot of man hath trod,
   Descend on our apostate race.

2.

Be darkness at thy coming light,
   Confusion, order in thy path ;
Souls without strength inspire with might ;
   Bid mercy triumph over wrath.

3.

O Spirit of the Lord ! prepare
   All the round earth her God to meet ;
Breathe thou abroad like morning air
   Till hearts of stone begin to beat.

4.

Baptize the nations ; far and nigh
   The triumphs of the cross record ;
The name of Jesus glorify
   Till every kindred calls him Lord.

JAMES MONTGOMERY, 1771-1854

HYMN 23.

ST. ANDREW. S. M.

JOSEPH BARNBY, 1838—1896.

A-MEN.

1.

HOW gentle God's commands !
　　How kind his precepts are !
Come, cast your burdens on the Lord,
　　And trust his constant care.

2.

While Providence supports
　　Let saints securely dwell ;
That hand which bears all nature up
　　Shall guide his children well.

3.

Why should this anxious load
　　Press down your weary mind?
Haste to your heavenly Father's throne,
　　And sweet refreshment find.

4.

His goodness stands approved
　　Down to the present day ;
I 'll drop my burden at his feet,
　　And bear a song away.

PHILIP DODDRIDGE, 1702-1751

HYMN 24.

LOVE DIVINE. 8.7.8.7.   JOHN STAINER, 1840—

A - MEN.

1.

GOD is love; his mercy brightens
  All the path in which we rove;
Bliss he wakes, and woe he lightens:
  God is wisdom, God is love.

2.

Chance and change are busy ever,
  Man decays, and ages move;
But his mercy waneth never:
  God is wisdom, God is love.

3.

E'en the hour that darkest seemeth
  Will his changeless goodness prove;
From the mist his brightness streameth:
  God is wisdom, God is love.

4.

He with earthly cares entwineth
  Hope and comfort from above;
Everywhere his glory shineth:
  God is wisdom, God is love.

JOHN BOWRING, 1792-1872.

HYMN 25.

DALEHURST. C. M.   ARTHUR COTTMAN, 1842—1879.

A-MEN.

1.

THOU Grace divine, encircling all,
   A soundless, shoreless sea,
Wherein at last our souls must fall, —
   O love of God most free !

2.

When over dizzy heights we go,
   One soft hand blinds our eyes,
The other leads us safe and slow, —
   O love of God most wise !

3.

And though we turn us from thy face,
   And wander wide and long,
Thou hold'st us still in thine embrace,
   O love of God most strong !

4.

And, filled and quickened by thy breath,
   Our souls are strong and free
To rise o'er sin and fear and death,
   O love of God, to thee.

ELIZA SCUDDER, 1821 –

HYMN 26.

FAITH. C. M.

JOHN BACCHUS DYKES, 1823—1876.

A - MEN.

1.

IMMORTAL Love, forever full,
  Forever flowing free,
Forever shared, forever whole,
  A never-ebbing sea !

2.

Our outward lips confess the name
  All other names above ;
Love only knoweth whence it came,
  And comprehendeth love.

3.

Blow, winds of God, awake and blow
  The mists of earth away !
Shine out, O Light divine, and show
  How wide and far we stray !

4.

The letter fails, and systems fall,
  And every symbol wanes :
The Spirit over-brooding all,
  Eternal Love, remains.

JOHN GREENLEAF WHITTIER, 1807-1892.

HYMN 27.

ST. SEPULCHRE. L. M.   GEORGE COOPER, 1820—1876.

A - MEN.

1.

ETERNAL and immortal King,
   Thy peerless splendors none can bear ;
But darkness veils seraphic eyes
   When God with all his lustre 's there.

2.

Yet faith can pierce the awful gloom,
   The great Invisible can see,
And with its tremblings mingle joy,
   In fixed regards, great God, to thee.

3.

Then every tempting form of sin,
   Shamed in thy presence, disappears,
And all the glowing, raptured soul
   The likeness it contemplates wears.

4.

O ever conscious to my heart,
   Witness to its supreme desire,
Behold, it presseth on to thee,
   For it hath caught the heavenly fire ;

5.

This one petition would it urge :
   To bear thee ever in its sight,
In life, in death, in worlds unknown,
   Its only portion and delight.

PHILIP DODDRIDGE, 1702-1751.

HYMN 28.

ABENDS. L. M.   HERBERT STANLEY OAKELEY, 1830—

A - MEN.

1.

O SOURCE divine, and Life of all,
   The Fount of being's fearful sea,
Thy depth would every heart appall
   That saw not love supreme in thee.

2.

We shrink before thy vast abyss,
   Where worlds on worlds eternal brood;
We know thee truly but in this, —
   That thou bestowest all our good.

3.

And so, mid boundless time and space,
   O, grant us still in thee to dwell,
And through thy ceaseless web to trace
   Thy presence working all things well;

4.

Nor let thou life's delightful play
   Thy truth's transcendent vision hide,
Nor strength and gladness lead astray
   From thee, our nature's only guide.

5.

Bestow on every joyous thrill
   Thy deeper tone of reverent awe,
Make pure thy creature's erring will,
   And teach his heart to love thy law.

JOHN STERLING, 1806–1844.

HYMN 29.

AURELIA. 7. 6. 7. 6. 7. 6. 7. 6.　　　　SAMUEL SEBASTIAN WESLEY, 1810—1876.

A-MEN.

29.

1.

O GOD, the Rock of Ages,
   Who evermore hast been
What time the tempest rages
   Our dwelling-place serene,
Before thy first creations,
   O Lord, the same as now,
To endless generations
   The everlasting thou,

2.

Our years are like the shadows
   On sunny hills that lie,
Or grasses in the meadows,
   That blossom but to die :
A sleep, a dream, a story
   By strangers quickly told,
An unremaining glory
   Of things that soon are old.

3.

O thou, who canst not slumber,
   Whose light grows never pale,
Teach us aright to number
   Our years before they fail ;
On us thy mercy lighten,
   On us thy goodness rest,
And let thy spirit brighten
   The hearts thyself hast blessed.

EDWARD HENRY BICKERSTETH, 1825.

HYMN 30.

BETHSAIDA. 10. 10. 10. 10.   JOSEPH BARNBY, 1838—1896.

A - MEN.

30.

FATHER, thy wonders do not singly stand,
  Nor far removed where feet have seldom strayed :
Around us ever lies the enchanted land,
  In marvels rich to thine own sons displayed.

2.

In finding thee, are all things round us found ;
  In losing thee, are all things lost beside.
Ears have we, but in vain sweet voices sound,
  And to our eyes the vision is denied.

3.

Open our eyes that we that world may see,
  Open our ears that we thy voice may hear,
And in the spirit-land may ever be,
  And feel thy presence with us always near, —

4.

No more to wander mid the things of time,
  No more to suffer death or earthly change,
But with the Christian's joy and faith sublime
  Through all thy vast eternal scenes to range.

JONES VERY, 1813-1880.

HYMN 31.

CLOISTERS. 11. 11. 11. 5.   JOSEPH BARNBY, 1838—1896.

A · MEN.

31.

1.

LORD of our life, and God of our salvation,
 Star of our night, and hope of every nation,
Hear and receive thy Church's supplication,
 Lord God almighty !

2.

Lord, thou canst help when earthly armor faileth,
Lord, thou canst save when sin itself assaileth,
Christ, o'er thy rock nor death nor hell prevaileth :
 Grant us thy peace, Lord, —

3.

Peace in our hearts, our evil thoughts assuaging,
Peace in thy Church, where brothers are engaging,
Peace, when the world its busy war is waging ;
 Calm thy foes raging !

4.

Grant us thy help till backward they are driven,
Grant them thy truth, that they may be forgiven,
Grant peace on earth, or, after we have striven,
 Peace in thy heaven.

Matthäus Apelles von Löwenstern, 1594–1648.
Tr. Philip Pusey, 1799–1855.

Hymn 32.

ST. ANNE. C. M.　　　　　　　　　WILLIAM CROFT, 1678—1727.

A - MEN.

1.

OUR God, our help in ages past,
　Our hope for years to come,
Our shelter from the stormy blast,
　And our eternal home,

2.

Before the hills in order stood,
　Or earth received her frame,
From everlasting thou art God,
　To endless years the same.

3.

A thousand ages in thy sight
　Are like an evening gone,
Short as the watch that ends the night
　Before the rising sun.

4.

Time, like an ever-rolling stream,
　Bears all its sons away :
They fly forgotten, as a dream
　Dies at the opening day.

5.

Our God. our help in ages past,
　Our hope for years to come,
Be thou our guard while troubles last,
　And our eternal home.

ISAAC WATTS, 1674-1748.

HYMN 33.

DOMENICA. S. M.   HERBERT STANLEY OAKELEY, 1830—

A - MEN.

1.

THIS is the day of light:
  Let there be light to-day;
O Day-spring, rise upon our night,
  And chase its gloom away!

2.

This is the day of rest:
  Our failing strength renew,
On weary brain and troubled breast
  Shed thou thy freshening dew.

3.

This is the day of peace:
  Thy peace our spirits fill,
Bid thou the blasts of discord cease,
  The waves of strife be still.

4.

This is the first of days:
  Send forth thy quickening breath,
And wake dead souls to love and praise,
  O Vanquisher of death!

JOHN ELLERTON, 1826-1893.

HYMN 34.

SPOHR. C. M.

LOUIS SPOHR, 1784—1859.

A - MEN.

1.

HOW lovely are thy dwellings fair !
　O Lord of hosts, how dear
The pleasant tabernacles are
　Where thou dost dwell so near !

2.

My soul doth long and almost die
　Thy courts, O Lord, to see ;
My heart and flesh aloud do cry,
　O living God, for thee.

3.

Happy who in thy house reside,
　Where thee they ever praise ;
Happy whose strength in thee doth bide,
　And in their hearts thy ways.

4.

They journey on from strength to strength,
　With joy and gladsome cheer,
Till all before our God at length
　In Zion do appear.

JOHN MILTON, 1608-1674.

HYMN 35.

ANGELS' HYMN. L. M.　　　　　　　ORLANDO GIBBONS, 1583 — 1625.

A . MEN.

1.

O THOU whose perfect goodness crowns
　With peace and joy this sacred day,
Our hearts are glad for all the years
　Thy love has kept us in thy way.

2.

For common tasks of help and cheer,
　For quiet hours of thought and prayer,
For moments when we seemed to feel
　The breath of a diviner air,

3.

For mutual love and trust that keep
　Unchanged through all the changing time,
For friends within the veil who thrill
　Our spirits with a hope sublime :

4.

For this, and more than words can say,
　We praise and bless thy holy name.
Come life or death, enough to know
　That thou art evermore the same.

JOHN WHITE CHADWICK, 1840-

HYMN 36.

FORGIVENESS. 7. 7. 7. 7.   GEORGE MURSELL GARRETT, 1834 —

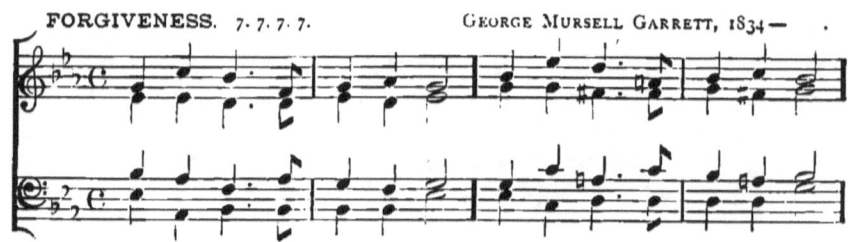

A · MEN.

1.

SOVEREIGN and transforming Grace,
  We invoke thy quickening power;
Reign, the spirit of this place,
  Bless the purpose of this hour.

2.

Holy and creative Light,
  We invoke thy kindling ray;
Dawn upon our spirits' night,
  Turn our darkness into day.

3.

Give the struggling peace for strife,
  Give the doubting light for gloom,
Speed the living into life,
  Warn the dying of their doom.

4.

Work in all : in all renew
  Day by day the life divine,
All our wills to thee subdue,
  All our hearts to thee incline.

FREDERIC HENRY HEDGE, 1805-1890.

HYMN 37.

BELMONT. C M.

A - MEN.

1.

THE offerings to thy throne which rise
    Of mingled praise and prayer
Are but a worthless sacrifice,
    Unless the heart is there.

2.

Upon thine all-discerning ear
    Let no vain words intrude,
No tribute but the vow sincere,
    The tribute of the good.

3.

My offerings will indeed be blest
    If sanctified by thee,
If thy pure spirit touch my heart
    With its own purity.

4.

O, may that spirit warm my heart
    To piety and love,
And to life's lowly vale impart
    Some ray from heaven above.

JOHN BOWRING, 1792-1872

HYMN 38.

SALZBURG. 7. 7. 7. 7. 7. 7. 7. 7.　　　　JOHANN ROSENMÜLLER, 1615—1686.

A·MEN.

38.

1.

FATHER of our feeble race,
   Wise, beneficent, and kind,
Spread o'er nature's ample face
   Flows thy goodness unconfined.
Musing in the silent grove
   Or the busy walks of men,
Still we trace thy wondrous love
   Claiming large returns again.

2.

Lord, what offering shall we bring,
   At thine altars when we bow?
Hearts, the pure unsullied spring
   Whence the kind affections flow;
Soft compassion's feeling soul,
   By the melting eye expressed;
Sympathy, at whose control
   Sorrow leaves the wounded breast;

3.

Willing hands to lead the blind,
   Bind the wounded, feed the poor;
Love, embracing all our kind;
   Charity, with liberal store.
Teach us, O thou heavenly King,
   Thus to show our grateful mind,
Thus the accepted offering bring,
   Love to thee and all mankind.

JOHN TAYLOR, 1750-1826

Hymn 39.

ST. CHRYSOSTOM. 8.8.8 8.8.8   JOSEPH BARNBY, 1838 — 1896.

A - MEN.

1.

GREAT God, this sacred day of thine
  Demands our souls' collected powers.
May we employ in work divine
  These solemn, these devoted hours ;
O may our souls, adoring, own
The grace which calls us to thy throne.

2.

Thy Spirit's powerful aid impart !
  O may thy word with life divine
Engage the ear and warm the heart.
  Then shall the day indeed be thine ;
Then shall our souls, adoring, own
The grace which calls us to thy throne.

ANNE STEELE, 1716-1778.

HYMN 40.

SOUTHWELL. C. M.   HERBERT STEPHEN IRONS, 1834 —

A-MEN.

1.

BEHOLD us, Lord, a little space
   From daily tasks set free,
And met within thy holy place
   To rest awhile with thee.

2.

Around us rolls the ceaseless tide
   Of business, toil, and care ;
And scarcely can we turn aside
   For one brief hour of prayer.

3.

Yet these are not the only walls
   Wherein thou mayest be sought ;
On homeliest work thy blessing falls,
   In truth and patience wrought.

4.

Thine is the loom, the forge, the mart,
   The wealth of land and sea,
The worlds of science and of art
   Revealed and ruled by thee.

5.

Work shall be prayer, if all be wrought
   As thou wouldst have it done,
And prayer, by thee inspired and taught,
   Itself with work be one.

JOHN ELLERTON, 1826-1893.

Hymn 41.

MAIDSTONE. 7. 7. 7. 7. 7. 7. 7. 7. WALTER BOND GILBERT, 1829—   .

A · MEN.

41.

1.

PLEASANT are thy courts above
   In the land of light and love ;
Pleasant are thy courts below
In this land of sin and woe :
O, my spirit longs and faints
For the converse of thy saints,
For the brightness of thy face,
King of glory, God of grace !

2.

Happy birds that sing and fly
Round thy altars, O Most High,
Happier souls that find a rest
In a heavenly Father's breast,
Like the wandering dove that found
No repose on earth around,
They can to their ark repair,
And enjoy it ever there.

3.

Happy souls, their praises flow
Even in this vale of woe ;
Waters in the desert rise,
Manna feeds them from the skies ;
On they go from strength to strength
Till they reach thy throne at length,
At thy feet adoring fall
Who hast led them safe through all.

HENRY FRANCIS LYTE, 1793-1847.

HYMN 42.

WAREHAM. L. M. WILLIAM KNAPP, 1698 — 1768.

A · MEN.

1.

GREAT God, the followers of thy Son,
  We bow before thy mercy-seat
To worship thee, the Holy One,
  And pour our wishes at thy feet.

2.

O grant thy blessing here to-day,
  O give thy people joy and peace,
The tokens of thy love display,
  And favor that shall never cease.

3.

We seek the truth that Jesus brought,
  His path of light we long to tread :
Here be his holy doctrines taught,
  And here their purest influence shed.

4.

May faith and hope and love abound,
  Our sins and errors be forgiven,
And we, in thy great day, be found
  Children of God and heirs of heaven.

HENRY WARE, JR., 1794-1843.

HYMN 43.

ST. SEPULCHRE. L. M.   GEORGE COOPER, 1820—1876.

A - MEN.

1.

L ORD God of morning and of night,
    We thank thee for thy grace of light;
As in the dawn the shadows fly,
Thy presence shines on us more nigh.

2.

Fresh hopes have wakened in the heart,
Fresh force to take the loftier part;
Thy slumber-balms our strength restore,
Throughout the day to serve thee more.

3.

Yet whilst thy will we would pursue,
Oft what we would we cannot do;
The sun may stand in zenith skies,
But on the soul thick midnight lies.

4.

O Lord of lights, 't is thou alone
Canst make our darkened hearts thine own,
Though this new day with joy we see,
Great dawn of God, we cry for thee.

FRANCIS TURNER PALGRAVE, 1824—

HYMN 44.

RATISBON. 7. 7. 7. 7. 7. 7.   JOHANN GOTTLOB WERNER'S CHORALBUCH, 1815.

A - MEN.

44.

1.

GRACIOUS Spirit, dwell with me !
   I myself would gracious be,
And with words that help and heal
Would thy life in mine reveal,
And with actions bold and meek
Would for Christ my Saviour speak.

2.

Truthful Spirit, dwell with me !
I myself would truthful be,
And with wisdom kind and clear
Let thy life in mine appear,
And with actions brotherly
Speak my Lord's sincerity.

3.

Mighty Spirit, dwell with me !
I myself would mighty be, —
Mighty so as to prevail
Where unaided man must fail,
Ever by a mighty hope
Pressing on and bearing up.

4.

Holy Spirit, dwell with me !
I myself would holy be :
Separate from sin, I would
Choose and cherish all things good,
And whatever I can be
Give to him who gave me thee.

THOMAS TOKE LYNCH, 1818-1871.

HYMN 45.

GRACE CHURCH. L. M.   IGNAZ JOSEPH PLEYEL, 1757—1831.

A · MEN.

1.

SPIRIT of power, and truth, and love,
 Who sitt'st enthroned in light above,
Descend, and bear us on thy wings
Far from these low and fleeting things.

2.

Compassed by foes on every side,
By sin and sore temptation tried,
Where can we look or whither flee
If not, great Strengthener, to thee?

3.

Come, Holy Spirit, like the fire,
With burning zeal our souls inspire,
Come like the south wind breathing balm,
Our joys refresh, our passions calm.

4.

Come like the sun's enlightening beam,
Come like the cooling, cleansing stream,
With all thy graces present be :
Spirit of God, we wait for thee.

WILLIAM LINDSAY ALEXANDER, 1808-1884.

HYMN 46.

ST. HUGH. C.M.   EDWARD JOHN HOPKINS, 1818—

A - MEN.

1.

THE Lord be with us as we bend
  His blessing to receive ;
His gift of peace on us descend
  Before his courts we leave.

2.

The Lord be with us as we walk
  Along our homeward road ;
In silent thought, or friendly talk,
  Our hearts be near to God.

3.

The Lord be with us till the night
  Enfold our day of rest ;
Be he of every heart the light,
  Of every home the guest.

4.

The Lord be with us through the hours
  Of slumber calm and deep,
Protect our homes, renew our powers,
  And guard his people's sleep.

JOHN ELLERTON, 1826-1893.

Hymn 47.

LONDON NEW. C. M.

Scottish Psalter, 1635.
John Playford's Psalter, 1671.

A-MEN.

1.

G OD moves in a mysterious way
   His wonders to perform ;
He plants his footsteps in the sea,
   And rides upon the storm.

2.

Deep in unfathomable mines
   Of never-failing skill,
He treasures up his bright designs,
   And works his sovereign will.

3.

Judge not the Lord by feeble sense,
   But trust him for his grace ;
Behind a frowning providence
   He hides a smiling face.

4.

Blind unbelief is sure to err,
   And scan his work in vain ;
God is his own interpreter,
   And he will make it plain.

WILLIAM COWPER, 1731-1800

HYMN 48.

BEN RHYDDING. S. M.   ALEXANDER ROBERT REINAGLE, 1799 — 1877.

A-MEN.

1.

COME, sound his praise abroad,
  And hymns of glory sing :
Jehovah is the sovereign God,
  The universal king.

2.

He formed the deeps unknown,
  He gave the seas their bound :
The watery worlds are all his own,
  And all the solid ground.

3.

Come, worship at his throne,
  Come, bow before the Lord :
We are his works, and not our own :
  He formed us by his word.

4.

To-day attend his voice,
  Nor dare provoke his rod :
Come, like the people of his choice,
  And own your gracious God.

ISAAC WATTS, 1674-1748.

HYMN 49.

ST. CLEMENT DANES. C. M.　　　　　SAMUEL HOWARD, 1710—1782.

A-MEN.

1.

THE harp at Nature's advent strung
　　Has never ceased to play ;
The song the stars of morning sung
　　Has never died away.

2.

And prayer is made, and praise is given
　　By all things near and far :
The ocean looketh up to heaven
　　And mirrors every star ;

3.

The green earth sends her incense up
　　From many a mountain shrine,
From folded leaf and dewy cup
　　She pours her sacred wine ;

4.

The blue sky is the temple's arch,
　　Its transept earth and air,
The music of its starry march
　　The chorus of a prayer :

5.

So Nature keeps the reverent frame
　　With which her years began,
And all her signs and voices shame
　　The prayerless heart of man.

JOHN GREENLEAF WHITTIER, 1807–1892.

HYMN 50.

ST. FLAVIAN. C. M.   JOHN DAY'S PSALTER, 1562.

A - MEN.

1.

THERE is a book who runs may read
    Which heavenly truth imparts,
And all the lore its scholars need
    Pure eyes and Christian hearts.

2.

The works of God, above, below,
    Within us and around,
Are pages in that book to show
    How God himself is found.

3.

The glorious sky, embracing all,
    Is like the Maker's love,
Wherewith encompassed, great and small
    In peace and order move.

4.

Two worlds are ours : 't is only sin
    Forbids us to descry
The mystic heaven and earth within,
    Plain as the sea and sky.

5.

Thou, who hast given me eyes to see
    And love this sight so fair,
Give me a heart to find out thee,
    And read thee everywhere.

JOHN KEBLE, 1792-1866.

HYMN 51.

CREATION. L. M. D.

FRANZ JOSEPH HAYDN, 1732—1809.

51.

A-MEN.

1.

THE spacious firmament on high,
  With all the blue ethereal sky,
And spangled heavens, a shining frame,
Their great Original proclaim.
The unwearied sun from day to day
Does his Creator's power display,
And publishes to every land
The work of an almighty hand.

2.

Soon as the evening shades prevail
The moon takes up the wondrous tale,
And nightly to the listening earth
Repeats the story of her birth;
Whilst all the stars that round her burn,
And all the planets in their turn,
Confirm the tidings as they roll,
And spread the truth from pole to pole.

3.

What though in solemn silence all
Move round the dark terrestrial ball?
What though no real voice nor sound
Amid their radiant orbs be found?
In reason's ear they all rejoice
And utter forth a glorious voice,
Forever singing as they shine,
"The hand that made us is divine."

JOSEPH ADDISON, 1672-1719.

HYMN 52.

SWEDEN. L. M.　　　　　　　　　　　HENRY HILES, 1826—

A - MEN.

1.

FATHER and Friend, thy light, thy love,
　Beaming through all thy works, we see ;
Thy glory gilds the heavens above,
　And all the earth is full of thee.

2.

Thy voice we hear, thy presence feel,
　Whilst thou, too pure for mortal sight,
Involved in clouds, invisible,
　Reignest the Lord of life and light.

3.

We know not in what hallowed part
　Of the wide heavens thy throne may be ;
But this we know, that where thou art
　Strength, wisdom, goodness, dwell with
　　thee.

4.

Thy children shall not faint nor fear,
　Sustained by this delightful thought,
Since thou, their God, art everywhere,
　They cannot be where thou art not.

JOHN BOWRING, 1792-1872.

HYMN 53.

DUKE STREET. L. M.   JOHN HATTON,   —1793.

A-MEN.

1.

GOD of the earth, the sky, the sea,
   Maker of all above, below,
Creation lives and moves in thee ;
   Thy present life through all doth flow.

2.

Thy love is in the sunshine's glow,
   Thy life is in the quickening air ;
When lightnings flash and storm-winds
      blow,
   There is thy power, thy law is there.

3.

We feel thy calm at evening's hour,
   Thy grandeur in the march of night,
And when the morning breaks in power,
   We hear thy word, " Let there be light."

4.

But higher far, and far more clear,
   Thee in man's spirit we behold,
Thine image and thyself are there, —
   The indwelling God, proclaimed of old.

SAMUEL LONGFELLOW, 1819–1892.

HYMN 54.

ST. AGNES. C. M.   JOHN BACCHUS DYKES, 1823 — 1876.

A - MEN.

1.

SPIRIT divine, attend our prayers,
 And make this house thy home :
Descend with all thy gracious powers,
 O, come, great Spirit, come !

2.

Come as the fire, and purge our hearts,
 Like sacrificial flame :
Let our whole soul an offering be
 To our Redeemer's name.

3.

Come as the dew, and sweetly bless
 This consecrated hour :
May barrenness rejoice to own
 Thy fertilizing power.

4.

Come as the dove, and spread thy wings,
 The wings of peaceful love,
And let thy church on earth become
 Blest as the church above.

5.

Come as the wind with rushing sound
 And pentecostal grace,
That all of woman born may see
 The glory of thy face.

ANDREW REED, 1788-1862.

HYMN 55.

ST. ALBAN. L. M.

ST. ALBAN'S TUNE BOOK, 1866.

A·MEN.

1.

SPIRIT of truth, who makest bright
All souls that long for heavenly light,
Appear, and on my darkness shine,
Descend, and be my guide divine.

2.

Spirit of power, whose might doth dwell
Full in the souls thou lovest well,
Unto this fainting heart draw near,
And be my daily quickener.

3.

Spirit of joy, who makest glad
Each broken heart by sin made sad,
Pour on this mourning soul thy cheer,
Give me to bless my comforter.

4.

Come mightier down, thyself impart
More largely to this longing heart,
My comforter more dearly be,
More sweetly guide and hallow me,

5.

Till thou shalt make me meet to bear
The sweetness of heaven's holy air,
The light wherein no darkness is,
The eternal, overflowing bliss.

THOMAS HORNBLOWER GILL, 1819—

Hymn 56.

LUDBOROUGH. L. M. TIMOTHY RICHARD MATTHEWS, 1826—

A - MEN.

1.

THAT God is love, unchanging love,—
  This truth of truths, do I not know?
Unnumbered blessings from above
  Forever come to tell me so.

2.

What have I done, what can I do,
  To purchase this perpetual feast?
Of all the proofs he loves me so,
  I am not worthy of the least.

3.

Forgive, dear God, forgive, forgive!
  Set free this self-bound heart of mine,
That I may learn for thee to live
  The self-renouncing life divine.

4.

There's no return that I can make
  For all thy goodness, God, to me,
But, doing all things for thy sake,
  To lose, and find, myself in thee.

WILLIAM HENRY FURNESS, 1802–1896.

HYMN 57.

ST. CLEMENT DANES. C. M.   SAMUEL HOWARD, 1710—1782.

A · MEN.

1.

COME, mighty Spirit, penetrate
　This heart and soul of mine,
And my whole being with thy grace
　Pervade, O Life divine !

2.

As this clear air surrounds the earth,
　Thy grace around me roll ;
As the fresh light pervades the air,
　So pierce and fill my soul ;

3.

As from these clouds drops down in love
　The precious summer rain,
So from thyself pour down the flood
　That freshens all again :

4.

Thus life within our lifeless hearts
　Shall make its glad abode,
And we shall shine in beauteous light,
　Filled with the light of God.

HORATIUS BONAR, 1808-1889

HYMN 58.

TALLIS'S ORDINAL. C. M.   THOMAS TALLIS, 1520—1585.

A-MEN.

1.

LET me no more my comfort draw
    From my frail hold of thee,
In this alone rejoice with awe, —
    Thy mighty grasp of me.

2.

Out of that weak, unquiet drift
    That comes but to depart,
To that pure heaven my spirit lift
    Where thou unchanging art.

3.

Lay hold of me with thy strong grasp,
    Let thy almighty arm
In its embrace my weakness clasp,
    And I shall fear no harm.

4.

Thy purpose of eternal good
    Let me but surely know,
On this I 'll lean, let changing mood
    And feeling come or go,

5.

Glad when thy sunshine fills my soul,
    Not lorn when clouds o'ercast,
Since thou within thy sure control
    Of love dost hold me fast.

JOHN CAMPBELL SHAIRP, 1819-1885.

Hymn 59.

DOMINUS REGIT ME. 8.7.8.7. JOHN BACCHUS DYKES, 1823—1876.

A · MEN.

1.

THE King of love my shepherd is,
    Whose goodness faileth never:
I nothing lack if I am his,
    And he is mine forever.

2.

Where streams of living water flow
    My ransomed soul he leadeth,
And where the verdant pastures grow
    With food celestial feedeth.

3.

Perverse and foolish oft I strayed,
    But yet in love he sought me
And on his shoulder gently laid
    And home rejoicing brought me.

4.

In death's dark vale I fear no ill
    With thee, dear Lord, beside me,
Thy rod and staff my comfort still,
    Thy cross before to guide me.

5.

Thou spread'st a table in my sight,
    Thy unction grace bestoweth,
And O! what transport of delight
    From thy pure chalice floweth!

6.

And so through all the length of days
    Thy goodness faileth never;
Good Shepherd, may I sing thy praise
    Within thy house forever.

HENRY WILLIAMS BAKER, 1821-1877.

HYMN 60.

NEUMARK. 8. 8. 4. 4. 8. 8. 8.　　　　　　　　　　GEORG NEUMARK, 1621—1681.

A-MEN.

60.

1.

O LORD, in me there lieth naught
But to thy search revealèd lies;
  For when I sit
  Thou markest it,
No less thou notest when I rise;
Yea closest closet of my thought
Hath open windows to thine eyes.

2.

Thou walkest with me when I walk;
When to my bed for rest I go,
  I find thee there,
  And everywhere:
Not youngest thought in me doth grow,
No, not one word I cast to talk
But, yet unuttered, thou dost know.

MARY SIDNEY, 1552–1621

HYMN 61.

BENEDICTION. 10. 10. 10. 10.   EDWARD JOHN HOPKINS, 1818 —

A - MEN.

61.

1.

THOU Life within my life, than self more near,
Thou veilèd Presence infinitely clear,
From all illusive shows of sense I flee,
To find my centre and my rest in thee.

2.

Below all depths thy saving mercy lies,
Through thickest glooms I see thy light arise;
Above the highest heavens thou art not found
More surely than within this earthly round.

3.

Take part with me against these doubts that rise
And seek to throne thee far in distant skies;
Take part with me against this self that dares
Assume the burden of these sins and cares.

4.

How shall I call thee who art always here?
How shall I praise thee who art still most dear?
What may I give thee, save what thou hast given,
And whom but thee have I in earth or heaven?

ELIZA SCUDDER, 1821–

HYMN 62.

STRENGTH AND STAY. 11. 10. 11. 10.   JOHN BACCHUS DYKES, 1823—1876.

A · MEN.

62.

1.

FATHER, to us thy children, humbly kneeling,
   Conscious of weakness, ignorance, sin, and shame,
Give such a force of holy thought and feeling,
  That we may live to glorify thy name,

2.

That we may conquer base desire and passion,
  That we may rise from selfish thought and will,
O'ercome the world's allurement, threat, and fashion,
  Walk humbly, gently, leaning on thee still.

3.

Let all thy goodness by our minds be seen,
  Let all thy mercy on our souls be sealed.
Lord, if thou wilt, thy power can make us clean;
  O, speak the word, thy servants shall be healed.

JAMES FREEMAN CLARKE, 1810–1888.

HYMN 63.

ST. MATTHIAS. 8. 8. 8. 8. 8. 8.   WILLIAM HENRY MONK, 1823 — 1889.

A - MEN.

63.

1.

THOU hidden love of God, whose height,
  Whose depth unfathomed, no man knows,
I see from far thy beauteous light,
  Inly I sigh for thy repose;
My heart is pained, nor can it be
At rest till it finds rest in thee.

2.

Thy secret voice invites me still
  The sweetness of thy yoke to prove,
And fain I would; but though my will
  Seem fixed, yet wide my passions rove,
Yet hindrances strew all the way:
I aim at thee, yet from thee stray.

3.

'T is mercy all that thou hast brought
  My mind to seek her peace in thee;
Yet, while I seek, but find thee not,
  No peace my wandering soul shall see.
O, when shall all my wanderings end,
And all my steps to thee-ward tend?

4.

Is there a thing beneath the sun
  That strives with thee my heart to share?
Ah, tear it thence, and reign alone,
  The Lord of every motion there!
Then shall my heart from earth be free,
When it has found repose in thee.

GERHARD TERSTEEGEN, 1697-1769.
Tr. JOHN WESLEY, 1703-1791.

HYMN 64.

BACH. 7. 8. 7. 8. 7 7. 7. 7.   JOHANN SEBASTIAN BACH, 1685 — 1750.

A - MEN.

64.

1.

MAKER of the human heart,
 Scorn not thou thine own creation,
Onward guide its nobler part,
 Train it for its high vocation;
From the long infected grain
Cleanse and purge each sinful stain,
Kindle with a kindred fire
Every good and great desire.

2.

When, in ruin and in gloom,
 Falls to dust our earthly mansion,
Give us ample verge and room
 For the measureless expansion,
Clear our clouded mental sight
To endure thy piercing light,
Open wide our narrow thought
To embrace thee as we ought.

3.

When the shadows melt away
 And the eternal day is breaking,
Judge most just, be thou our stay
 In that strange and solemn waking;
Thou to whom the heart sincere
Is thy best of temples here,
May thy faithfulness and love
Be our long last home above!

ARTHUR PENRHYN STANLEY, 1815-1881.

HYMN 65.

NEWLAND. S. M.

HENRY JOHN GAUNTLETT, 1805 — 1876.

A-MEN.

1.

SEND down thy truth, O God !
  Too long the shadows frown,
Too long the darkened way we 've trod,
  Thy truth, O Lord, send down !

2.

Send down thy spirit free,
  Till wilderness and town
One temple for thy worship be,
  Thy spirit, O, send down !

3.

Send down thy love, thy life,
  Our lesser lives to crown,
And cleanse them of their hate and strife,
  Thy living love send down !

4.

Send down thy peace, O Lord !
  Earth's bitter voices drown
In one deep ocean of accord,
  Thy peace, O God, send down !

EDWARD ROWLAND SILL, 1841–1887.

HYMN 66.

FARRANT. C. M.

RICHARD FARRANT, 1530—1580.

A - MEN.

1.

G O not, my soul, in search of him ;
 Thou wilt not find him there,
Or in the depths of shadow dim,
 Or heights of upper air.

2.

For not in far-off realms of space
 The spirit hath its throne ;
In every heart it findeth place
 And waiteth to be known.

3.

O gift of gifts, O grace of grace,
 That God should condescend
To make thy heart his dwelling-place
 And be thy daily friend.

4.

Then go not thou in search of him,
 But to thyself repair ;
Wait thou within the silence dim,
 And thou shalt find him there.

FREDERICK LUCIAN HOSMER, 1840—

HYMN 67.

ALL HALLOWS. 8. 6. 8. 6. 8. 6.   ARTHUR HENRY BROWN, 1830 — .

A - MEN.

67.

1.

BEYOND, beyond that boundless sea,
  Above that dome of sky,
Further than thought itself can flee,
  Thy dwelling is on high:
Yet dear the awful thought to me
  That thou, my God, art nigh.

2.

We hear thy voice when thunders roll
  Through the wide fields of air,
The waves obey thy dread control,
  But still thou art not there:
Where shall I find him, O my soul,
  Who yet is everywhere?

3.

O, not in circling depth nor height,
  But in the conscious breast,
Present to faith, though veiled from sight,
  There doth his spirit rest.
O, come, thou Presence infinite,
  And make thy creature blest.

JOSIAH CONDER, 1789-1855.

Hymn 68.

MOUNT CALVARY. C. M.   ROBERT PRESCOTT STEWART, 1825—1894.

A-MEN.

1.

O HELP us, Lord ! each hour of need
    Thy heavenly succor give,
Help us in thought, and word, and deed,
    Each hour on earth we live.

2.

O help us when our spirits bleed,
    With contrite anguish sore,
And when our hearts are cold and dead,
    O help us, Lord, the more !

3.

O help us, through the prayer of faith,
    More firmly to believe ;
For still, the more the servant hath,
    The more shall he receive.

HENRY HART MILMAN, 1791–1868.

HYMN 69.

WARD. L. M.   LOWELL MASON, 1792—1872.

A-MEN.

1.

H ATH not thy heart within thee burned
    At evening's calm and holy hour,
As if its inmost depths discerned
    The presence of a loftier power?

2.

It was the voice of God that spake
    In silence to thy silent heart,
And bade each worthier thought awake,
    And every dream of earth depart.

3.

Voice of our God, O, yet be near!
    In low, sweet accents, whisper peace,
Direct us on our pathway here,
    Then bid in heaven our wanderings cease.

STEPHEN GREENLEAF BULFINCH, 1809-1870.

HYMN 70.

ROCKINGHAM. L. M.　　　　　　　EDWARD MILLER, 1731 — 1807.

A - MEN.

1.

MY God, permit me not to be
　A stranger to myself and thee.
Amidst a thousand thoughts I rove,
Forgetful of my highest love.

2.

Why should my passions mix with earth,
And thus debase my heavenly birth?
Why should I cleave to things below,
And let my God, my Saviour, go?

3.

Call me away from flesh and sense;
One sovereign word can draw me thence:
I would obey the voice divine,
And all inferior joys resign.

4.

Be earth, with all her scenes, withdrawn,
Let noise and vanity be gone.
In secret silence of the mind,
My heaven, and there my God, I find.

ISAAC WATTS, 1674-1748

HYMN 71.

GRACE CHURCH. L. M.

IGNAZ JOSEPH PLEYEL, 1757—1831.

A - MEN.

1.

G OD of my life, whose gracious power
   Through varied deaths my soul hath led,
Or turned aside the fatal hour,
   Or lifted up my sinking head, —

2.

In all my ways thy hand I own,
   Thy ruling providence I see.
O help me still my course to run,
   And still direct my paths to thee !

3.

I have no might to oppose the foe,
   But everlasting strength is thine ;
Show me the way that I should go,
   Show me the path I should decline.

4.

Foolish and impotent and blind,
   Lead me a way I have not known,
Bring me where I my heaven may find,—
   The heaven of loving thee alone.

CHARLES WESLEY, 1708-1788.

HYMN 72.

BEATITUDO. C. M.   JOHN BACCHUS DYKES, 1823—1876.

A - MEN.

1.

WHEN I survey life's varied scene,
    Amid the darkest hours
Sweet rays of comfort shine between,
    And thorns are mixed with flowers.

2.

Is health and ease my happy share?
    O may I bless my God !
Thy kindness let my songs declare,
    And spread thy praise abroad.

3.

And O, whate'er of earthly bliss
    Thy sovereign hand denies,
Accepted at thy throne of grace,
    Let this petition rise, —

4.

"Give me a calm, a thankful heart,
    From every murmur free,
The blessings of thy grace impart,
    And let me live to thee,

5.

" Let the sweet hope that thou art mine
    My path of life attend,
Thy presence through my journey shine,
    And bless its happy end. "

ANNE STEELE, 1716-1778.

HYMN 73.

UNIVERSITY COLLEGE. 7.7.7.7.   HENRY JOHN GAUNTLETT, 1805—1876.

A-MEN.

1.

L IFE of ages, richly poured,
    Love of God, unspent and free,
Flowing in the prophet's word
    And the people's liberty, —

2.

Never was to chosen race
    That unstinted tide confined ;
Thine is every time and place,
    Fountain sweet of heart and mind.

3.

Breathing in the thinker's creed,
    Pulsing in the hero's blood,
Nerving simplest thought and deed,
    Freshening time with truth and good,

4.

Consecrating art and song,
    Holy book and pilgrim track,
Hurling floods of tyrant wrong
    From the sacred limits back, —

5.

Life of ages, richly poured,
    Love of God, unspent and free,
Flow still in the prophet's word
    And the people's liberty !

SAMUEL JOHNSON, 1822-1882.

HYMN 74.

DUNDEE. C. M.

SCOTTISH PSALTER, 1615.

A - MEN.

1.

A UTHOR of good, to thee I turn ;
   Thy ever-wakeful eye
Alone can all my wants discern,
   Thy hand alone supply.

2.

O let thy fear within me dwell,
   Thy love my footsteps guide ;
That love shall vainer loves expel,
   That fear all fears beside.

3.

And O. by error's force subdued,
   Since oft my stubborn will
Preposterous shuns the latent good,
   And grasps the specious ill,

4.

Not to my wish, but to my want,
   Do thou thy gifts apply ;
Unasked, what good thou knowest grant,
   What ill, though asked, deny.

JAMES MERRICK, 1720-1769.

HYMN 75.

ST. STEPHEN. C. M.

WILLIAM JONES, 1726—1800.

A-MEN.

1.

I WORSHIP thee, sweet will of God,
  And all thy ways adore ;
And every day I live I seem
  To love thee more and more.

2.

Man's weakness waiting upon God
  Its end can never miss ;
For men on earth no work can do
  More angel-like than this.

3.

He always wins who sides with God,
  To him no chance is lost ;
God's will is sweetest to him when
  It triumphs at his cost.

4.

Ill that he blesses is our good,
  And unblest good is ill ;
And all is right that seems most wrong,
  If it be his sweet will.

FREDERICK WILLIAM FABER, 1814-1863.

HYMN 76.

KEBLE. L. M.

JOHN BACCHUS DYKES, 1823 — 1876.

A-MEN.

1.

L ORD, thou hast searched and seen
    me through :
Thine eye commands, with piercing view,
My rising and my resting hours,
My heart and flesh with all their powers.

2.

My thoughts, before they are my own,
Are to my God distinctly known :
He knows the words I mean to speak,
Ere from my opening lips they break.

3.

Within thy circling power I stand ;
On every side I find thy hand :
Awake, asleep, at home, abroad,
I am surrounded still with God.

4.

O, may these thoughts possess my breast,
Where'er I rove, where'er I rest,
Nor let my weaker passions dare
Consent to sin, for God is there.

ISAAC WATTS, 1674-1748.

HYMN 77.

POSEN. 7. 7 7. 7.   GEORG CHRISTOPH STRATTNER, 1650 — 1705.

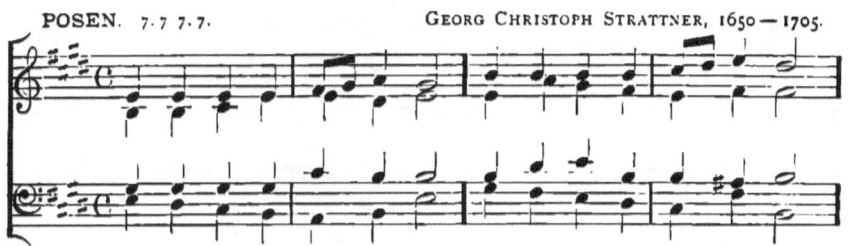

A · MEN.

1.

T AKE my life, and let it be
    Consecrated, Lord, to thee ;
Take my moments and my days,
Let them flow in ceaseless praise.

2.

Take my voice, and let me sing
Always, only, for my King ;
Take my lips, and let them be
Filled with messages from thee.

3.

Take my silver and my gold,
Not a mite would I withhold :
Take my intellect, and use
Every power as thou shalt choose.

4.

Take my will, and make it thine,
It shall be no longer mine ;
Take my heart, it is thine own,
It shall be thy royal throne.

FRANCES RIDLEY HAVERGAL, 1836—1879

Hymn 78.

STRENGTH AND STAY. 11. 10. 11. 10.   John Bacchus Dykes, 1823 — 1876.

A - MEN.

78.

FATHER, in thy mysterious presence kneeling,
   Fain would our souls feel all thy kindling love ;
For we are weak, and need some deep revealing
   Of trust and strength and calmness from above.

2.

Lord, we have wandered forth through doubt and sorrow,
   And thou hast made each step an onward one ;
And we will ever trust each unknown morrow, —
   Thou wilt sustain us till its work is done.

3.

In the heart's depths a peace serene and holy
   Abides ; and when pain seems to have its will,
Or we despair, O, may that peace rise slowly,
   Stronger than agony, and we be still !

4.

Now, Father, now, in thy dear presence kneeling,
   Our spirits yearn to feel thy kindling love, —
Now make us strong ; we need thy deep revealing
   Of trust and strength and calmness from above.

SAMUEL JOHNSON, 1822-1882

HYMN 79.

CONISTON. C. M.　　　　　　　　　　　　JOSEPH BARNBY, 1838—1896.

A-MEN.

1.

THE bird let loose in eastern skies,
　When hastening fondly home,
Ne'er stoops to earth her wing, nor flies
　Where idle warblers roam ;

2.

But high she shoots through air and light,
　Above all low delay,
Where nothing earthly bounds her flight,
　Nor shadow dims her way.

3.

So grant me, God, from every care
　And stain of passion free,
Aloft, through virtue's purer air,
　To hold my course to thee, —

4.

No sin to cloud, no lure to stay
　My soul as home she springs,
Thy sunshine on her joyful way,
　Thy freedom in her wings !

THOMAS MOORE, 1779-1852.

HYMN 80.

HERMANN. C. M.   NICOLAUS HERMANN, —1561.

A·MEN.

1.

THE Lord descended from above,
　And bowed the heavens high,
And underneath his feet he cast
　The darkness of the sky;

2.

On Cherubs and on Cherubins
　Full royally he rode,
And on the wings of all the winds
　Came flying all abroad.

3.

Unspotted are the ways of God,
　His word is purely tried,
He is a sure defence to such
　As in his faith abide.

4.

For who is God except the Lord?
　For other there is none;
Or else who is omnipotent,
　Saving our God alone?

THOMAS STERNHOLD,   —1549.

HYMN 81.

RIVAULX. L. M.

JOHN BACCHUS DYKES, 1823 — 1876.

A · MEN.

1.

WHAT secret place, what distant star,
 Is like, dread Lord, to thine abode?
Why dwellest thou from us so far?
 We yearn for thee, thou hidden God!

2.

Vain searchers! but we need not mourn,
 We need not stretch our weary wings;
Thou meetest us where'er we turn,
 Thou beamest, Lord, from all bright
  things.

3.

To us, vain searchers after God,
 To us the Holy Ghost doth come;
From us thou hidest thine abode,
 But thou wilt make our souls thy
  home.

4.

O Glory that no eye may bear!
 O Presence bright, our souls' sweet
  guest!
O farthest off, O ever near,
 Most hidden and most manifest!

THOMAS HORNBLOWER GILL, 1819–

Hymn 82.

LUDBOROUGH. L. M.   Timothy Richard Matthews, 1826—

A - MEN.

1.

I LOVE, I love thee, Lord most high,
  Because thou first hast lovèd me ;
I seek no other liberty
  But that of being bound to thee.

2.

May memory no thought suggest
  But shall to thy pure glory tend,
My understanding find no rest
  Except in thee, its only end.

3.

All mine is thine : say but the word,
  Whate'er thou willest shall be done ;
I know thy love, all-gracious Lord ;
  I know it seeks my good alone.

4.

Apart from thee all things are naught :
  Then grant, O my supremest bliss,
Grant me to love thee as I ought, —
  Thou givest all in giving this.

Tr. Edward Caswall, 1814-1878

HYMN 83.

PENTECOST. L. M.   WILLIAM BOYD, 1846—

A - MEN.

1.

ONE Lord there is, all lords above ;
   His name is truth, his name is love,
His name is beauty, it is light,
His will is everlasting right.

2.

But ah, to wrong what is his name ?
This Lord is a consuming flame
To every wrong beneath the sun ;
He is one Lord, the holy one.

3.

Lord of the everlasting name, —
Truth, beauty, light, consuming flame, —
Shall I not lift my heart to thee,
And ask thee, Lord, to rule in me ?

4.

If I be ruled in other wise,
My lot is cast with all that dies,
With things that harm, and things that hate,
And roam by night, and miss the gate, —

5.

The happy gate, which leads to where
Love is like sunshine in the air,
And love and law are both the same,
Named with an everlasting name.

WILLIAM BRIGHTY RANDS, 1827-1882.

HYMN 84.

ST. BERNARD. C. M.   JOHN RICHARDSON, 1816—1879.

A-MEN.

1.

MY God, I feel thy wondrous might
  In nature's various shows, —
The whirlwind's breath, the tender light
  Of the rejoicing rose.

2.

For doth not that same power enfold
  Whatever things are new,
Which shone about the saints of old
  And struck the seas in two?

3.

Ashamed, I veil my fearful eyes
  From this, thy earthly reign;
What shall I do when I arise
  From death, but die again?

4.

What shall I do but prostrate fall
  Before the splendor there,
That here so dazzles me through all
  The dusty robes I wear?

5.

I dare not pray to thee to give
  That heaven which shall appear;
My cry is, help me, thou, to live
  Within the heaven that 's here!

ALICE CARY, 1820—1871.

HYMN 85.

First Tune.

ST. EDMUND.   6. 4. 6. 4. 6. 6. 4.   ARTHUR SEYMOUR SULLIVAN, 1842—   .

A - MEN.

85.

1.

NEARER, my God, to thee,
  Nearer to thee !
E'en though it be a cross
  That raiseth me,
Still all my song would be,
Nearer, my God, to thee,
  Nearer to thee !

2.

Though like the wanderer,
  The sun gone down,
Darkness be over me,
  My rest a stone,
Yet in my dreams I'd be
Nearer, my God, to thee,
  Nearer to thee.

3.

There let the way appear
  Steps unto heaven ;
All that thou send'st to me
  In mercy given ;
Angels to beckon me
Nearer, my God, to thee,
  Nearer to thee.

4.

Then, with my waking thoughts
  Bright with thy praise,
Out of my stony griefs
  Bethel I 'll raise ;
So by my woes to be
Nearer, my God, to thee,
  Nearer to thee.

5.

Or if on joyful wing
  Cleaving the sky,
Sun, moon, and stars forgot,
  Upwards I fly,
Still all my song shall be,
Nearer, my God, to thee,
  Nearer to thee !

SARAH FLOWER ADAMS, 1805-1848.

HYMN 85.

Second Tune.

BETHANY. 6. 4. 6. 4. 6. 6. 4.

LOWELL MASON, 1792—1872.

A-MEN.

85.

1.

NEARER, my God, to thee,
    Nearer to thee !
E'en though it be a cross
    That raiseth me,
Still all my song would be,
Nearer, my God, to thee,
    Nearer to thee !

2.

Though like the wanderer,
    The sun gone down,
Darkness be over me,
    My rest a stone,
Yet in my dreams I 'd be
Nearer, my God, to thee,
    Nearer to thee.

3.

There let the way appear
    Steps unto heaven ;
All that thou send'st to me
    In mercy given ;
Angels to beckon me
Nearer, my God, to thee,
    Nearer to thee.

4.

Then, with my waking thoughts
    Bright with thy praise,
Out of my stony griefs
    Bethel I 'll raise ;
So by my woes to be
Nearer, my God, to thee,
    Nearer to thee.

5.

Or if on joyful wing
    Cleaving the sky,
Sun, moon, and stars forgot,
    Upwards I fly,
Still all my song shall be,
Nearer, my God, to thee,
    Nearer to thee !

SARAH FLOWER ADAMS, 1805-1848.

Hymn 86.

EMS. S. M. GERMAN CHORAL.

A - MEN.

1.

WHERE is thy God, my soul?
　Is he within thy heart?
Or ruler of a distant realm
　In which thou hast no part?

2.

Where is thy God, my soul?
　Only in stars and sun?
Or have the holy words of truth
　His light in every one?

3.

Where is thy God, my soul?
　Confined to scripture's page?
Or does his Spirit check and guide
　The spirit of each age?

4.

O Ruler of the sky,
　Rule thou within my heart!
O great Adorner of the world,
　Thy light of life impart!

5.

Giver of holy words,
　Bestow thy holy power,
And aid me, whether work or thought
　Engage the varying hour.

6.

In thee have I my help,
　As all my fathers had;
I'll trust thee when I'm sorrowful,
　And serve thee when I'm glad.

THOMAS TOKE LYNCH, 1818-1871.

HYMN 87.

CORONATION. C. M.

OLIVER HOLDEN, 1765—1844.

A-MEN.

1.

ALL hail the power of Jesus' name !
　Let angels prostrate fall ;
Bring forth the royal diadem,
　And crown him Lord of all.

2.

Let every kindred, every tribe,
　On this terrestrial ball,
To him all majesty ascribe,
　And crown him Lord of all.

3.

O that, with yonder sacred throng,
　We at his feet may fall ;
We 'll join the everlasting song,
　And crown him Lord of all.

EDWARD PERRONET, 1726-1792.
JOHN RIPPON, 1751-1836.

Hymn 88.

HOREB. L. M. D.   Joseph Barnby, 1838 — 1896.

A - MEN.

88.

1.

THE Lord is come. On Syrian soil
The child of poverty and toil,
The man of sorrows, born to know
Each varying shade of human woe,
His joy, his glory, to fulfil
In earth and heaven his Father's will;
On lonely mount, by festive board,
On bitter cross, — despised, adored.

2.

The Lord is come. Dull hearts to wake,
He speaks, as never man yet spake,
The truth which makes his servants free,
The royal law of liberty.
Though heaven and earth shall pass away,
His living words our spirits stay,
And from his treasures, new and old,
The eternal mysteries unfold.

3.

The Lord is come. In him we trace
The fulness of God's truth and grace;
Throughout those words and acts divine,
Gleams of the eternal splendor shine;
And from his inmost spirit flow,
As from a height of sunlit snow,
The rivers of perennial life,
To heal and sweeten nature's strife.

4.

The Lord is come. In every heart
Where truth and mercy claim a part,
In every land where right is might,
And deeds of darkness shun the light,
In every church where faith and love
Lift earthward thoughts to things above,
In every holy, happy home, —
We bless thee, Lord, that thou hast come.

ARTHUR PENRHYN STANLEY, 1815-1881

HYMN 89.

ST. GEORGE'S, WINDSOR.   7.7.7.7.7.7.7.7.   GEORGE JOB ELVEY, 1816 — 1893.

A - MEN.

89.

1.

WATCHMAN! tell us of the night,
    What its signs of promise are.
Traveller! o'er yon mountain's height
    See that glory-beaming star.
Watchman! doth its beauteous ray
    Aught of hope or joy foretell?
Traveller! yes, it brings the day,
    Promised day of Israel.

2.

Watchman! tell us of the night,
    Higher yet that star ascends.
Traveller! blessedness and light,
    Peace and truth its course portends.
Watchman! will its beams alone
    Gild the spot that gave them birth?
Traveller! ages are its own,
    And it bursts o'er all the earth.

3.

Watchman! tell us of the night,
    For the morning seems to dawn.
Traveller! darkness takes its flight,
    Doubt and terror are withdrawn.
Watchman! let thy wanderings cease,
    Hie thee to thy quiet home.
Traveller! lo! the Prince of Peace,
    Lo! the Son of God is come!

JOHN BOWRING, 1792-1872.

Hymn 90.

HERMANN. C. M.

Nicolaus Hermann, — 1561.

A - MEN.

1.

Hark the glad sound, the Saviour comes,
The Saviour promised long:
Let every heart prepare a throne,
And every voice a song.

2.

He comes, the broken heart to bind,
The bleeding soul to cure,
And with the treasures of his grace
To enrich the humble poor.

3.

Our glad hosannas, Prince of Peace,
Thy welcome shall proclaim,
And heaven's eternal arches ring
With thy beloved name.

Philip Doddridge, 1702-1751.

HYMN 91.

NATIVITY. C. M.

HENRY LAHEE, 1826 —

A-MEN.

1.

JOY to the world! the Lord is come:
   Let earth receive her King,
Let every heart prepare him room,
   And heaven and nature sing.

2.

Joy to the earth! the Saviour reigns:
   Let men their songs employ,
While fields and floods, rocks, hills, and
     plains
Repeat the sounding joy.

3.

He rules the world with truth and grace,
   And makes the nations prove
The glories of his righteousness,
   And wonders of his love.

ISAAC WATTS, 1674-1748.

HYMN 92.

VENI EMMANUEL. 8.8.8.8.8.9.

FRENCH MISSAL,
MELODY OF THE 13TH CENTURY.

92.

1.

D RAW nigh, draw nigh, Emmanuel,
And ransom captive Israel,
That mourns in lonely exile here
Until the Son of God appear.
Rejoice! rejoice! Emmanuel
Shall be born for thee, O Israel!

2.

Draw nigh, draw nigh, O David's Key, —
The heavenly gate will ope to thee, —
Make safe the way that leads on high,
And close the path to misery.
Rejoice! rejoice! Emmanuel
Shall be born for thee, O Israel!

3.

Draw nigh, draw nigh, O Lord of might,
Who to thy tribe from Sinai's height,
In ancient time didst give the law,
In cloud, and majesty, and awe.
Rejoice! rejoice! Emmanuel
Shall be born for thee, O Israel!

Tr. JOHN MASON NEALE, 1818-1866.

Hymn 93.

BETHLEHEM. 8. 6. 8. 6. 7. 6. 8. 6.　　　　　JOSEPH BARNBY, 1838—1896.

A-MEN.

93.

1.

O LITTLE town of Bethlehem,
How still we see thee lie!
Above thy deep and dreamless sleep
The silent stars go by:
Yet in thy dark streets shineth
The everlasting Light;
The hopes and fears of all the years
Are met in thee to-night.

2.

For Christ is born of Mary,
And gathered all above,
While mortals sleep, the angels keep
Their watch of wondering love.
O morning stars, together
Proclaim the holy birth!
And praises sing to God the King,
And peace to men on earth!

3.

How silently, how silently,
The wondrous gift is given!
So God imparts to human hearts
The blessings of his heaven.
No ear may hear his coming,
But in this world of sin,
Where meek souls will receive him, still
The dear Christ enters in.

4.

O holy Child of Bethlehem,
Descend to us, we pray,
Cast out our sin, and enter in,
Be born in us to-day!
We hear the Christmas angels
The great glad tidings tell;
O come to us, abide with us,
Our Lord Emmanuel!

PHILLIPS BROOKS, 1835-1893.

HYMN 94.

First Tune.

SEARS. C. M. D.

JOHN BACCHUS DYKES, 1823—1876.

To hear the an - gels sing. A-MEN.

To hear . . . . the an - gels sing.

94.

1.

IT came upon the midnight clear,
  That glorious song of old,
From angels bending near the earth
  To touch their harps of gold:
"Peace on the earth, good-will to men,
  From heaven's all-gracious King."
The world in solemn stillness lay
  To hear the angels sing.

2.

Still through the cloven skies they come,
  With peaceful wings unfurled,
And still their heavenly music floats
  O'er all the weary world;
Above its sad and lowly plains
  They bend on hovering wing,
And ever o'er its Babel sounds
  The blessed angels sing.

3.

And ye, beneath life's crushing load
  Whose forms are bending low,
Who toil along the climbing way,
  With painful steps and slow, —
Look now, for glad and golden hours
  Come swiftly on the wing:
O, rest beside the weary road,
  And hear the angels sing!

4.

For lo! the days are hastening on
  By prophet bards foretold,
When with the ever-circling years
  Comes round the age of gold,
When Peace shall over all the earth
  Its ancient splendors fling,
And the whole world give back the song
  Which now the angels sing.

EDMUND HAMILTON SEARS, 1810-1876.

HYMN 94.

Second Tune.

ANGELS' SONG. C. M. D.   FELIX MENDELSSOHN-BARTHOLDY, 1809—1847.

A-MEN.

94.

1.

IT came upon the midnight clear,
　That glorious song of old,
From angels bending near the earth
　To touch their harps of gold:
"Peace on the earth, good-will to men,
　From heaven's all-gracious King."
The world in solemn stillness lay
　To hear the angels sing.

2.

Still through the cloven skies they come,
　With peaceful wings unfurled,
And still their heavenly music floats
　O'er all the weary world;
Above its sad and lowly plains
　They bend on hovering wing,
And ever o'er its Babel sounds
　The blessed angels sing.

3.

And ye, beneath life's crushing load
　Whose forms are bending low,
Who toil along the climbing way,
　With painful steps and slow, —
Look now, for glad and golden hours
　Come swiftly on the wing:
O, rest beside the weary road,
　And hear the angels sing!

4.

For lo! the days are hastening on
　By prophet bards foretold,
When with the ever-circling years
　Comes round the age of gold,
When Peace shall over all the earth
　Its ancient splendors fling,
And the whole world give back the song
　Which now the angels sing.

EDMUND HAMILTON SEARS, 1810-1876

HYMN 95.

ST. AGNES. C. M.   JOHN BACCHUS DYKES, 1823—1876.

A · MEN.

1.

CALM on the listening ear of night
   Come heaven's melodious strains,
Where wild Judea stretches forth
   Her silver-mantled plains.

2.

Celestial choirs. from courts above,
   Shed sacred glories there,
And angels, with their sparkling lyres,
   Make music on the air.

3.

The answering hills of Palestine
   Send back the glad reply,
And greet, from all their holy heights,
   The day-spring from on high.

4.

O'er the blue depths of Galilee
   There comes a holier calm,
And Sharon waves, in solemn praise,
   Her silent groves of palm.

5.

" Glory to God," the sounding skies
   Loud with their anthems ring,
" Peace on the earth, good-will to men,
   From heaven's eternal King ! "

6.

Light on thy hills, Jerusalem !
   The Saviour now is born ;
And bright, on Bethlehem's joyous plains,
   Breaks the first Christmas morn.

EDMUND HAMILTON SEARS, 1810-1876.

HYMN 96.

ANGELUS. L. M.

GEORG JOSEPHI, *circa* 1657.

A · MEN.

1.

A̲T even, ere the sun was set,
　The sick, O Lord, around thee lay ;
O, in what divers pains they met !
　O, with what joy they went away !

2.

Once more 't is eventide, and we
　Oppressed with various ills draw near :
What if thy form we cannot see ?
　We know and feel that thou art here.

3.

O Saviour Christ, our woes dispel ;
　For some are sick, and some are sad,
And some have never loved thee well,
　And some have lost the love they had,

4.

And none, O Lord, have perfect rest,
　For none are wholly free from sin ;
And they who fain would serve thee best
　Are conscious most of wrong within.

5.

Thy touch has still its ancient power.
　No word from thee can fruitless fall ;
Hear, in this solemn evening hour.
　And in thy mercy heal us all.

HENRY TWELLS, 1823-

HYMN 97.

STANLEY. 7. 8. 8. 8. 8. 8. 8. 8.   JOHN GOSS, 1800 — 1880.

A - MEN.

97.

1.

MASTER! it is good to be
High on the mountain here with thee,
Where stand revealed to mortal gaze
The great old saints of other days,
Who once received on Horeb's height
The eternal laws of truth and right,
Or caught the still small whisper, higher
Than storm, than earthquake, or than fire.

2.

Master! it is good to be
With thee and with thy faithful three,
Here, where the apostle's heart of rock
Is nerved against temptation's shock,
Here, where the son of thunder learns
The thought that breathes, the word that burns;
Here, where on eagle's wings we move
With him whose last, best creed is love.

3.

Master! it is good to be
Entranced, enwrapt, alone with thee, —
Watching the glistering raiment glow,
Whiter than Hermon's whitest snow,
The human lineaments that shine
Irradiant with a light divine,
Till we too change from grace to grace
Gazing on that transfigured face.

4.

Master! it is good to be
Here on the holy mount with thee,
When, darkling in the depths of night,
When, dazzled with excess of light,
We bow before the heavenly voice
That bids bewildered souls rejoice,
Though love wax cold, and faith be dim —
"This is my Son — O hear ye him!"

ARTHUR PENRHYN STANLEY, 1815-1881.

HYMN 98.

INTERCESSION. L. M.   Arranged by JOHN BACCHUS DYKES, 1823—1876.

A - MEN.

1.

HOW sweetly flowed the gospel's sound
  From lips of gentleness and grace,
When listening thousands gathered round,
  And joy and reverence filled the place.

2.

From heaven he came, of heaven he spoke,
  To heaven he led his followers' way ;
Dark clouds of gloomy night he broke,
  Unveiling an immortal day.

3.

"Come, wanderers, to my Father's home,
  Come, all ye weary ones, and rest ! "
Yes, sacred Teacher, we will come,
  Obey thee, love thee, and be blest.

JOHN BOWRING, 1792-1872.

HYMN 99.

LABAN. S. M.   LOWELL MASON, 1792—1872.

A-MEN.

1.

A VOICE by Jordan's shore,
  A summons stern and clear :
Repent, be just, and sin no more ;
  God's judgment draweth near.

2.

A voice by Galilee,
  A holier voice I hear :
Love God, thy neighbor love ; for see,
  God's mercy draweth near.

3.

O voice of duty, still
  Speak forth, I hear with awe ;
In thee I own the sovereign will,
  Obey the sovereign law.

4.

Thou higher voice of love,
  Yet speak thy word in me ;
Through duty let me upward move
  To thy pure liberty.

SAMUEL LONGFELLOW, 1819-1892.

HYMN 100.

ST. AMBROSE. 6. 6. 4. 6. 6. 6. 4.   WILLIAM HENRY MONK, 1823—1889.

A - MEN.

100.

1.

MY faith looks up to thee,
Thou Lamb of Calvary,
Saviour divine !
Now hear me while I pray,
Take all my guilt away,
O let me from this day
Be wholly thine !

2.

May thy rich grace impart
Strength to my fainting heart,
My zeal inspire !
As thou hast died for me,
O may my love to thee
Pure, warm, and changeless be, —
A living fire !

3.

While life's dark maze I tread,
And griefs around me spread,
Be thou my guide ;
Bid darkness turn to day,
Wipe sorrow's tears away,
Nor let me ever stray
From thee aside.

4.

When ends life's transient dream,
When death's cold, sullen stream
Shall o'er me roll,
Blest Saviour, then, in love,
Fear and distrust remove !
O bear me safe above, —
A ransomed soul !

RAY PALMER, 1808-1887.

Hymn 101.

DAY OF REST. 7. 6. 7. 6. 7. 6. 7. 6.   James William Elliott, 1833—

101.

1.

O JESUS, I have promised
　　To serve thee to the end;
Be thou forever near me,
　My Master and my Friend!
I shall not fear the battle
　If thou art by my side,
Nor wander from the pathway,
　If thou wilt be my Guide.

2.

O, let me hear thee speaking
　In accents clear and still,
Above the storms of passion,
　The murmurs of self-will!
O, speak to reassure me,
　To hasten or control!
O, speak, and make me listen,
　Thou Guardian of my soul!

3.

O Jesus, thou hast promised
　To all who follow thee
That where thou art in glory
　There shall thy servant be;
And, Jesus, I have promised
　To serve thee to the end, —
O, give me grace to follow
　My Master and my Friend!

JOHN ERNEST BODE, 1816-1874.

HYMN 102.

LUX PRIMA. 7.7.7.7.7.7.   CHARLES FRANÇOIS GOUNOD, 1818—1893.

A - MEN.

102.

1.

CHRIST, whose glory fills the skies,
   Christ, the true, the only light,
Sun of Righteousness, arise !
   Triumph o'er the shades of night !
Day-spring from on high, be near !
Day-star, in my heart appear !

2.

Dark and cheerless is the morn,
   Unaccompanied by thee ;
Joyless is the day's return
   Till thy mercy's beams I see,
Till they inward light impart,
Glad my eyes, and warm my heart.

3.

Visit, then, this soul of mine,
   Pierce the gloom of sin and grief,
Fill me, Radiancy divine,
   Scatter all my unbelief,
More and more thyself display,
Shining to the perfect day !

CHARLES WESLEY, 1708-1788.

HYMN 103.

HOLLINGSIDE. 7.7.7.7.7.7.7.7.   JOHN BACCHUS DYKES, 1823—1876.

A · MEN.

103.

1.

JESUS, lover of my soul,
  Let me to thy bosom fly,
While the nearer waters roll,
  While the tempest still is high:
Hide me, O my Saviour, hide
  Till the storm of life is past,
Safe into the haven guide,
  O, receive my soul at last!

2.

Other refuge have I none,
  Hangs my helpless soul on thee;
Leave, ah, leave me not alone,
  Still support and comfort me:
All my trust on thee is stayed,
  All my help from thee I bring;
Cover my defenceless head
  With the shadow of thy wing.

3.

Plenteous grace with thee is found,
  Grace to cover all my sin;
Let the healing streams abound,
  Make and keep me pure within:
Thou of life the fountain art;
  Freely let me take of thee,
Spring thou up within my heart,
  Rise to all eternity!

CHARLES WESLEY, 1708-1788.

Hymn 104.

ST. BEES. 7.7.7.7.   JOHN BACCHUS DYKES, 1823—1876.

A-MEN.

1.

COME, said Jesus' sacred voice,
    Come, and make my paths your
       choice !
I will guide you to your home :
Weary pilgrim, hither come !

2.

Thou who, houseless, sole, forlorn,
Long hast borne the proud world's scorn,
Long hast roamed the barren waste,
Weary pilgrim, hither haste !

3.

Ye who, tossed on beds of pain,
Seek for ease but seek in vain,
Ye whose swoln and sleepless eyes
Watch to see the morning rise,

4.

Sinner, come ! for here is found
Balm that flows for every wound,
Peace that ever shall endure,
Rest eternal, sacred, sure.

ANNA LAETITIA BARBAULD, 1743-1825

HYMN 105.

First Tune.

ST. ANNE. C. M.

WILLIAM CROFT, 1678 — 1727.

A-MEN

1.

THE Son of God goes forth to war,
  A kingly crown to gain ;
His blood-red banner streams afar :
  Who follows in his train?

2.

Who best can drink his cup of woe,
  Triumphant over pain.
Who patient bears his cross below. —
  He follows in his train.

3.

The martyr first, whose eagle eye
  Could pierce beyond the grave.
Who saw his master in the sky,
  And called on him to save.

4.

Like him, with pardon on his tongue
  In midst of mortal pain,
He prayed for them that did the wrong :
  Who follows in his train?

5.

A noble army, men and boys,
  The matron and the maid,
Around the Saviour's throne rejoice,
  In robes of light arrayed

6.

They climbed the steep ascent of heaven
  Through peril, toil, and pain ;
O God ! to us may grace be given
  To follow in their train !

REGINALD HEBER, 1783-1826.

HYMN 105.

Second Tune.

ALL SAINTS. C. M. D.

HENRY STEPHEN CUTLER, 1825—

A-MEN.

105.

1.

THE Son of God goes forth to war,
   A kingly crown to gain;
His blood-red banner streams afar:
   Who follows in his train?

Who best can drink his cup of woe,
   Triumphant over pain,
Who patient bears his cross below, —
   He follows in his train.

2.

The martyr first, whose eagle eye
   Could pierce beyond the grave,
Who saw his master in the sky,
   And called on him to save.

Like him, with pardon on his tongue
   In midst of mortal pain,
He prayed for them that did the wrong:
   Who follows in his train?

3.

A noble army, men and boys,
   The matron and the maid,
Around the Saviour's throne rejoice,
   In robes of light arrayed.

They climbed the steep ascent of heaven
   Through peril, toil, and pain;
O God! to us may grace be given
   To follow in their train!

REGINALD HEBER, 1783-1826.

HYMN 106.

INNOCENTS. 7.7.7.7.

A-MEN.

1.

Songs of praise the angels sang,
    Heaven with alleluias rang,
When Jehovah's work begun,
When he spake and it was done.

2.

Songs of praise awoke the morn
When the prince of peace was born ;
Songs of praise arose when he
Captive led captivity.

3.

Heaven and earth must pass away ;
Songs of praise shall crown that day :
God will make new heavens, new earth ;
Songs of praise shall hail their birth.

4.

Saints below, with heart and voice,
Still in songs of praise rejoice,
Learning here, by faith and love,
Songs of praise to sing above.

JAMES MONTGOMERY, 1771-1854.

Hymn 107.

LOVE DIVINE. 8.7.8.7.　　　　　　　　　　　　JOHN STAINER, 1840—

A · MEN.

1.

LOVE divine, all loves excelling,
　Joy of heaven to earth come down,
Fix in us thy humble dwelling,
　All thy faithful mercies crown.

2.

Jesus, thou art all compassion,
　Pure, unbounded love thou art ;
Visit us with thy salvation,
　Enter every trembling heart.

3.

Breathe, O, breathe thy loving spirit
　Into every troubled breast ;
Let us all in thee inherit,
　Let us find that second rest.

4.

Come, almighty to deliver,
　Let us all thy life receive ;
Suddenly return, and never,
　Never more thy temples leave.

CHARLES WESLEY, 1708-1788

Hymn 108.

FAITH. C. M.

JOHN BACCHUS DYKES, 1823—1876.

A · MEN.

1.

O LORD and Master of us all,
    Whate'er our name or sign,
We own thy sway, we hear thy call,
    We test our lives by thine.

2.

Our thoughts lie open to thy sight;
    And, naked to thy glance,
Our secret sins are in the light
    Of thy pure countenance.

3.

To thee our full humanity,
    Its joys and pains belong;
The wrong of man to man on thee
    Inflicts a deeper wrong.

4.

Who hates hates thee, who loves becomes
    Therein to thee allied;
All sweet accords of hearts and homes
    In thee are multiplied.

5.

Deep strike thy roots, O heavenly Vine,
    Within our earthly sod,
Most human and yet most divine,
    The flower of man and God!

JOHN GREENLEAF WHITTIER, 1807-1892.

Hymn 109.

ROCKINGHAM. L. M. EDWARD MILLER, 1731 — 1807.

A · MEN.

1.

M^Y dear Redeemer and my Lord,
   I read my duty in thy word ;
But in thy life the law appears,
Drawn out in living characters.

2.

Such was thy truth, and such thy zeal,
Such deference to thy Father's will,
Such love and meekness so divine, —
I would transcribe, and make them mine.

3.

Cold mountains and the midnight air
Witnessed the fervor of thy prayer ;
The desert thy temptations knew,
Thy conflict and thy victory too.

4.

Be thou my pattern ! make me bear
More of thy gracious image here !
Then God, the Judge, shall own my name
Amongst the followers of the Lamb.

ISAAC WATTS, 1674-1748

Hymn 110.

HORSLEY. C. M.   William Horsley, 1774—1858.

A-MEN.

1.

O UR Father ! while our hearts unlearn
    The creeds that wrong thy name,
Still let our hallowed altars burn
    With faith's undying flame.

2.

Not by the lightning-gleams of wrath
    Our souls thy face shall see ;
The star of love must light the path
    That leads to heaven and thee.

3.

Help us to read our Master's will
    Through every darkening stain
That clouds his sacred image still,
    And see him once again,

4.

The brother man, the pitying friend,
    Who weeps for human woes,
Whose pleading words of pardon blend
    With cries of raging foes.

5.

If 'mid the gathering storms of doubt
    Our hearts grow faint and cold,
The strength we cannot live without
    Thy love will not withhold.

6.

Our prayers accept ; our sins forgive ;
    Our youthful zeal renew ;
Shape for us holier lives to live,
    And nobler work to do.

OLIVER WENDELL HOLMES, 1809-1894.

HYMN III.

A-MEN.

1.

O MASTER, let me walk with thee
  In lowly paths of service free,
Tell me thy secret, help me bear
The strain of toil, the fret of care.

2.

Help me the slow of heart to move
By some clear, winning word of love,
Teach me the wayward feet to stay,
And guide them in the homeward way.

3.

Teach me thy patience. Still with thee
In closer, dearer company,
In work that keeps faith sweet and strong,
In trust that triumphs over wrong,

4.

In hope that sends a shining ray
Far down the future's broadening way,
In peace that only thou canst give,
With thee, O Master, let me live.

WASHINGTON GLADDEN, 1836–   .

HYMN 112.

LANGRAN. 10. 10. 10. 10.   JAMES LANGRAN, 1835—

A · MEN.

112.

O THOU great Friend to all the sons of men,
   Who once appeared in humblest guise below,
Sin to rebuke, to break the captive's chain,
   To call thy brethren forth from want and woe, —

2.

Thee would I sing: thy truth is still the light
   Which guides the nations, groping on their way,
Stumbling and falling in disastrous night,
   Yet hoping ever for the perfect day.

3.

Yes: thou art still the life; thou art the way
   The holiest know, — light, life, and way of heaven;
And they who dearest hope and deepest pray,
   Toil by the truth, life, way, that thou hast given.

THEODORE PARKER, 1810–1860.

Hymn 113.

WEBER. 7.7.7.7.   CARL MARIA VON WEBER, 1786—1826.

A · MEN.

1.

FEEBLE, helpless, how shall I
   Learn to live, and learn to die?
Who, O God, my guide shall be?
Who shall lead thy child to thee?

2.

Heavenly Father, gracious one,
Thou hast sent thy blessed Son:
He will give the light I need,
He my trembling steps will lead.

3.

Through this world, uncertain, dim,
Let me ever learn of him,
From his precepts wisdom draw,
Make his life my solemn law.

4.

Thus in deed and thought and word,
Led by Jesus Christ the Lord,
In my weakness, thus shall I
Learn to live, and learn to die, —

5.

Learn to live in peace and love,
Like the perfect ones above;
Learn to die without a fear,
Knowing thee, my Father, near.

WILLIAM HENRY FURNESS. 1802-1896.

HYMN 114.

FAITH. C. M.   JOHN BACCHUS DYKES, 1823—1876.

A · MEN

1.

O LOVE ! O Life ! our faith and sight
   Thy presence maketh one.
As, through transfigured clouds of white,
   We trace the noon-day sun,

2.

So, to our mortal eyes subdued,
   Flesh-veiled but not concealed,
We know in thee the fatherhood
   And heart of God revealed.

3.

We faintly hear, we dimly see,
   In differing phrase we pray ;
But, dim or clear, we own in thee
   The light, the truth, the way.

4.

Our Friend, our Brother, and our Lord,
   What may thy service be ?
Nor name, nor form, nor ritual word,
   But simply following thee.

JOHN GREENLEAF WHITTIER, 1807–1892

HYMN 115.

PASSION CHORAL. 7.6.7.6.7.6.7.6.   HANS LEO HASSLER, 1564—1612.

A-MEN.

115.

1.

O SACRED head, now wounded,
   With grief and shame weighed down,
Now scornfully surrounded
   With thorns, thy only crown, —
How art thou pale with anguish,
   With sore abuse and scorn !
How does that visage languish
   Which once was bright as morn !

2.

What language shall I borrow
   To thank thee, dearest friend,
For this thy dying sorrow,
   Thy pity without end ?
O, make me thine forever !
   And, should I fainting be,
Lord, let me never, never,
   Outlive my love to thee !

3.

Be near me when I 'm dying,
   O, show thy cross to me !
And for my succor flying,
   Come, Lord, and set me free !
These eyes new faith receiving,
   From Jesus shall not move ;
For he who dies believing
   Dies safely through thy love.

BERNARD OF CLAIRVAUX, 1091-1153.
Tr. PAULUS GERHARDT, 1607-1676.
Tr. JAMES WADDELL ALEXANDER, 1804-1859.

Hymn 116.

LANCASHIRE. 7.6.7.6.7.6.7.6.　　　　　　　　　　HENRY SMART, 1813 — 1879.

A·MEN.

116.

1.

'TIS the day of resurrection, —
  Earth, tell it out abroad, —
The passover of gladness,
  The passover of God.
From death to life eternal,
  From this world to the sky,
Our Christ hath brought us over
  With hymns of victory.

2.

Our hearts be pure from evil,
  That we may see aright
The Lord in rays eternal
  Of resurrection-light,
And, listening to his accents,
  May hear, so calm and plain,
His own " All hail ! " and, hearing,
  May raise the victor-strain.

3.

Now let the heavens be joyful,
  Let earth her song begin,
Let the round world keep triumph
  And all that is therein,
Invisible and visible,
  Their notes let all things blend ;
For Christ the Lord hath risen,
  Our joy that hath no end.

SAINT JOHN OF DAMASCUS, *circa* 780.
Tr. JOHN MASON NEALE, 1818-1866.

Hymn 117.

JESUS, MEINE ZUVERSICHT. 7. 8. 7. 8. 7. 7.   Johann Crüger, 1598 — 1662.

A - MEN.

117.

1.

JESUS CHRIST, my sure defence
  And my Saviour, ever liveth.
Knowing this, my confidence
  Rests upon the hope it giveth,
Though the night of death be fraught
Still with many an anxious thought.

2.

Jesus, my Redeemer, lives;
  I too unto life must waken.
He will have me where he is:
  Shall my courage, then, be shaken?
Shall I fear? Or could the head
Rise and leave its members dead?

3.

Nay, too closely am I bound
  Unto him by hope forever;
Faith's strong hand the rock hath found,
  Grasped it, and will leave it never:
Not the ban of death can part
From its Lord the trusting heart.

LUISE HENRIETTE VON BRANDENBURG, 1627-1667.
Tr. CATHERINE WINKWORTH, 1829-1878.

HYMN 118.

WORGAN. 7. 4. 7. 4. 7. 4. 7. 4.   LYRA DAVIDICA, 1708.

A - MEN.

118.

1.

CHRIST the Lord is risen to-day,
> Alleluia !
Sons of men and angels say
> Alleluia !
Raise your joys and triumphs high,
> Alleluia !
Sing, ye heavens, and earth reply,
> Alleluia !

2.

Soar we now where Christ has led,
> Alleluia !
Following our exalted head,
> Alleluia !
Made like him, like him we rise,
> Alleluia !
Ours the cross, the grave, the skies !
> Alleluia !

CHARLES WESLEY, 1708-1788

HYMN 119.

ST. OSWALD. 8.7.8.7.   JOHN BACCHUS DYKES, 1823 — 1876.

A · MEN.

1.

IN the cross of Christ I glory,
　Towering o'er the wrecks of time ;
All the light of sacred story
　Gathers round its head sublime.

2.

When the woes of life o'ertake me,
　Hopes deceive, and fears annoy,
Never shall the cross forsake me ;
　Lo ! it glows with peace and joy.

3.

When the sun of bliss is beaming
　Light and love upon my way,
From the cross the radiance streaming
　Adds more lustre to the day.

4.

Bane and blessing, pain and pleasure,
　By the cross are sanctified ;
Peace is there that knows no measure,
　Joys that through all time abide.

JOHN BOWRING, 1792-1872.

Hymn 120.

STUTTGART. 8.7.8.7.   New Gotha Cantional, 1715.

A · MEN.

1.

HEAR what God, the Lord, hath spoken :
  O my people, faint and few,
Comfortless, afflicted, broken,
  Fair abodes I build for you.

2.

Themes of heart-felt tribulation
  Shall no more perplex your ways :
You shall name your walls "Salvation,"
  And your gates shall all be "Praise."

3.

Ye, no more your suns descending,
  Waning moons no more, shall see ;
But your griefs, forever ending,
  Find eternal noon in me.

4.

God shall rise, and, shining o'er you,
  Change to day the gloom of night :
He, the Lord, shall be your glory,
  God your everlasting light.

WILLIAM COWPER, 1731-1800.

HYMN 121.

SCOTTISH PSALTER, 1635.
JOHN PLAYFORD'S PSALTER, 1671.

A-MEN.

1.

IMMORTAL by their deed and word,
Like light around them shed,
Still speak the prophets of the Lord,
Still live the sainted dead.

2.

The voice of old by Jordan's flood
Yet floats upon the air ;
We hear it in beatitude,
In parable, and prayer.

3.

And still the beauty of that life
Shines star-like on our way,
And breathes its calm amid the strife
And burden of to-day.

4.

Earnest of life forevermore,
That life of duty here, —
The trust that in the darkest hour
Looked forth and knew no fear !

5.

Spirit of Jesus, still speed on !
Speed on thy conquering way
Till every heart the Father own,
And all his will obey !

FREDERICK LUCIAN HOSMER, 1840—

HYMN 122.

ST. CUTHBERT. 8.6.8.4.   JOHN BACCHUS DYKES, 1823 — 1876.

A - MEN.

1.

OUR blest Redeemer, ere he breathed
　His tender, last farewell,
A guide, a comforter, bequeathed
　With us to dwell.

2.

He came sweet influence to impart,
　A gracious, willing guest,
While he can find one humble heart
　Wherein to rest.

3.

And his that gentle voice we hear,
　Soft as the breath of even,
That checks each fault, that calms
　　each fear,
And speaks of heaven.

4.

And every virtue we possess,
　And every victory won,
And every thought of holiness,
　Are his alone.

5.

Spirit of purity and grace,
　Our weakness pitying see ;
O make our hearts thy dwelling place,
　And worthier thee !

HARRIET AUBER, 1773-1862.

HYMN 123.

HUMMEL. C. M.   HEINRICH CHRISTOPH ZEUNER, 1795 — 1857.

A - MEN.

1.

CITY of God, how broad and far
  Outspread thy walls sublime !
The true thy chartered freemen are,
  Of every age and clime.

2.

One holy Church, one army strong,
  One steadfast high intent,
One working band, one harvest-song,
  One King omnipotent !

3.

How purely hath thy speech come down
  From man's primeval youth !
How grandly hath thine empire grown
  Of freedom, love, and truth !

4.

How gleam thy watch-fires through the
    night,
  With never fainting ray !
How rise thy towers, serene and bright,
  To meet the dawning day !

5.

In vain the surge's angry shock,
  In vain the drifting sands ;
Unharmed upon the eternal rock,
  The eternal city stands.

SAMUEL JOHNSON, 1822-1882.

Hymn 124.

ST. STEPHEN. C. M.   WILLIAM JONES, 1726—1800.

A·MEN.

1.

ONE holy Church of God appears
   Through every age and race,
Unwasted by the lapse of years,
   Unchanged by changing place.

2.

From oldest time, on farthest shores,
   Beneath the pine or palm,
One unseen presence she adores,
   With silence or with psalm.

3.

Her priests are all God's faithful sons,
   To serve the world raised up;
The pure in heart, her baptized ones;
   Love, her communion-cup.

4.

The truth is her prophetic gift,
   The soul her sacred page;
And feet on mercy's errands swift
   Do make her pilgrimage.

5.

O living Church, thine errand speed,
   Fulfil thy task sublime,
With bread of life earth's hunger feed,
   Redeem the evil time !

SAMUEL LONGFELLOW, 1819-1892.

HYMN 125.

AUSTRIA. 8. 7. 8. 7. 8. 7. 8. 7.   Franz Joseph Haydn, 1732 — 1809.

A·MEN.

125.

1.

GLORIOUS things of thee are spoken,
   Zion, city of our God!
He, whose word cannot be broken,
   Formed thee for his own abode.
On the rock of ages founded,
   What can shake thy sure repose?
With salvation's walls surrounded,
   Thou mayest smile at all thy foes.

2.

See! the streams of living waters,
   Springing from eternal love,
Well supply thy sons and daughters,
   And all fear of want remove.
Who can faint while such a river
   Ever flows their thirst to assuage, —
Grace, which, like the Lord the giver,
   Never fails from age to age?

JOHN NEWTON, 1725-1807.

HYMN 126.

SOUTHWELL. C. M.   HERBERT STEPHEN IRONS, 1834 —

A-MEN.

1.

O LORD of life and truth and grace
    Ere nature was begun,
Make welcome to our erring race
    Thy Spirit and thy Son.

2.

We hail the Church, built high o'er all
    The heathens' rage and scoff, —
Thy providence its fencèd wall,
    " The Lamb the light thereof."

3.

Thy Christ hath reached his heavenly seat,
    Through sorrows and through scars ;
The golden lamps are at his feet,
    And in his hand the stars.

4.

O, may he walk among us here
    With his rebuke and love, —
A brightness o'er this lower sphere,
    A ray from worlds above !

. NATHANIEL LANGDON FROTHINGHAM, 1793-1870.

HYMN 127.

ST. PHILIP. S. M. EDWARD JOHN HOPKINS, 1818 — .

A - MEN.

1.

COME, kingdom of our God,
    Sweet reign of light and love,
Shed peace, and hope, and joy abroad,
    And wisdom from above.

3.

Come, kingdom of our God,
    And make the broad earth thine,
Stretch o'er her lands and isles the rod
    That flowers with grace divine.

2.

Over our spirits first
    Extend thy healing reign;
There raise and quench the sacred thirst
    That never pains again.

4.

Soon may all tribes be blest
    With fruit from life's glad tree,
And in its shade like brothers rest,
    Sons of one family.

JOHN JOHNS, 1801-1847.

Hymn 128.

DUKE STREET. L. M.

JOHN HATTON,　—1793.

A-MEN.

1.

JESUS shall reign where'er the sun
　Does his successive journeys run,
His kingdom stretch from shore to shore
Till moons shall wax and wane no more.

2.

People and realms of every tongue
Dwell on his love with sweetest song,
And infant voices shall proclaim
Their early blessings on his name.

3.

Blessings abound where'er he reigns ;
The prisoner leaps to lose his chains,
The weary find eternal rest,
And all the sons of want are blest.

4.

Let every creature rise, and bring
Peculiar honors to our King,
Angels descend with songs again,
And earth repeat the loud Amen !

ISAAC WATTS, 1674-1748.

HYMN 129.

CHRISTOPHER TYE, 1508 — 1572.
THOMAS ESTE'S PSALTER, 1592.

WINCHESTER OLD. C. M.

A · MEN.

1.

WHEN God of old came down
   from heaven,
In power and wrath he came ;
Before his feet the clouds were riven,
   Half darkness and half flame :

2.

So, when the Spirit of our God
   Came down his flock to find,
A voice from heaven was heard abroad,
   A rushing, mighty wind.

3.

It fills the Church of God, it fills
   The sinful world around ;
Only in stubborn hearts and wills
   No place for it is found.

4.

Come, Lord, come Wisdom, Love, and
   Power,
   Open our ears to hear,
Let us not miss the accepted hour,
   Save, Lord, by love or fear !

JOHN KEBLE, 1792-1866.

HYMN 130.

DUNFERMLINE. C. M.   SCOTTISH PSALTER, 1615.

A · MEN.

1.

R ISE, God ! judge thou the earth in
     might,
  This wicked earth redress !
For thou art he who shall by right
  The nations all possess.

2.

Before him righteousness shall go,
  His royal harbinger.
Then will he come, and not be slow ;
  His footsteps cannot err.

3.

Truth from the earth, like to a flower,
  Shall bud and blossom then,
And justice, from her heavenly bower,
  Look down on mortal men.

4.

The nations all whom thou hast made
  Shall come, and all shall frame
To bow them low before thee, Lord,
  And glorify thy name.

5.

For great thou art, and wonders great
  By thy strong hand are done :
Thou, in thy everlasting seat,
  Remainest God alone.

JOHN MILTON, 1608-1674.

HYMN 131.

ST. CECILIA. 6. 6. 6. 6.   LEIGHTON GEORGE HAYNE, 1836 — 1883.

A · MEN.

1.

THY kingdom come, O God !
   Thy rule, O Christ, begin !
Break with thine iron rod
   The tyrannies of sin !

2.

Where is thy reign of peace,
   And purity, and love?
When shall all hatred cease,
   As in the realms above?

3.

When comes the promised time
   That war shall be no more,
Oppression, lust, and crime
   Shall flee thy face before?

4.

We pray thee, Lord, arise
   And come in thy great might ,
Revive our longing eyes,
   Which languish for thy sight.

5.

O'er heathen lands afar
   Thick darkness broodeth yet :
Arise, O morning star, —
   Arise, and never set !

LEWIS HENSLEY, 1827 –

Hymn 132.

WALTHAM. 6.6.6.6.6.6.   William Henry Monk, 1823—1889.

A-MEN.

132.

1.

O THOU not made with hands,
 Not throned above the skies,
Nor walled with shining walls,
 Nor framed with stones of price,
More bright than gold or gem,
God's own Jerusalem !

2.

Where'er the gentle heart
 Finds courage from above,
Where'er the heart forsook
 Warms with the breath of love,
Where faith bids fear depart,
City of God, thou art.

3.

Where in life's common ways
 With cheerful feet we go,
When in his steps we tread
 Who trod the way of woe,
Where he is in the heart,
City of God, thou art.

4.

Not throned above the skies,
 Nor golden-walled afar,
But where Christ's two or three
 In his name gathered are,
Be in the midst of them,
God's own Jerusalem.

Francis Turner Palgrave, 1824–

HYMN 133.

HAMBURG. L. M.   LOWELL MASON, 1792—1872.

A-MEN.

1.

YET sometimes glimpses on my sight
 Through present wrong the eternal
  right ;
And step by step, since time began,
I see the steady gain of man,—

2.

That all of good the past hath had
Remains to make our own time glad,
Our common, daily life divine,
And every land a Palestine.

3.

Through the harsh noises of our day
A low, sweet prelude finds its way ;
Through clouds of doubt and creeds of
 fear
A light is breaking calm and clear.

4.

Henceforth my heart shall sigh no more
For olden time and holier shore :
God's love and blessing, then and there,
Are now and here and everywhere.

JOHN GREENLEAF WHITTIER, 1807–1892.

HYMN 134.

ELY. L. M.　　　　　　　　　　　　　　THOMAS TURTON, 1780—1864.

A-MEN.

1.

THE past is dark with sin and shame,
　The future dim with doubt and fear ;
But, Father, yet we praise thy name,
　Whose guardian love is always near.

2.

For man has striven, ages long,
　With faltering steps, to come to thee ;
And, in each purpose high and strong,
　The influence of thy grace could see.

3.

He could not breathe an earnest prayer
　But thou wast kinder than he dreamed,
As age by age brought hopes more fair,
　And nearer still thy kingdom seemed.

4.

But never rose within his breast
　A trust so calm and deep as now :
Shall not the weary find a rest ?
　Father, Preserver, answer thou !

5.

'Tis dark around, 'tis dark above,
　But through the shadow streams the sun ;
We cannot doubt thy certain love ;
　And man's true aim shall yet be won !

THOMAS WENTWORTH HIGGINSON, 1823—

Hymn 135.

LÜBECK. 7.7.7.7.   Johann Anastasius Freylinghausen, 1670—1739.

A·MEN.

1.

FATHER, let thy kingdom come, —
　Let it come with living power,
Speak at length the final word,
　Usher in the triumph-hour.

2.

As it came in days of old,
　In the deepest hearts of men,
When thy martyrs died for thee,
　Let it come, O God, again.

3.

Tyrant thrones and idol shrines,
　Let them from their place be hurled.
Enter on thy better reign,
　Wear the crown of this poor world.

4.

O what long, sad years have gone
　Since thy Church was taught this prayer!
O what eyes have watched and wept
　For the dawning everywhere!

5.

Break, triumphant day of God,
　Break at last, our hearts to cheer!
Eager souls and earnest songs
　Wait to hail thy dawning here.

6.

Empires, temples, sceptres, thrones, —
　May they all for God be won;
And on earth made one with heaven
　Father, may thy will be done.

John Page Hopps, 1834—   .

HYMN 136.

FERNSHAW. C. M.

JOSIAH BOOTH, 1852—

A - MEN.

1.

THY kingdom come, on bended
   knee
  The passing ages pray,
And faithful souls have yearned to see
  On earth that kingdom's day.

2.

But the slow watches of the night
  Not less to God belong,
And for the everlasting right
  The silent stars are strong.

3.

And lo ! already on the hills
  The flags of dawn appear;
Gird up your loins, ye prophet souls,
  Proclaim the day is near, —

4.

The day in whose clear-shining light
  All wrong shall stand revealed,
When justice shall be throned in might,
  And every hurt be healed,

5.

When knowledge hand in hand with peace
  Shall walk the earth abroad, —
The day of perfect righteousness,
  The promised day of God.

FREDERICK LUCIAN HOSMER, 1840— .

Hymn 137.

INTERCESSION. L. M.   Arranged by JOHN BACCHUS DYKES, 1823—1876.

A - MEN.

137.

1.

FATHER, we humbly would repose
    Our souls on thee who dwell'st above,
And bless· thee for the peace which flows
    From faith in thine all-pitying love.

2.

Though every earthly trust may break,
    Infinite might belongs to thee;
Though friends may die and friends forsake,
    Unchangeable thou still wilt be.

3·

Though griefs may gather darkly round,
    They cannot veil us from thy sight;
Though vain all human aid be found,
    Thou every one canst turn to light.

4·

All things thy wise designs fulfil,
    In earth beneath and heaven above;
And good breaks out from every ill,
    Through faith in thine all-pitying love.

WILLIAM GASKELL, 1805–1884.

HYMN 138.

PLEYEL. 7. 7. 7. 7.   IGNAZ JOSEPH PLEYEL, 1757 — 1831.

A - MEN.

1.

DAY by day the manna fell :
   O to learn this lesson well !
Still by constant mercy fed,
Give me, Lord, my daily bread.

2.

Day by day, the promise reads,
Daily strength for daily needs :
Cast foreboding fears away,
Take the manna of to-day.

3.

Lord, my times are in thy hand :
All my sanguine hopes have planned
To thy wisdom I resign,
And would make thy purpose mine.

4.

Thou my daily task shalt give ;
Day by day to thee I live ;
So shall added years fulfil
Not my own, my Father's will.

JOSIAH CONDER, 1789-1855.

Hymn 139.

RIVAULX. L. M.   JOHN BACCHUS DYKES, 1823 — 1876.

A - MEN.

I.

THROUGH all the various shifting
    scene
Of life's mistaken ill or good,
Thy hand, O God, conducts, unseen,
    The beautiful vicissitude.

2.

Thou portion'st with parental care,
    Howe'er unjustly we complain,
To each his necessary share
    Of joy and sorrow, health and pain.

3.

All things on earth and all in heaven
    On thine eternal will depend ;
And all for greater good were given,
    Would man pursue the appointed end.

4.

Be this our care : to all beside
    Indifferent let our wishes be, —
Passion be calm, and dumb be pride,
    And fixed our souls, O God, on thee.

SAMUEL COLLETT, *circa* 1763.

HYMN 140.

MOUNT CALVARY. C. M.   ROBERT PRESCOTT STEWART, 1825—1894.

A·MEN.

1.

O FOR a faith that will not shrink,
   Though pressed by many a foe,
That will not tremble on the brink
   Of poverty or woe,

2.

That will not murmur nor complain
   Beneath the chastening rod,
But, in the hour of grief or pain,
   Can lean upon its God, —

3.

A faith that shines more bright and clear
   When tempests rage without,
That when in danger knows no fear,
   In darkness feels no doubt.

4.

Lord, give me such a faith as this,
   And then, whate'er may come,
I taste e'en now the hallowed bliss
   Of an eternal home.

WILLIAM HILEY BATHURST, 1796–1877

HYMN 141.

TRUST. 8.7.8.7.   FELIX MENDELSSOHN-BARTHOLDY, 1809—1847.

A-MEN.

1.

CALL Jehovah thy salvation,
  Rest beneath the Almighty's shade,
In his secret habitation
  Dwell, nor ever be dismayed.

2.

There no tumult can alarm thee,
  Thou shalt dread no hidden snare,
Guilt nor violence can harm thee
  In eternal safeguard there.

3.

Since, with pure and firm affection,
  Thou on God hast set thy love,
With the wings of his protection
  He will shield thee from above.

4.

Thou shalt call on him in trouble ;
  He will hearken, he will save,
Here for grief reward thee double,
  Crown with life beyond the grave.

JAMES MONTGOMERY, 1771-1854

Hymn 142.

GERMANY. L. M.   Ludwig van Beethoven, 1770—1827.

A · MEN.

142.

1.

WHEN Israel, of the Lord beloved,
  Out of the land of bondage came,
Her fathers' God before her moved,
  An awful guide, in smoke and flame.

2.

By day, along the astonished lands
  The cloudy pillar glided slow;
By night, Arabia's crimsoned sands
  Returned the fiery column's glow.

3.

But present still, though now unseen,
  When brightly shines the prosperous day,
Be thoughts of thee a cloudy screen
  To temper the deceitful ray.

4.

And O, when stoops on Judah's path,
  In shade and storm, the frequent night,
Be thou, long-suffering, slow to wrath,
  A burning and a shining light.

WALTER SCOTT, 1771-1832.

HYMN 143.

LANCASHIRE. 7.6.7.6.7.6.7.6.   HENRY SMART, 1813—1879.

A - MEN.

143.

1.

IN heavenly love abiding,
   No change my heart shall fear;
And safe is such confiding,
   For nothing changes here.
The storm may roar without me,
   My heart may low be laid;
But God is round about me,
   And can I be dismayed?

2.

Wherever he may guide me,
   No want shall turn me back;
My Shepherd is beside me,
   And nothing can I lack.
His wisdom ever waketh,
   His sight is never dim,
He knows the way he taketh,
   And I will walk with him.

3.

Green pastures are before me,
   Which yet I have not seen;
Bright skies will soon be o'er me
   Where the dark clouds have been.
My hope I cannot measure,
   My path to life is free,
My Saviour has my treasure,
   And he will walk with me.

ANNA LAETITIA WARING, 1823-

HYMN 144.

VULPIUS. C. M.

MELCHIOR VULPIUS, 1560—1616.

A · MEN.

1.

UP to those bright and gladsome hills
  Whence flows my weal and mirth
I look, and sigh for him who fills,
  Unseen, both heaven and earth.

2.

He is alone my help and hope
  That I shall not be moved;
His watchful eye is ever ope,
  And guardeth his beloved.

3.

The glorious God is my sole stay,
  He is my sun and shade:
The cold by night, the heat by day,
  Neither shall me invade.

4.

He keeps me from the spite of foes,
  Doth all their plots control,
And is a shield, not reckoning those,
  Unto my very soul.

5.

Whether abroad amidst the crowd,
  Or else within my door,
He is my pillar and my cloud,
  Now and for evermore.

HENRY VAUGHAN, 1621-1695.

Hymn 145.

ST. FULBERT. C. M.   HENRY JOHN GAUNTLETT, 1805 — 1876.

A·MEN.

1.

O NOT alone in saddest plight
  My Lord do I require,
Not only in the thickest fight,
  And in the sevenfold fire.

2.

Not only for some task sublime
  Thy succor I implore;
Not only on some solemn time
  Thy holy spirit pour.

3.

Lord, for each daily task of mine
  I want thy quickening power:
I want thy smile away to shine
  The trouble of each hour.

4.

I want each joy from thee to spring,
  Each joy for thee more bright,
Each footstep of thine ordering,
  All light seen in thy light.

5.

I want thee through the vale of tears,
  All up the heavenly road,
Each moment of the eternal years
  Shall I possess my God.

THOMAS HORNBLOWER GILL, 1819—

HYMN 146.

ANGELUS. L. M.   GEORG JOSEPHI, *circa* 1657.

A - MEN.

1.

NOT always on the mount may we
 Rapt in the heavenly vision be :
The shores of thought and feeling know
The spirit's tidal ebb and flow.

2.

"Lord, it is good abiding here,"
We cry, the heavenly presence near ;
The vision vanishes, our eyes
Are lifted into vacant skies.

3.

Yet hath one such exalted hour
Upon the soul redeeming power,
And in its strength through after days
We travel our appointed ways,

4.

Till all the lowly vale grows bright,
Transfigured in remembered light,
And in untiring souls we bear
The freshness of the upper air.

5.

The mount for vision : but below
The paths of daily duty go,
And nobler life therein shall own
The pattern on the mountain shown.

FREDERICK LUCIAN HOSMER, 1840–   .

Hymn 147.

ST. PETER. C. M.   ALEXANDER ROBERT REINAGLE, 1799 — 1877.

A-MEN.

1.

WHILE thee I seek, protecting
    Power,
  Be my vain wishes stilled,
And may this consecrated hour
  With better hopes be filled.

2.

Thy love the powers of thought bestowed,
  To thee my thoughts would soar;
Thy mercy o'er my life has flowed,
  That mercy I adore.

3.

In each event of life how clear
  Thy ruling hand I see,
Each blessing to my soul more dear
  Because conferred by thee.

4.

In every joy that crowns my days,
  In every pain I bear,
My heart shall find delight in praise,
  Or seek relief in prayer.

5.

When gladness wings my favored hour,
  Thy love my thoughts shall fill;
Resigned, when storms of sorrow lower,
  My soul shall meet thy will.

6.

My lifted eye without a tear
  The lowering storm shall see;
My steadfast heart shall know no fear,
  That heart will rest on thee.

HELEN MARIA WILLIAMS, 1762–1827

HYMN 148.

EIN' FESTE BURG.   8. 7. 8. 7. 6. 6. 6. 6. 7.   MARTIN LUTHER, 1483 — 1546.

AMEN.

148.

A MIGHTY fortress is our God,
  A bulwark never failing;
Our helper he, amid the flood
Of mortal ills prevailing.
    For still our ancient foe
    Doth seek to work us woe;
    His craft and power are great;
    And, armed with cruel hate,
On earth is not his equal.

2.

Did we in our own strength confide,
  Our striving would be losing, —
Were not the right man on our side,
  The man of God's own choosing.
    Dost ask who that may be?
    Christ Jesus, it is he,
    Lord Sabaoth his name,
    From age to age the same,
And he must win the battle.

3.

And though this world, with devils filled,
  Should threaten to undo us;
We will not fear, for God hath willed
  His truth to triumph through us.
    The prince of darkness grim, —
    We tremble not for him;
    His rage we can endure,
    For lo! his doom is sure, —
One little word shall fell him.

4.

That word above all earthly powers —
  No thanks to them — abideth;
The Spirit and the gifts are ours
  Through him who with us sideth.
    Let goods and kindred go,
    This mortal life also;
    The body they may kill:
    God's truth abideth still,
His kingdom is forever.

MARTIN LUTHER, 1483-1546.
Tr. FREDERICK HENRY HEDGE, 1805-1890.

HYMN 149.

MARLBOROUGH. 11.10.11.10. Arr. by ARTHUR SEYMOUR SULLIVAN, 1842—

A - MEN.

149.

1.

I CANNOT find thee. Still on restless pinion
   My spirit beats the void where thou dost dwell,
I wander lost through all thy vast dominion,
   And shrink beneath thy light ineffable.

2.

I cannot find thee. E'en when most adoring,
   Before thy throne I bend in lowliest prayer;
Beyond these bounds of thought my thought upsoaring
   From farthest quest comes back: thou art not there.

3.

Yet high above the limits of my seeing,
   And folded far within the inmost heart,
And deep below the deeps of conscious being,
   Thy splendor shineth: there, O God, thou art.

4.

I cannot lose thee. Still in thee abiding,
   The end is clear, how wide soe'er I roam;
The hand that holds the worlds my steps is guiding,
   And I must rest at last in thee, my home.

ELIZA SCUDDER, 1821–

HYMN 150.

WESSEX. 8. 6. 8. 6. 8. 8.   EDWARD JOHN HOPKINS, 1818 — .

A · MEN.

150.

1.

I LOOK to thee in every need,
 And never look in vain;
I feel thy strong and tender love,
 And all is well again:
The thought of thee is mightier far
Than sin and pain and sorrow are.

2.

Discouraged in the work of life,
 Disheartened by its load,
Shamed by its failures or its fears,
 I sink beside the road:
But let me only think of thee,
And then new heart springs up in me.

3.

Thy calmness bends serene above,
 My restlessness to still;
Around me flows thy quickening life,
 To nerve my faltering will;
Thy presence fills my solitude;
Thy providence turns all to good.

4.

Embosomed deep in thy dear love,
 Held in thy law, I stand;
Thy hand in all things I behold,
 And all things in thy hand;
Thou leadest me by unsought ways,
And turn'st my mourning into praise.

SAMUEL LONGFELLOW, 1819–1892

HYMN 151.

CAREYS. 8. 8. 8. 8. 8. 8.   HENRY CAREY, 1685 — 1743.

A - MEN.

151.

1.

THE Lord my pasture shall prepare,
And feed me with a shepherd's care;
His presence shall my wants supply,
And guard me with a watchful eye;
My noonday walks he shall attend,
And all my midnight hours defend.

2.

When in the sultry glebe I faint,
Or on the thirsty mountain pant,
To fertile vales and dewy meads
My weary, wandering steps he leads,
Where peaceful rivers, soft and slow,
Amid the verdant landscape flow.

3.

Though in the paths of death I tread,
With gloomy horrors overspread,
My steadfast heart shall fear no ill,
For thou, O Lord, art with me still;
Thy friendly crook shall give me aid,
And guide me through the dreadful shade.

JOSEPH ADDISON, 1672-1719.

HYMN 152.

VERITAS. 10. 10. 10. 10.　　　　　　　　　　JOSEPH BARNBY, 1838—1896.

A · MEN.

152.

1.

LEAD us, O Father, in the paths of peace;
   Without thy guiding hand we go astray,
And doubts appall, and sorrows still increase;
   Lead us through Christ, the true and living way.

2.

Lead us, O Father, in the paths of truth;
   Unhelped by thee, in error's maze we grope,
While passion stains and folly dims our youth,
   And age comes on uncheered by faith or hope.

3.

Lead us, O Father, in the paths of right;
   Blindly we stumble when we walk alone,
Involved in shadows of a moral night;
   Only with thee we journey safely on.

4.

Lead us, O Father, to thy heavenly rest,
   However rough and steep the pathway be,
Through joy or sorrow, as thou deemest best,
   Until our lives are perfected in thee.

WILLIAM HENRY BURLEIGH, 1812-1871.

HYMN 153.

INNSBRUCK. 8. 8. 6. 8. 8. 6.   HEINRICH ISAAC, *circa* 1500.

A - MEN.

153.

1.

OFT as we run the weary way
  That leads through shadows unto day,
    With trial sore amazed,
We deem our sorrows are unknown,
Our battle joined and fought alone,
    Our victory unpraised.

2.

Faithless and blind, we cannot trace
The witnesses who watch our race
    Beyond our senses' ken:
The mighty cloud of all who died
With faithful rapture, humble pride,
    For love of God and man,—

3.

Who, from the battlements above,
Follow our course with eager love,
    And cheer our contest on,
Who cry at every faithful blow
Struck at the old usurping foe,
    "Servant of God, well done!"

4.

And one, the conqueror of death,
Beginner, finisher of faith,
    Who, for the joy of love,
Endured the cross, despised the shame,
Awakes in us the battle flame,
    And waits for us above.

5.

With patience, then, we run the race,
With joy and confidence and grace,
    In quiet hope and power,
Cast off the sins that check our speed,
The weights that faith and love impede,
    Withstand the evil hour.

6.

For heaven is round us as we move:
Our days are compassed with its love,
    Its light is on our road;
And when the knell of death is rung,
Sweet alleluias shall be sung
    To welcome us to God.

STOPFORD AUGUSTUS BROOKE, 1832-

Hymn 154.

ADESTE FIDELES. 11.11.11.11.   JOHN READING, 1677 — 1764.

154.

A - MEN.

1.

THE Lord is my shepherd, no want shall I know:
    I feed in green pastures, safe-folded I rest;
He leadeth my soul where the still waters flow,
    Restores me when wandering, redeems when oppressed.

2.

Through the valley and shadow of death though I stray,
    Since thou art my guardian, no evil I fear:
Thy rod shall defend me, thy staff be my stay;
    No harm can befall, with my comforter near.

3.

In the midst of affliction, my table is spread;
    With blessings unmeasured my cup runneth o'er;
With perfume and oil thou anointest my head:
    O, what shall I ask of thy providence more?

4.

Let goodness and mercy, my bountiful God,
    Still follow my steps till I meet thee above.
I seek, by the path which my forefathers trod
    Through the land of their sojourn, thy kingdom of love.

JAMES MONTGOMERY, 1771-1854.

Hymn 155.

PRAETORIUS. C. M.

MICHAEL PRAETORIUS, 1571 — 1621.

A·MEN.

1.

NOW it belongs not to my care
   Whether I die or live :
To love and serve thee is my share,
   And this thy grace must give.

2.

If life be long, I will be glad
   That I may long obey ;
If short, yet why should I be sad
   That shall have the same pay ?

3.

Christ leads me through no darker rooms
   Than he went through before ;
He that into God's kingdom comes
   Must enter by this door.

4.

Come, Lord, when grace has made me meet
   Thy blessèd face to see ;
For, if thy work on earth be sweet,
   What will thy glory be ?

RICHARD BAXTER, 1615-1691.

HYMN 156.

GRACE CHURCH. L. M.   IGNAZ JOSEPH PLEYEL, 1757 — 1831.

A - MEN.

1.

O THOU to whose all-searching sight
The darkness shineth as the light,
Search, prove, my heart ; it pants for thee :
O, burst these bands, and set it free !

2.

If in this darksome wild I stray,
Be thou my light, be thou my way :
No foes, no violence, I fear,
No fraud, while thou, my God, art near.

3.

If rough and thorny be my way,
My strength proportion to my day
Till toil and grief and pain shall cease
Where all is calm and joy and peace.

NICOLAUS LUDWIG VON ZINZENDORF, 1700-1760.
Tr. JOHN WESLEY, 1703-1791.

HYMN 157.

OBERLIN. 8.8.8.8.6. MAGDEBURG CHORALBUCH, 1540.

A - MEN.

157.

1.

O LORD, thy heavenly grace impart,
   And fix my frail, inconstant heart!
Henceforth my chief desire shall be
To dedicate myself to thee,
    To thee, my God, to thee.

2.

Whate'er pursuits my time employ,
One thought shall fill my soul with joy:
That silent, secret thought shall be
That all my hopes are fixed on thee,
    On thee, my God, on thee.

3.

Thy glorious eye pervadeth space;
Thou 'rt present, Lord, in every place;
And, wheresoe'er my lot may be,
Still shall my spirit cleave to thee,
    To thee, my God, to thee.

4.

Renouncing every worldly thing,
Safe 'neath the covert of thy wing,
My sweetest thought henceforth shall be
That all I want I find in thee,
    In thee, my God, in thee.

Tr. LUCY WILSON, 1802-1863.

HYMN 158.

FERNSHAW. C. M.   JOSIAH BOOTH, 1852 —

A - MEN.

1.

O THOU, in all thy might so far,
 In all thy love so near,
Beyond the range of sun and star,
 And yet beside us here, —

2.

What heart can comprehend thy name,
 Or, searching, find thee out,
Who art within, a quickening flame,
 A presence round about?

3.

Yet though I know thee but in part,
 I ask not, Lord, for more:
Enough for me to know thou art,
 To love thee and adore.

4.

O, sweeter than aught else besides,
 The tender mystery
That like a veil of shadow hides
 The light I may not see!

5.

And dearer than all things I know
 Is childlike faith to me,
That makes the darkest way I go
 An open path to thee.

FREDERICK LUCIAN HOSMER, 1840–

Hymn 159.

ST. CLARE. 8. 7. 8. 5.

ALFRED JAMES EYRE, 1853 —

A - MEN.

1.

HAST thou, 'midst life's empty noises,
   Heard the solemn steps of time
And the low, mysterious voices
   Of another clime?

2.

Early hath life's mighty question
   Thrilled within thy heart of youth,
With a deep and strong beseeching, —
   What, and where, is truth?

3.

Not to ease and aimless quiet
   Doth that inward answer tend,
But to works of love and duty
   As our being's end :

4.

Earnest toil and strong endeavor
   Of a spirit which within
Wrestles with familiar evil
   And besetting sin,

5.

And without, with tireless vigor,
   Steady heart, and weapon strong,
In the power of truth assailing
   Every form of wrong.

JOHN GREENLEAF WHITTIER, 1807–1892.

HYMN 160.

DALEHURST. C. M. ARTHUR COTTMAN, 1842—1879.

A-MEN.

1.

YET, in the maddening maze of things,
  And tossed by storm and flood,
To one fixed stake my spirit clings, —
  I know that God is good.

2.

Not mine to look where cherubim
  And seraphs may not see ;
But nothing can be good in him
  Which evil is in me.

3.

The wrong that pains my soul below
  I dare not throne above ;
I know not of his hate, — I know
  His goodness and his love.

4.

And thou, O Lord, by whom are seen
  Thy creatures as they be,
Forgive me, if too close I lean
  My human heart on thee.

JOHN GREENLEAF WHITTIER, 1807-1892.

HYMN 161.

MELCOMBE. L. M.   SAMUEL WEBBE, 1740—1816.

A - MEN.

1.

O THOU who hast at thy command
   The hearts of all men in thy hand,
Our wayward, erring hearts incline
To have no other will but thine.

2.

Our wishes, our desires, control,
Mould every purpose of the soul ;
O'er all may we victorious be
That stands between ourselves and thee.

3.

Thrice blest will all our blessings be
When we can look through them to thee,
When each glad heart its tribute pays
Of love and gratitude and praise.

4.

And, while we to thy glory live,
May we to thee all glory give
Until the joyful summons come
That calls thy willing servants home !

JANE COTTERILL, 1790-1825.

HYMN 162.

ST. BEDE. 8. 6. 8. 6. 8. 6.

JOHN BACCHUS DYKES, 1823 — 1876.

A - MEN.

162.

1.

FATHER, I know that all my life
  Is portioned out for me,
And the changes that are sure to come
  I do not fear to see;
But I ask thee for a present mind
  Intent on pleasing thee.

2.

I ask thee for a thoughtful love,
  Through constant watching wise,
To meet the glad with joyful smiles,
  And to wipe the weeping eyes;
And a heart at leisure from itself
  To soothe and sympathize.

3.

I would not have the restless will
  That hurries to and fro,
Seeking for some great thing to do,
  Or secret thing to know:
I would be treated as a child,
  And guided where I go.

4.

Wherever in the world I am,
  In whatsoe'er estate,
I have a fellowship with hearts
  To keep and cultivate,
And a work of lowly love to do
  For the Lord on whom I wait.

ANNA LAETITIA WARING, 1823.

HYMN 163.

BEDFORD. C. M.   WILLIAM WEALE,   — 1727.

A · MEN.

1.

IN thee my powers, my treasures, live ;
  To thee my life must tend :
Giving thyself, thou all dost give,
  O soul-sufficing Friend !

2.

And wherefore should I seek above
  The city in the sky,
Since firm in faith and deep in love
  Its broad foundations lie,

3.

Since in a life of peace and prayer,
  Nor known on earth, nor praised,
By humblest toil, by ceaseless care,
  Its holy towers are raised?

4.

Where pain the soul hath purified,
  And penitence hath shriven,
And truth is crowned and glorified, —
  There, only there, is heaven.

ELIZA SCUDDER, 1821–

HYMN 164.

ST. FRANCIS XAVIER. C. M.

JOHN STAINER, 1840 —

A · MEN.

1.

M Y God, I love thee : not because
    I hope for heaven thereby,
Nor because they who love thee not
    Must burn eternally ;

2.

Not with the hope of gaining aught,
    Not seeking a reward ;
But as thyself hast loved me,
    O ever-loving Lord !

3.

E'en so I love thee and will love,
    And in thy praise will sing,
Solely because thou art my God,
    And my eternal King.

Tr. EDWARD CASWALL, 1814-1878.

HYMN 165.

CARMEL. 10. 10. 10. 10. 10. 10.   HENRY SMART, 1813—1879.

165.

A - MEN.

1.

ETERNAL Ruler of the ceaseless round
    Of circling planets singing on their way,
Guide of the nations from the night profound
    Into the glory of the perfect day,
Rule in our hearts, that we may ever be
Guided, and strengthened, and upheld by thee.

2.

We would be one in hatred of all wrong,
    One in our love of all things sweet and fair,
One with the joy that breaketh into song,
    One with the grief that trembles into prayer,
One in the power that makes thy children free
To follow truth, and thus to follow thee.

JOHN WHITE CHADWICK, 1840–

Hymn 166.

TALLIS'S ORDINAL. C. M.   THOMAS TALLIS, 1520—1585.

A - MEN.

1.

O GOD, whose dread and dazzling brow
    Love never yet forsook,
On those who seek thy presence now,
    In deep compassion look.

2.

For many a frail and erring heart
    Is in thy holy sight,
And feet too willing to depart
    From the plain way of right.

3.

Yet, pleased the humble prayer to hear
    And kind to all that live,
Thou, when thou seest the contrite tear,
    Art ready to forgive.

WILLIAM CULLEN BRYANT, 1794-1878.

HYMN 167.

MAINZER. L. M.   JOSEPH MAINZER, 1801 — 1851.

A - MEN.

1.

FORTH in thy name, O Lord, I go
  My daily labor to pursue,
Thee, only thee, resolved to know
  In all I think, or speak, or do.

2.

Thee may I set at my right hand,
  Whose eyes mine inmost substance see,
And labor on at thy command,
  And offer all my works to thee.

3.

Give me to bear thy easy yoke,
  And every moment watch and pray,
And still to things eternal look,
  And hasten to thy glorious day.

CHARLES WESLEY, 1708-1788.

HYMN 168.

ANGELS' HYMN. L. M.   ORLANDO GIBBONS, 1583—1625.

1.

O BLESSÈD life ! the heart at rest
   When all without tumultuous seems,
   That trusts a higher will, and deems
That higher will, not hers, is best.

2.

O blessèd life ! the mind that sees —
   Whatever change the years may bring —
   A mercy still in everything,
And shining through all mysteries.

3.

O blessèd life ! the soul that soars,
   When sense of mortal sight is dim,
   Beyond the sense, — beyond, to him
Whose love unlocks the heavenly doors.

4.

O blessèd life ! heart, mind, and soul
   From self-born aims and wishes free,
   In all at one with Deity,
And loyal to the Lord's control.

5.

O life ! how blessèd, how divine !
   High life, the earnest of a higher !
   Saviour, fulfil my deep desire,
And let this blessèd life be mine !

WILLIAM TIDD MATSON, 1833–

HYMN 169.

BRISTOL. C. M.   EDWARD HODGES, 1796 — 1867.

A - MEN.

1.

My heart is resting, O my God !
  I will give thanks and sing ;
My heart is at the secret source
  Of every precious thing.

2.

I thirst for springs of heavenly life,
  And here all day they rise ;
I seek the treasure of thy love,
  And close at hand it lies.

3.

Glory to thee for strength withheld,
  For want and weakness known,
And the fear that sends me to thy breast
  For what is most my own.

4.

Mine be the reverent listening love
  That waits all day on thee,
With the service of a watchful heart
  Which no one else can see.

5.

The faith that in a hidden way
  No other eye may know
Finds all its daily work prepared,
  And loves to have it so.

ANNA LAETITIA WARING, 1823–

HYMN 170.

VIENNA. 7.7.7.7.

JUSTIN HEINRICH KNECHT, 1752 — 1817.

A · MEN.

1.

WHAT is this that stirs within,
    Loving goodness, hating sin,
Always craving to be blest,
Finding here below no rest?

2.

Naught that charms the ear or eye
Can its hunger satisfy ;
Active, restless, it would pierce
Through the outward universe.

3.

What is it? and whither, whence,
This unsleeping, secret sense,
Longing for its rest and food
In some hidden, untried good?

4.

'T is the soul, — mysterious name, —
Him it seeks from whom it came :
When we muse we feel the fire
Burning on and mounting higher.

5.

Onward, upward to thy throne,
O thou infinite Unknown !
We would press until we see
Thee in all and all in thee.

WILLIAM HENRY FURNESS, 1802-1896.

Hymn 171.

MORNINGTON. S. M.   GARRET WELLESLEY, 1735 — 1781.

A - MEN.

1.

Teach me, my God and King,
 In all things thee to see,
And what I do in any thing,
 To do it as for thee,

2.

To scorn the senses' sway
 While still to thee I tend.
In all I do, be thou the way,
 In all be thou the end.

3.

All may of thee partake :
 Nothing so mean can be
But draws, when acted for thy sake,
 Greatness and worth from thee.

4.

If done to obey thy laws,
 Even servile labors shine :
Hallowed all toil if this the cause,
 The meanest work divine.

GEORGE HERBERT, 1593-1632.
JOHN WESLEY, 1703-1791.

HYMN 172.

MARTYRDOM. C. M.   HUGH WILSON, 1764—1824.

A - MEN.

1.

O WHEREFORE hath my spirit leave
 To come so near my God,
And yet so soon must gaze and grieve
 O'er the abandoned road?

2.

I feel my God almost possessed,
 The heavenly land half won,
The blissful greeting of the blest,
 The eternal song, begun.

3.

Ah, wings that droop! Ah, strains that die!
 Ah, light that fades away!
Ah, fleeting people of the sky!
 Ah, heaven, that will not stay!

4.

What glory in thy presence, Lord!
 What sweetness in thy smile!
Thine awful voice, how quickly heard!
 Ah, wherefore but a while?

5.

Lord, help this earnest, helpless will;
 Lay thine own hand on me:
Shall I not climb thy holy hill?
 Shall I not dwell with thee?

THOMAS HORNBLOWER GILL, 1819.

HYMN 173.

SEBASTIAN. 7.7.7.7.

A · MEN.

1.

MIGHTY God, the first, the last,
  What are ages in thy sight
But as yesterday when past,
  Or a watch within the night?

2.

All that being ever knew,
  Down, far down, ere time had birth,
Stands as clear within thy view
  As the present things of earth.

3.

All that being e'er shall know,
  On, still on, through farthest years,
All eternity can show,
  Bright before thee now appears.

4.

In thine all-embracing sight
  Every change its purpose meets,
Every cloud floats into light,
  Every woe its glory greets.

5.

Whatsoe'er our lot may be,
  Calmly in this thought we 'll rest, —
Could we see as thou dost see,
  We should choose it as the best.

WILLIAM GASKELL, 1805-1884.

HYMN 174.

BEATITUDO. C. M.

JOHN BACCHUS DYKES, 1823—1876.

A - MEN.

1.

O FOR a closer walk with God,
A calm and heavenly frame,
A light to shine upon the road
That leads me to the Lamb !

2.

What peaceful hours I once enjoyed !
How sweet their memory still !
But they have left an aching void
The world can never fill.

3.

Return, O holy Dove ! return,
Sweet messenger of rest !
I hate the sins that made thee mourn,
And drove thee from my breast.

4.

The dearest idol I have known,
Whate'er that idol be,
Help me to tear it from thy throne,
And worship only thee.

5.

So shall my walk be close with God,
Calm and serene my frame ;
So purer light shall mark the road
That leads me to the Lamb.

WILLIAM COWPER, 1731-1800.

HYMN 175.

REST. 8.8.8.4.   GEORGE JOB ELVEY, 1816—1893.

A - MEN.

1.

ONE thing I of the Lord desire, —
   For all my way hath miry been, —
Be it by water or by fire,
    O make me clean !

2.

Erewhile I strove for perfect truth,
   And thought it was a worthy strife ;
But now I leave that aim of youth
    For perfect life.

3.

If clearer vision thou impart,
   Grateful and glad my soul shall be ;
But yet to have a purer heart
    Is more to me.

4.

Yea, only as the heart is clean
   May larger vision yet be mine,
For mirrored in its depths are seen
    The things divine.

5.

So wash thou me without, within ;
   Or purge with fire, if that must be ;
No matter how, if only sin
    Die out in me.

WALTER CHALMERS SMITH, 1824-   .

HYMN 176.

ST. FLAVIAN. C. M.   JOHN DAY'S PSALTER, 1562.

A - MEN.

1.

UNWORTHY to be called thy son,
  I come with shame to thee,
Father, O more than father thou
  Hast always been to me.

2.

Help me to break the heavy chains
  The world has round me thrown,
And know the glorious liberty
  Of an obedient son.

3.

That I may henceforth heed whate'er
  Thy voice within me saith,
Fix deeply in my heart of hearts
  The mighty power of faith, —

4.

Faith that, like armor to my soul,
  Shall keep all evil out,
More mighty than an angel host
  Encamping round about.

WILLIAM HENRY FURNESS, 1802 1896.

Hymn 177.

ST. BERNARD. C. M.   JOHN RICHARDSON, 1816—1879.

A - MEN.

1.

BENEATH thine hammer, Lord, I lie
   With contrite spirit prone :
O, mould me till to self I die,
   And live to thee alone.

2.

With frequent disappointments sore
   And many a bitter pain,
Thou laborest at my being's core
   Till I be formed again.

3.

Smite, Lord : thine hammer's needful
   wound
My baffled hopes confess ;
Thine anvil is the sense profound
   Of mine own nothingness.

4.

Smite, till, from all its idols free,
   And filled with love divine,
My heart shall know no good but thee,
   And have no will but thine.

FREDERIC HENRY HEDGE, 1805-1890

HYMN 178.

ST. ANSELM.   7. 6. 7. 6. 7. 6. 7. 6.   JOSEPH BARNBY, 1838—1896.

A - MEN.

178.

1.

SOMETIMES a light surprises
   The Christian while he sings:
It is the Lord, who rises
   With healing in his wings.
When comforts are declining,
   He grants the soul again
A season of clear shining,
   To cheer it after rain.

2.

In holy contemplation,
   We sweetly then pursue
The theme of God's salvation,
   And find it ever new.
Set free from present sorrow,
   We cheerfully can say, —
"E'en let the unknown to-morrow
   Bring with it what it may.

3.

"It can bring with it nothing
   But he will bear us through;
Who gives the lilies clothing
   Will clothe his people too;
Beneath the spreading heavens
   No creature but is fed,
And he who feeds the ravens
   Will give his children bread.

4.

"The vine nor fig-tree neither
   Their wonted fruit should bear,
Though all the fields should wither,
   Nor flocks nor herds be there,
Yet God the same abiding,
   His praise shall tune my voice;
For, while in him confiding,
   I cannot but rejoice."

WILLIAM COWPER, 1731-1800.

HYMN 179.

ST. CECILIA. 6. 6. 6. 6.   LEIGHTON GEORGE HAYNE, 1836—1883.

A - MEN.

1.

THY way, not mine, O Lord,
　　However dark it be :
Lead me by thine own hand ;
　　Choose out the path for me.

2.

Smooth let it be or rough,
　　It will be still the best :
Winding or straight, it leads
　　Right onward to thy rest.

3.

I dare not choose my lot ;
　　I would not, if I might :
Choose thou for me, my God ;
　　So shall I walk aright.

4.

Take thou my cup, and it
　　With joy or sorrow fill
As best to thee may seem :
　　Choose thou my good and ill.

5.

Choose thou for me my friends,
　　My sickness or my health ;
Choose thou my cares for me,
　　My poverty or wealth.

6.

Not mine, not mine, the choice,
　　In things or great or small :
Be thou my guide, my strength,
　　My wisdom, and my all.

HORATIUS BONAR, 1808-1889.

HYMN 180.

WILTSHIRE. C. M.　　　　　　　　GEORGE THOMAS SMART, 1776—1867.

A · MEN.

1.

ALL as God wills, who wisely heeds
　To give or to withhold,
And knoweth more of all my needs
　Than all my prayers have told.

2.

Enough that blessings undeserved
　Have marked my erring track ;
That, wheresoe'er my feet have swerved,
　His chastening turned me back ;

3.

That more and more a providence
　Of love is understood,
Making the springs of time and sense
　Sweet with eternal good ;

4.

That death seems but a covered way
　Which opens into light,
Wherein no blinded child can stray
　Beyond the Father's sight.

5.

No longer forward nor behind
　I look, in hope or fear,
But grateful take the good I find,
　The best of now and here.

JOHN GREENLEAF WHITTIER, 1807-1892.

HYMN 181.

FEDERAL STREET. L. M.

HENRY KEMBLE OLIVER, 1800 — 1885.

A·MEN.

1.

MY God, I thank thee! may no
    thought
E'er deem thy chastisements severe,
But may this heart, by sorrow taught,
    Calm each wild wish, each idle fear.

2.

Thy mercy bids all nature bloom,
    The sun shines bright, and man is gay;
Thine equal mercy spreads the gloom
    That darkens o'er his little day.

3.

Full many a throb of grief and pain
    Thy frail and erring child must
    know;
But not one prayer is breathed in vain,
    Nor does one tear unheeded flow.

4.

Thy various messengers employ,
    Thy purposes of love fulfil,
And, 'mid the wreck of human joy,
    May kneeling faith adore thy will!

ANDREWS NORTON, 1786-1853

HYMN 182.

HANFORD. 8. 8. 8. 4.　　　　　　　　ARTHUR SEYMOUR SULLIVAN, 1842 —

A · MEN.

1.

MY God and Father, while I stray,
　　Far from my home, in life's rough
　　　　way,
O, teach me from my heart to say,
　　" Thy will be done."

2.

Though thou hast called me to resign
What most I prized, it ne'er was mine :
I have but yielded what was thine, —
　　" Thy will be done."

3.

Let but my fainting heart be blest
With thy sweet spirit for its guest,
My God, to thee I leave the rest, —
　　" Thy will be done."

4.

Renew my will from day to day,
Blend it with thine, and take away
All that now makes it hard to say,
　　"Thy will be done."

CHARLOTTE ELLIOTT, 1789-1871.

HYMN 183.

CANONBURY. L. M.

ROBERT SCHUMANN, 1810—1856.

A - MEN.

1.

O LOVE divine, that stooped to share
Our sharpest pang, our bitterest tear,
On thee we cast each earth-born care ;
We smile at pain while thou art near.

2.

Though long the weary way we tread,
And sorrow crown each lingering year,
No path we shun, no darkness dread, —
Our hearts still whispering, thou art
near !

3.

When drooping pleasure turns to grief,
And trembling faith is changed to fear,
The murmuring wind, the quivering leaf,
Shall softly tell us, thou art near !

4.

On thee we fling our burdening woe,
O Love divine, forever dear !
Content to suffer while we know,
Living and dying, thou art near.

OLIVER WENDELL HOLMES, 1809-1894.

HYMN 184.

ST. AGNES. C. M.   JOHN BACCHUS DYKES, 1823—1876.

A - MEN.

1.

PRAYER is the soul's sincere desire,
  Uttered or unexpressed,
The motion of a hidden fire,
  That trembles in the breast.

2.

Prayer is the burden of a sigh,
  The falling of a tear,
The upward glancing of an eye,
  When none but God is near.

3.

Prayer is the simplest form of speech
  That infant lips can try,
Prayer the sublimest strains that reach
  The Majesty on high.

4.

O thou by whom we come to God, —
  The life, the truth, the way, —
The path of prayer thyself hast trod,
  Lord, teach us how to pray !

JAMES MONTGOMERY, 1771-1851

HYMN 185.

DIX. 7. 7. 7. 7. 7. 7.

CONRAD KOCHER, 1786 — 1872.

A · MEN.

1.

A S the hart, with eager looks,
    Panteth for the water-brooks,
So my soul, athirst for thee,
Pants the living God to see.
When, O when, with filial fear,
Lord, shall I to thee draw near?

2.

Why art thou cast down, my soul?
God, thy God, shall make thee whole.
Why art thou disquieted?
God shall lift thy fallen head,
And his countenance benign
Be the saving health of thine.

JAMES MONTGOMERY, 1771-1854.

Hymn 186.

ST. HUGH. C. M.   EDWARD JOHN HOPKINS, 1818 —

A - MEN.

1.

ONE prayer I have — all prayers
in one —
When I am wholly thine :
Thy will, my God, thy will be done,
And let that will be mine.

2.

All-wise, almighty, and all-good,
In thee I firmly trust ;
Thy ways, unknown or understood,
Are merciful and just.

3.

Thy gifts are only then enjoyed
When used as talents lent,
Those talents only well employed
When in thy service spent.

4.

And, though thy wisdom takes away,
Shall I arraign thy will?
No : let me bless thy name, and say,
"The Lord is gracious still."

JAMES MONTGOMERY, 1771-1854.

HYMN 187.

NASSAU.   7. 6. 7. 6. 3. 3. 6. 6.   JOHANN ROSENMÜLLER, 1615—1686.

A - MEN.

187.

1.

NOT in anger, mighty God,
 Not in anger smite us!
We must perish if thy rod
 Justly should requite us.
  We are nought,
  Sin hath brought,
 Lord, thy wrath upon us,
 Yet have mercy on us!

2.

Show me now a father's love
 And his tender patience,
Heal my wounded soul, remove
 These too sore temptations.
  I am weak;
  Father, speak
 Thou of peace and gladness,
 Comfort thou my sadness!

JOHANN GEORG ALBINUS, 1624–1679.
Tr. CATHERINE WINKWORTH, 1829–1878

Hymn 188.

GERMANY. L. M.

LUDWIG VAN BEETHOVEN, 1770—1827.

188.

TO thine eternal arms, O God,
   Take us, thine erring children, in,
From dangerous paths too boldly trod,
   From wandering thoughts and dreams of sin.

2.

Those arms were round our childish ways,
   A guard through helpless years to be ;
O, leave not our maturer days,
   We still are helpless without thee.

3.

We trusted hope and pride and strength :
   Our strength proved false, our pride was vain,
Our dreams have faded all at length, —
   We come to thee, O Lord, again.

4.

A guide to trembling steps yet be,
   Give us of thine eternal powers ;
So shall our paths all lead to thee,
   And life smile on like childhood's hours.

THOMAS WENTWORTH HIGGINSON, 1823-

HYMN 189.

VENTNOR. II. IO. II. IO.   JOSEPH BARNBY, 1838—1896.

A - MEN.

189.

1.

WHEN winds are raging o'er the upper ocean,
    And billows wild contend with angry roar,
'Tis said, far down beneath the wild commotion
    That peaceful stillness reigneth evermore.

2.

Far, far beneath, the noise of tempest dieth,
    And silver waves chime ever peacefully;
And no rude storm, how fierce soe'er he flieth,
    Disturbs the sabbath of that deeper sea.

3.

So to the soul that knows thy love, O Purest,
    There is a temple, peaceful evermore;
And all the babble of life's angry voices
    Dies in hushed stillness at its sacred door.

4.

Far, far away, the noise of passion dieth,
    And loving thoughts rise ever peacefully;
And no rude storm, how fierce soe'er he flieth,
    Disturbs that deeper rest, O Lord, in thee.

HARRIET BEECHER STOWE, 1812–

HYMN 190.

JOY.   7. 6. 7. 6. 7. 7. 7. 6.   LUDWIG VAN BEETHOVEN, 1770 — 1827.

A - MEN.

190.

1.

OPEN, Lord, my inward ear,
  And bid my heart rejoice,
Bid my quiet spirit hear
  Thy comfortable voice.
Never in the whirlwind found,
  Or where earthquakes rock the place.
Still and silent is the sound,
  The whisper of thy grace.

2.

Lord, my time is in thy hand,
  My soul to thee convert;
Thou canst make me understand,
  Though I am slow of heart.
Thine in whom I live and move,
  Thine the work, the praise is thine;
Thou art wisdom, power and love,
  And all thou art is mine.

3.

From the world of sin and noise
  And hurry I withdraw;
For the small and inward voice
  I wait with humble awe:
Silent am I now and still,
  Dare not in thy presence move;
To my waiting soul reveal
  The secret of thy love.

CHARLES WESLEY, 1708–1788.

Hymn 191.

CREDO.   8. 8. 8. 8. 8. 8.   John Stainer, 1840 —   .

191.

1.

SURROUNDED by unnumbered foes,
    Against my soul the battle goes;
Yet, though I weary sore. distressed,
I know that I shall reach my rest.
I lift my tearful eyes above,
His banner over me is love.

2.

Its sword my spirit will not yield,
Though flesh may faint upon the field;
He waves before my fading sight
The branch of palm — the crown of light.
I lift my brightening eyes above,
His banner over me is love.

3.

My cloud of battle-dust may dim,
His veil of splendor curtain him,
And in the midnight of my fear
I may not feel him standing near;
But, as I lift mine eyes above,
His banner over me is love.

GERALD MASSEY, 1828-

Hymn 192.

ST. WERBURG 8. 8. 8. 8. 8. 8. John Bacchus Dykes, 1823—1876.

A - MEN.

192.

1.

WITH open eyes that look on God,
My daily journey I pursue.
I do not dread his lifted rod:
Why should I fear what love can do?
And if I need that he chastise,
Is he not good, as he is wise?

2.

I know, if I but follow him,
I shall be safe from harm, and make,
Albeit all the way be dim,
Nor slip nor failure nor mistake;
Or, making such, he will ordain
What seems my loss shall prove my gain.

3.

And though I look to careless eyes
A waif on pathless waters cast,
His faithful promise shall suffice
For stay and comfort to the last.
When, all my guarded wanderings o'er,
Let my safe feet but touch the shore,

4.

And like a child with home in sight
I 'll fall into his open arms,
Glad that I never felt affright,
Nor thought of him as one who harms, —
I, his dear child, or here, or there,
And he my Father everywhere.

CAROLINE ATHERTON MASON, 1823-1890

HYMN 193.

ADOLPHUS. 8. 8. 7. 8. 8. 7.   GERMAN CHORAL, 1540.

A · MEN.

193.

1.

BE not dismayed, thou little flock,
    Although the foe's fierce battle-shock,
  Loud on all sides, assail thee.
Though o'er thy fall they laugh secure,
Their triumph cannot long endure :
    Let not thy courage fail thee.

2.

Thy cause is God's : go at his call,
And to his hand commit thy all.
    Fear thou no ill impending.
His Gideon shall arise for thee,
God's word and people manfully,
    In God's own time, defending.

3.

Our hope is sure in Jesus' might ;
Against themselves the godless fight,
    Themselves, not us, distressing.
Shame and contempt their lot shall be ;
God is with us, with him are we ;
    To us belongs his blessing.

GUSTAVUS ADOLPHUS, 1594-1632.
Tr. ELIZABETH CHARLES, 1828-1896.

HYMN 194.

PENTECOST. L. M.   WILLIAM BOYD, 1846 —

A - MEN

1.

FIGHT the good fight,
   With all thy might !
Christ is thy strength, and Christ thy right ;
Lay hold on life, and it shall be
Thy joy and crown eternally !

2.

Run the straight race
Through God's good grace,
Lift up thine eyes and seek his face !
Life with its way before us lies,
Christ is the path, and Christ the prize.

3.

Cast care aside,
Upon thy guide
Lean, and his mercy will provide ;
Lean, and the trusting soul shall prove
Christ is its life, and Christ its love.

JOHN SAMUEL BEWLEY MONSELL, 1811-1875.

Hymn 195.

FESTUS. L. M.

GERMAN CHORAL.

A-MEN.

1.

THE God of glory walks his round,
From day to day, from year to year ;
And warns us each with awful sound,
" No longer stand ye idle here ! "

2.

O, as the griefs you would assuage
That wait on life's declining year,
Secure a blessing for your age,
And work your Maker's business here.

3.

O thou, by all thy works adored,
To whom the sinner's soul is dear,
Recall us to thy vineyard, Lord,
And grant us grace to please thee here.

REGINALD HEBER, 1783-1826.

HYMN 196.

DAY OF PRAISE. S. M.   CHARLES STEGGALL, 1826—

A - MEN.

1.

G IVE forth thine earnest cry,
   O conscience, voice of God;
To young and old, to low and high,
   Proclaim his will abroad.

2.

Within the human breast
   Thy strong monitions plead;
Still thunder thy divine protest
   Against the unrighteous deed.

3.

Show the true way of peace,
   O thou, our guiding light;
From bondage of the wrong release
   To service of the right.

HYMNS OF THE SPIRIT, 1864.

HYMN 197.

OLMÜTZ. S. M.

LOWELL MASON, 1792—1872.

A · MEN.

1.

A CHARGE to keep I have,
  A God to glorify,
A never-dying soul to save,
  And fit it for the sky;

2.

To serve the present age,
  My calling to fulfil:
O, may it all my powers engage
  To do my Master's will.

3.

Arm me with jealous care,
  As in thy sight to live,
And, O, thy servant, Lord, prepare
  A strict account to give.

CHARLES WESLEY, 1708-1788.

HYMN 198.

ST. TIMOTHY. C. M.   HENRY WILLIAMS BAKER, 1821—1877.

A · MEN.

1.

I WANT a principle within
    Of jealous, godly fear,
A sensibility of sin,
    A pain to feel it near.

2.

I want the first approach to feel
    Of pride, or fond desire,
To catch the wanderings of my will,
    And quench the kindling fire.

3.

From thee that I no more may part,
    No more thy goodness grieve,
The filial awe, the fleshly heart,
    The tender conscience, give.

4.

Quick as the apple of an eye,
    O God, my conscience make :
Awake my soul when sin is nigh,
    And keep it still awake !

CHARLES WESLEY, 1708-1788.

HYMN 199.

CAMBRIDGE. S. M.

RALPH HARRISON, 1748 — 1810.

A - MEN.

1.

Y E servants of the Lord,
  Each in his office wait,
Observant of his heavenly word,
  And watchful at his gate.

2.

Let all your lamps be bright,
  And trim the golden flame,
Gird up your loins, as in his sight;
  For awful is his name.

3.

Watch! 't is your Lord's command;
  And, while we speak, he 's near;
Mark the first signal of his hand,
  And ready all appear.

4.

O happy servant he,
  In such a posture found!
He shall his Lord with rapture see,
  And be with honor crowned.

PHILIP DODDRIDGE, 1702-1751

HYMN 200.

INTERCESSION. L. M.   Arranged by JOHN BACCHUS DYKES, 1823—1876.

A - MEN.

200.

1.

MAY I resolve with all my heart,
    With all my powers, to serve the Lord,
Nor from his precepts e'er depart,
    Whose service is a rich reward.

2.

Be this the purpose of my soul,
    My solemn, my determined choice, —
To yield to his supreme control,
    And in his kind commands rejoice.

3.

O, may I never faint nor tire,
    Nor, wandering, leave his sacred ways!
Great God, accept my soul's desire,
    And give me strength to live thy praise!

ANNE STEELE, 1716-1778.

HYMN 201.

DUNDEE. C. M.

SCOTTISH PSALTER, 1615.

A-MEN.

1.

THY way is in the deep, O Lord;
 E'en there we 'll go with thee :
We 'll meet the tempest at thy word,
 And walk upon the sea.

2.

Poor tremblers at his rougher wind,
 Why do we doubt him so?
Who gives the storm a path will find
 The way our feet shall go.

3.

A moment may his hand be lost,
 Drear moment of delay ;
We cry, "Lord, help the tempest-tost,"
 And safe we 're borne away.

4.

O happy soul of faith divine,
 Thy victory how sure !
The love that kindles joy is thine,
 The patience to endure.

5.

Come, Lord of peace, our griefs dispel,
 And wipe our tears away.
'T is thine to order all things well,
 And ours to bless the sway.

JAMES MARTINEAU, 1805- .

Hymn 202.

VULPIUS. C. M.   MELCHIOR VULPIUS, 1560—1616.

A-MEN.

1.

O GOD of truth, whose living word
  Upholds whate'er hath breath,
Look down on thy creation, Lord,
  Enslaved by sin and death.

2.

Set up thy standard, Lord, that we
  Who claim a heavenly birth
May march with thee to smite the lies
  That vex thy groaning earth.

3.

We fight for truth, we fight for God,
  Poor slaves of lies and sin.
He who would fight for thee on earth
  Must first be true within.

4.

Thou God of truth, for whom we long,
  Thou who wilt hear our prayer,
Do thine own battle in our hearts,
  And slay the falsehood there.

5.

Yea, come! then tried as in the fire,
  From every lie set free,
Thy perfect truth shall dwell in us,
  And we shall live in thee.

THOMAS HUGHES, 1823-1896.

HYMN 203.

GILBERTS. 8. 7. 8. 7. 4. 4. 7.

WALTER BOND GILBERT, 1829 —

UNISON.

HARMONY.

A · MEN.

203.

1.

GUIDE me, O thou great Jehovah,
　　Pilgrim through this barren land!
I am weak, but thou art mighty;
　　Hold me with thy powerful hand!
Bread of heaven, bread of heaven,
Feed me till I want no more!

2.

Open now the crystal fountain,
　　Whence the healing stream doth flow,
Let the fire and cloudy pillar
　　Lead me all my journey through,
Strong Deliverer, strong Deliverer,
Be thou still my strength and shield!

3.

When I tread the verge of Jordan,
　　Bid my anxious fears subside!
Death of deaths, and hell's destruction,
　　Land me safe on Canaan's side!
Songs of praises, songs of praises,
I will ever give to thee.

WILLIAM WILLIAMS, 1717-1791.

HYMN 204.

CHRISTMAS. C. M.
Georg Friedrich Händel, 1685—1759.

A - MEN.

204.

1.

AWAKE, my soul, stretch every nerve,
　And press with vigor on !
A heavenly race demands thy zeal,
　And an immortal crown.

2.

A cloud of witnesses around
　Hold thee in full survey:
Forget the steps already trod,
　And onward urge thy way !

3.

'T is God's all-animating voice
　That calls thee from on high;
'T is his own hand presents the prize
　To thine aspiring eye, —

4.

That prize, with peerless glories bright,
　Which shall new lustre boast
When victors' wreaths and monarchs' gems
　Shall blend in common dust.

PHILIP DODDRIDGE, 1702-1751.

HYMN 205.

DONCASTER. S. M.   SAMUEL WESLEY, 1766—1837.

A - MEN.

1.

O MASTER of my soul,
    To whom the lives of men,
That floated once upon thy breath,
    Shall yet return again,

2.

Give me the eyes to see,
    Give me the ears to hear,
Give me the spiritual sense
    To feel that thou art near:

3.

So when this earthly mist
    Fades in the azure sky,
My soul shall still be close to thee,
    And in thee cannot die.

EDWIN HATCH, 1835-1889.

HYMN 206.

CAMDEN. L. M.

JOHN BAPTISTE CALKIN, 1827 —

A · MEN.

1.

PRESS on ! press on ! ye sons of light,
Untiring in your holy fight,
Still treading each temptation down,
And battling for a brighter crown.

2.

Press on ! press on ! through toil and woe,
Calmly resolved to triumph go,
And make each dark and threatening ill
Yield but a higher glory still.

3.

Press on ! press on ! still look in faith
To him who vanquished sin and death,
And, till you hear his high " Well done,"
True to the last, press on ! press on !

WILLIAM GASKELL, 1805-1884.

HYMN 207.

AMSTERDAM. 7. 6. 7. 6. 7. 7. 7. 6.   GERMAN CHORAL.

A -MEN.

207.

1.

RISE, my soul, and stretch thy wings,
   Thy better portion trace,
Rise from transitory things
   Towards heaven, thy native place!
Sun and moon and stars decay,
   Time shall soon this earth remove:
Rise, my soul, and haste away
   To seats prepared above!

2.

Rivers to the ocean run,
   Nor stay in all their course;
Fire, ascending, seeks the sun;
   Both speed them to their source:
So my soul, derived from God,
   Pants to view his glorious face,
Forward tends to his abode
   To rest in his embrace.

ROBERT SEAGRAVE, 1693-

Hymn 208.

TRURO. L. M.   Charles Burney, 1726—1814.

A · MEN.

208.

1.

AWAKE, our souls! away, our fears!
Let every trembling thought be gone!
Awake, and run the heavenly race,
And put a cheerful courage on!

2.

True, 't is a strait and thorny road,
And mortal spirits tire and faint;
But they forget the mighty God
That feeds the strength of every saint, —

3.

The mighty God, whose matchless power
Is ever new and ever young,
And firm endures while endless years
Their everlasting circles run.

4.

From thee, the overflowing spring,
Our souls shall drink a fresh supply,
While such as trust their native strength
Shall melt away, and drop, and die.

5.

Swift as an eagle cuts the air,
We 'll mount aloft to thine abode;
On wings of love our souls shall fly,
Nor tire amidst the heavenly road.

ISAAC WATTS, 1674-1748.

HYMN 209.

ST. GERTRUDE. 6.5.6.5.6.5.6.5.6.5.6.5.   ARTHUR SEYMOUR SULLIVAN, 1842 —

With the cross of Je-sus,

With the cross of   Je - sus,   A · MEN.

With the cross of Je-sus.

209.

1.

ONWARD, Christian soldiers,
  Marching as to war,
With the cross of Jesus
  Going on before!
Christ, the royal Master,
  Leads against the foe:
Forward into battle
  Do his banners go.

    Onward, Christian soldiers,
      Marching as to war,
    With the cross of Jesus
      Going on before!

2.

Like a mighty army
  Moves the Church of God:
Brothers, we are treading
  Where the saints have trod;
We are not divided,
  All one body we,
One in hope, in doctrine,
  One in charity.

    Onward, Christian soldiers,
      Marching as to war,
    With the cross of Jesus
      Going on before!

3.

Onward, then, ye people,
  Join our happy throng,
Blend with ours your voices
  In the triumph-song, —
Glory, laud, and honor
  Unto Christ the King!
This through countless ages
  Men and angels sing.

    Onward, Christian soldiers,
      Marching as to war,
    With the cross of Jesus
      Going on before!

SABINE BARING-GOULD. 1834–

HYMN 210.

ERFURT. L. M.

MARTIN LUTHER, 1483—1546.

A - MEN.

210.

1.

GO forth to life, O child of earth !
    Still mindful of thy heavenly birth.
Thou art not here for ease or sin,
But manhood's noble crown to win.

2.

Though passion's fires are in thy soul,
Thy spirit can their flames control ;
Though tempters strong beset thy way,
Thy spirit is more strong than they.

3.

Go on from innocence of youth
To manly pureness, manly truth !
God's angels still are near to save,
And God himself doth help the brave.

4.

Then forth to life, O child of earth !
Be worthy of thy heavenly birth !
For noble service thou art here ;
Thy brothers help, thy God revere !

SAMUEL LONGFELLOW, 1819–1892.

HYMN 211.

GARRETT. S. M.

GEORGE MURSELL GARRETT, 1834—

A - MEN.

1

GIVE to the winds thy fears,
    Hope, and be undismayed !
God hears thy sighs and counts thy tears ;
    God shall lift up thy head.

2.

Through waves and clouds and storms,
    He gently clears thy way :
Wait thou his time ; so shall this night
    Soon end in joyous day.

3.

What though thou rulest not ?
    Yet heaven, and earth, and hell
Proclaim, God sitteth on the throne
    And ruleth all things well.

4

Leave to his sovereign sway
    To choose and to command !
So shalt thou wondering own, his way
    How wise, how strong his hand.

PAULUS GERHARDT, 1607–1676.
Tr. JOHN WESLEY, 1703–1791.

HYMN 212.

NATIVITY. C M.   HENRY LAHEE, 1826—

A - MEN.

1.

A M I a soldier of the cross,
   A follower of the Lamb, —
And shall I fear to own his cause,
   Or blush to speak his name?

2.

Must I be carried to the skies
   On flowery beds of ease,
While others fought to win the prize,
   And sailed through bloody seas?

3.

Are there no foes for me to face?
   Must I not stem the flood?
Is this vile world a friend to grace,
   To help me on to God?

4.

Sure I must fight, if I would reign;
   Increase my courage, Lord !
I 'll bear the toil, endure the pain,
   Supported by thy word.

ISAAC WATTS, 1674-1748.

HYMN 213.

SALVATOR. 8. 7. 8. 7. 8. 7. 8. 7.　　　　　JOHN GOSS, 1800 — 1880.

Take, my soul, thy full sal - va - tion, Rise o'er sin and fear and care,

Joy to find, in ev - ery sta - tion, Something still to do or bear!

Think what spir-it dwells with-in thee, What a fa-ther's smile is thine,

What thy Sav-iour died to win thee,— Child of heaven, shouldst thou re-pine?

2D STANZA.

Haste, then, on from grace to glo - ry, Armed by faith and winged by prayer;

Heaven's e - ter - nal day 's be - fore thee, God's own hand shall guide thee there.

Soon shall close thy earth - ly mis-sion, Swift shall pass thy pil - grim days,

Hope soon change to glad fru - i - tion, Faith to sight, and prayer to praise. A-men.

HENRY FRANCIS LYTE, 1793-1847.

HYMN 214.

WEBB. 7 . 6 . 7 . 6 . 7 . 6 . 7 . 6. GEORGE JAMES WEBB, 1803 — 1887.

A - MEN.

214.

1.

GOD is my strong salvation:
   What foe have I to fear?
In darkness and temptation,
   My light, my help, is near.
Though hosts encamp around me,
   Firm to the fight I stand:
What terror can confound me
   With God at my right hand?

2.

Place on the Lord reliance,
   My soul, with courage wait,
His truth be thine affiance,
   When faint and desolate.
His might thine heart shall strengthen,
   His love thy joy increase,
Mercy thy days shall lengthen,
   The Lord will give thee peace.

JAMES MONTGOMERY, 1771-1854.

HYMN 215.

SAMSON. L. M.   GEORG FRIEDRICH HÄNDEL, 1685 — 1759.

A - MEN.

1.

THE Christian warrior, — see him
  stand
In the whole armor of his God !
The Spirit's sword is in his hand,
 His feet are with the gospel shod,

2.

In panoply of truth complete,
 Salvation's helmet on his head,
With righteousness, a breastplate meet,
 And faith's broad shield before him
  spread.

3.

With this omnipotence he moves,
 From this the alien armies flee,
Till more than conqueror he proves,
 Through Christ, who gives him victory.

JAMES MONTGOMERY, 1771-1854.

HYMN 216.

HESPERUS. L. M.   HENRY BAKER, 1835—

A · MEN.

1.

G O, labor on, spend and be spent, —
  Thy joy to do the Father's will !
It is the way the Master went ;
  Should not the servant tread it still ?

2.

Go, labor on ! 't is not for nought ;
  Thy earthly loss is heavenly gain.
Men heed thee, love thee, praise thee not ;
  The Master praises, — what are men ?

3.

Go, labor on ! enough while here
  If he shall praise thee, if he deign
Thy willing heart to mark and cheer ;
  No toil for him shall be in vain.

4.

Toil on, and in thy toil rejoice !
  For toil comes rest, for exile home :
Soon shalt thou hear the Bridegroom's
    voice,
  The midnight peal, "Behold, I come !"

HORATIUS BONAR, 1808–1889.

HYMN 217.

DEDHAM. C. M. WILLIAM GARDINER, 1770 — 1853.

A·MEN.

1.

GOD'S glory is a wondrous thing,
 Most strange in all its ways,
And, of all things on earth, least like
 What men agree to praise.

2.

Workman of God, O, lose not heart,
 But learn what God is like,
And, in the darkest battlefield,
 Thou shalt know where to strike.

3.

Thrice blest is he to whom is given
 The instinct that can tell
That God is on the field when he
 Is most invisible.

4.

Blest too is he who can divine
 Where real right doth lie,
And dares to take the side that seems
 Wrong to man's blindfold eye.

5.

For right is right, since God is God,
 And right the day must win;
To doubt would be disloyalty,
 To falter would be sin.

FREDERICK WILLIAM FABER, 1814-1863.

Hymn 218.

ANGELUS. L. M.

GEORG JOSEPH, *circa* 1657.

A-MEN.

1.

AMIDST a world of hopes and fears,
A wild of cares and toils and tears,
Where foes alarm, and dangers threat,
And pleasures kill, and glories cheat;

2.

Shed, Lord of light, a heavenly ray
To guide me in the doubtful way;
And o'er me hold thy shield of power
To guard me in the dangerous hour.

3.

Teach me the flattering paths to shun
In which the sons of folly run;
Who for a shade the substance miss,
And grasp their ruin in their bliss.

4.

Each sacred principle impart, —
The faith that sanctifies the heart,
Hope that to heaven's high vault aspires,
And love that warms with holy fires.

5.

Afflicted, may I not repine,
My will submissive bend to thine;
And through this maze of mortal ill,
Safe lead me to thy heavenly hill.

HENRY MOORE, 1732-1802

HYMN 219.

ROCKINGHAM. L. M.   EDWARD MILLER, 1731 — 1807.

A - MEN.

1.

ASSIST me, Lord, to act, to be,
   What nature and thy laws decree,
Worthy that intellectual flame
Which from thy breathing spirit came, —

2.

My mortal freedom to maintain,
Bid passion serve, and reason reign,
Self-poised, and independent still
On this world's varying good or ill.

3.

May my expanded soul disclaim
The narrow view, the selfish aim,
But with a Christian zeal embrace
Whate'er is friendly to my race.

4.

O Father, grace and virtue grant !
No more I wish, no more I want.
To know, to serve thee, and to love,
Is peace below, — is bliss above.

HENRY MOORE, 1732-1802

HYMN 220.

WAREHAM. L. M.

WILLIAM KNAPP, 1698 — 1768.

A . MEN.

1.

H OW happy is he born and taught
That serveth not another's will,
Whose armor is his honest thought,
And simple truth his utmost skill,

2.

Whose passions not his masters are,
Whose soul is still prepared for death,
Untide unto the world by care
Of public fame or private breath,

3.

Who hath his life from rumors freed,
Whose conscience is his strong retreat,
Whose state can neither flatterers feed,
Nor ruin make oppressors great.

4.

This man is freed from servile bands
Of hope to rise, or fear to fall, —
Lord of himself, though not of lands,
And, having nothing, yet hath all.

HENRY WOTTON, 1568-1639.

HYMN 221.

ST. FULBERT. C. M.   HENRY JOHN GAUNTLETT, 1805—1876.

A·MEN.

1.

ALMIGHTY God, in humble prayer
  To thee our souls we lift;
Do thou our waiting minds prepare
  For thy most needful gift.

2.

We ask not golden streams of wealth
  Along our path to flow;
We ask not undecaying health,
  Nor length of years below.

3.

We ask not honors which an hour
  May bring, or take away;
We ask not pleasure, pomp, nor power,
  Lest we should go astray.

4.

We ask for wisdom. Lord, impart
  The knowledge how to live:
A wise and understanding heart
  To all before thee give.

JAMES MONTGOMERY, 1771-1854.

HYMN 222.

NOX PRAECESSIT. C. M.   JOHN BAPTISTE CALKIN, 1827 —

A - MEN.

1.

WALK in the light! so shalt thou
    know
  That fellowship of love
His spirit only can bestow,
  Who reigns in light above.

2.

Walk in the light! and thou shalt find
  Thy heart made truly his,
Who dwells in cloudless light enshrined,
  In whom no darkness is.

3.

Walk in the light! and thou shalt own
  Thy darkness passed away,
Because that light hath on thee shone
  In which is perfect day.

4.

Walk in the light! and thine shall be
  A path, though thorny, bright;
For God, by grace, shall dwell in thee,
  And God himself is light.

BERNARD BARTON, 1784-1849.

HYMN 223.

HORSLEY. C. M.   WILLIAM HORSLEY, 1774—1858.

A-MEN

1.

BENEATH the shadow of the cross,
  As earthly hopes remove,
His new commandment Jesus gives, —
  His blessed word of love.

2.

O bond of union, strong and deep !
  O bond of perfect peace !
Not even the lifted cross can harm
  If we but hold to this.

3.

Then, Jesus, be thy spirit ours,
  And swift our feet shall move
To deeds of pure self-sacrifice,
  And the sweet tasks of love.

SAMUEL LONGFELLOW, 1819-1892.

HYMN 224.

ST. MAGNUS. C. M.   JEREMIAH CLARK, 1670—1707.

A · MEN.

1.

POUR forth the oil, pour boldly forth ;
  It will not fail until
Thou failest vessels to provide
  Which it may freely fill.

2.

Dig channels for the streams of love,
  Where they may broadly run,
And love has overflowing streams
  To fill them every one.

3.

But if, at any time, thou cease
  Such channels to provide,
The very founts of love for thee
  Will soon be parched and dried.

4.

For we must share, if we would keep,
  That good thing from above ;
Ceasing to give, we cease to have :
  Such is the law of love.

RICHARD CHENEVIX TRENCH, 1807–1886.

HYMN 225.

ST. ALBAN. L. M.   ST. ALBAN'S TUNE BOOK, 1866.

A - MEN.

1.

O FOR that flame of living fire
  Which shone so bright in saints of
    old,
Which bade their souls to heaven aspire,
  Calm in distress, in danger bold, —

2.

That spirit which, from age to age,
  Proclaimed thy love and taught thy
    ways,
Brightened Isaiah's vivid page
  And breathed in David's hallowed lays !

3.

Is not thy grace as mighty now
  As when Elijah felt its power,
When glory beamed from Moses' brow,
  Or Job endured the trying hour?

4.

Remember, Lord, the ancient days,
  Renew thy work, thy grace restore,
Warm our cold hearts to prayer and
    praise,
  And teach us how to love thee more !

WILLIAM HILEY BATHURST, 1796-1877.

HYMN 226.

ALBANO. C. M.

VINCENT NOVELLO, 1781 — 1861.

A · MEN.

1.

WE pray no more, made lowly wise,
　For miracle and sign ;
Anoint our eyes to see within
　The common, the divine.

2.

" Lo here ! lo there ! " no more we cry,
　Dividing with our call
The mantle of thy presence, Lord,
　That seamless covers all.

3.

We turn from seeking thee afar,
　And in unwonted ways,
To build from out our daily lives
　The temples of thy praise.

4.

And if thy casual comings, Lord,
　To hearts of old were dear,
What joy shall dwell within the faith
　That feels thee ever near !

5.

And nobler yet shall duty grow,
　And more shall worship be,
When thou art found in all our life,
　And all our life in thee.

FREDERICK LUCIAN HOSMER, 1840-

HYMN 227.

INNSBRUCK. 8. 8. 6. 8. 8. 6. HEINRICH ISAAC, *circa* 1500.

A · MEN.

227.

LORD God, by whom all change is wrought,
By whom new things to birth are brought,
In whom no change is known,
Whate'er thou dost, whate'er thou art,
Thy people still in thee have part,
Still, still, thou art our own.

Spirit who makest all things new,
Thou leadest onward; we pursue
The heavenly march sublime :
'Neath thy renewing fire we glow,
And still from strength to strength we go,
From height to height we climb.

Darkness and dread we leave behind ;
New light, new glory, still we find,
New realms divine possess,
New births of grace new raptures bring ;
Triumphant the new song we sing,
The great Renewer bless.

THOMAS HORNBLOWER GILL, 1819

Hymn 228.

DALEHURST C. M   ARTHUR COTTMAN, 1842 — 1879.

A-MEN.

1.

NOW that the day-star glimmers bright,
  We suppliantly pray
That he, the uncreated Light,
  May guide us on our way.

2.

No sinful word, nor deed of wrong,
  Nor thoughts that idly rove,
But simple truth be on our tongue,
  And in our hearts be love.

3.

And grant that to thine honor, Lord,
  Our daily toil may tend,
That we begin it at thy word,
  And in thy favor end.

Tr. JOHN HENRY NEWMAN, 1801-1890.

Hymn 229.

MAINZER. L M.

JOSEPH MAINZER, 1801 — 1851.

A·MEN.

1.

TRUE Sun, upon our souls arise,
    Shining in beauty evermore,
And through each sense the quickening
    beam
    Of thy eternal spirit pour.

2.

Confirm us in each good resolve,
    The tempter's envious rage subdue,
Turn each misfortune to our good,
    Direct us right in all we do.

3.

Still, ever pure as morn's first ray,
    May modesty our steps attend,
Our faith be fervent as the noon,
    Upon our souls no night descend.

St. Ambrose, 340-397.
Tr Edward Caswall, 1814-1878.

HYMN 230.

First Tune.

MATINS. 8. 4. 7. 8. 4. 7.　　　　　JOHN SEBASTIAN BACH HODGES, 1830—

A - MEN.

230.

1.

COME, my soul, thou must be waking;
　　Now is breaking
　O'er the earth another day;
Come to him who made this splendor,
　　See thou render
　All thy feeble powers can pay.

2.

Thou, too, hail the light returning;
　　Ready burning
　Be the incense of thy powers;
For the night is safely ended:
　　God hath tended
　With his care thy helpless hours.

3.

Pray that he may prosper ever
　　Each endeavor
　When thine aim is good and true,
But that he may ever thwart thee,
　　And convert thee,
　When thou evil wouldst pursue.

4.

Round the gifts his bounty showers,
　　Walls and towers
　Girt with flames thy God shall rear.
Angel legions to defend thee
　　Shall attend thee,
　Hosts whom Satan's self shall fear.

Friedrich Rudolph Ludwig von Canitz, 1654-1699.
Tr. Henry James Buckoll, 1803-1871.

HYMN 230.

Second Tune.

CANITZ. 8. 4. 7. 8. 4. 7.

JOHN STAINER, 1840 —

A · MEN.

230.

1.

COME, my soul, thou must be waking;
　　Now is breaking
O'er the earth another day;
Come to him who made this splendor,
　　See thou render
All thy feeble powers can pay.

2.

Thou, too, hail the light returning;
　　Ready burning
Be the incense of thy powers;
For the night is safely ended:
　　God hath tended
With his care thy helpless hours.

3.

Pray that he may prosper ever
　　Each endeavor
When thine aim is good and true,
But that he may ever thwart thee,
　　And convert thee,
When thou evil wouldst pursue.

4.

Round the gifts his bounty showers,
　　Walls and towers
Girt with flames thy God shall rear.
Angel legions to defend thee
　　Shall attend thee,
Hosts whom Satan's self shall fear.

FRIEDRICH RUDOLPH LUDWIG VON CANITZ, 1654-1699.
Tr. HENRY JAMES BUCKOLL, 1803-1871.

Hymn 231.

CONFIDENCE. 10. 10. 10. 10.   JOSEPH BARNBY, 1838—1896.

A · MEN.

231.

1.

FATHER, there is no change to live with thee
     Save that in Christ I grow from day to day;
In each new word I hear, each thing I see,
     I but rejoicing hasten on my way.

2.

The morning comes, with blushes overspread,
     And I, new-wakened, find a morn within;
And in its modest dawn around me shed,
     Thou hear'st the prayer and the ascending hymn.

3.

Hour follows hour, the lengthening shades descend;
     Yet they could never reach as far as me,
Did not thy love its kind protection lend
     That I, thy child, might sleep in peace with thee.

JONES VERY, 1813-1880.

HYMN 232.

BAYNARD. 8.8.8.8.8.8.

JOSIAH BOOTH, 1852—

UNISON.

HARMONY.

A-MEN.

232.

THOU art, O God, the life and light
  Of all this wondrous world we see ;
Its glow by day, its smile by night,
  Are but reflections caught from thee :
Where'er we turn thy glories shine,
And all things fair and bright are thine.

2.

When day, with farewell beam, delays
  Among the opening clouds of even,
And we can almost think we gaze
  Through golden vistas into heaven,
Those hues that make the sun's decline
So soft, so radiant, Lord, are thine.

3.

When youthful spring around us breathes,
  Thy spirit warms her fragrant sigh ;
And every flower the summer wreathes
  Is born beneath that kindling eye :
Where'er we turn, thy glories shine,
And all things fair and bright are thine.

THOMAS MOORE, 1779-1852

HYMN 233.

MEAR. C. M.

A - MEN.

1.

O LORD of life, thy quickening voice
  Awakes my morning song ;
In gladsome words I would rejoice
  That I to thee belong.

2.

I see thy light, I feel thy wind,
  The world, it is thy word ;
Whatever wakes my heart and mind,
  Thy presence is, my Lord.

3.

Therefore, I choose my highest part,
  And turn my face to thee ;
Therefore, I stir my inmost heart
  To worship fervently.

4.

Within my heart, speak, Lord, speak on,
  My heart alive to keep
Till comes the night, and, labor done,
  In thee I fall asleep.

GEORGE MACDONALD, 1824-

HYMN 234.

WINCHESTER NEW. L. M.   HAMBURGER MUSIKALISCHES HANDBUCH, 1690.

A · MEN

1.

NOW with the rising golden dawn,
   Let us, the children of the day,
Cast off the darkness which so long
   Has led our guilty souls astray.

2.

O, may the morn, so pure, so clear,
   Its own sweet calm in us instil, —
A guileless mind, a heart sincere,
   Simplicity of word and will, —

3.

And ever, as the day glides by,
   May we the busy senses rein,
Keep guard upon the hand and eye,
   Nor let the body suffer stain.

4.

For all day long, on heaven's high tower,
   There stands a sentinel, who spies
Our every action, hour by hour,
   From early dawn till daylight dies.

AURELIUS CLEMENS PRUDENTIUS, 348 - *circa* 413
Tr. EDWARD CASWALL, 1814-1878.

HYMN 235.

VENTNOR. 11. 10. 11. 10.   JOSEPH BARNBY, 1838—1896.

A - MEN.

235.

STILL, still with thee, when purple morning breaketh,
When the bird waketh, and the shadows flee;
Fairer than morning, lovelier than the daylight,
Dawns the sweet consciousness, I am with thee.

2.

As in the dawning, o'er the waveless ocean,
The image of the morning star doth rest,
So in this stillness, thou beholdest only
Thine image in the waters of my breast.

3.

When sinks the soul, subdued by toil, to slumber,
Its closing eye looks up to thee in prayer;
Sweet the repose beneath the wings o'ershading,
But sweeter still to wake and find thee there.

4.

So shall it be at last, in that bright morning
When the soul waketh, and life's shadows flee:
O, in that hour, fairer than daylight dawning,
Shall rise the glorious thought, I am with thee.

HARRIET BEECHER STOWE. 1812-

HYMN 236.

ELY. L M.

THOMAS TURTON, 1780 — 1864.

A - MEN.

1.

EXPECTANT of my Lord's command,
    Till he my work appoint, I wait,—
Some work with which my powers may
    mate
Divinely suited to my hand,

2.

Some work by which my soul may grow
    In health and sinew, and acquire
    Strength to fulfil her large desire
That from the flower the fruit may show,

3.

Some work by which my heart may
    prove
On whom her steadfast wishes rest,
And undeniably attest
Her deep sincerity of love,

4.

Some work whose end shall make my
    days
Nor useless nor ignoble glide, —
A work whose influence shall abide,
Redounding to the Master's praise.

5.

O Master, I would yield to thee
    Of life's great energies the whole,
    E'en as the lavish rivers roll
Their wealth of waters to the sea.

WILLIAM TIDD MATSON, 1833

HYMN 237.

UNIVERSITY COLLEGE. 7.7.7.7.   HENRY JOHN GAUNTLETT, 1805—1876.

A · MEN.

1.

IN the morning I will raise
　To my God the voice of praise ;
With his kind protection blest,
Sweet and deep has been my rest.

2.

In the morning I will pray
For his blessing on the day ;
What this day shall be my lot,
Light or darkness, know I not.

3.

Should it be with clouds o'ercast,
Clouds of sorrow gathering fast,
Thou, who givest light divine,
Shine within me, Lord, O, shine !

4.

Show me, if I tempted be,
How to find all strength in thee,
And a perfect triumph win
Over every bosom sin.

5.

Then, when fall the shades of night,
All within shall still be light,
Thou wilt peace around diffuse,
Gently as the evening dews.

WILLIAM HENRY FURNESS, 1802-1896.

HYMN 238.

PENTECOST. L. M.   WILLIAM BOYD, 1846 —

A · MEN.

1.

GOD of the morning, at whose voice
    The cheerful sun makes haste to rise,
And like a giant doth rejoice
    To run his journey through the skies, —

2.

O, like the sun may I fulfil
    The appointed duties of the day,
With ready mind and active will
    March on, and keep my heavenly way !

3.

Lord, thy commands are clean and pure,
    Enlightening our beclouded eyes,
Thy threatenings just, thy promise sure ;
    Thy gospel makes the simple wise.

4.

Give me thy counsel for my guide,
    And then receive me to thy bliss :
All my desires and hopes beside
    Are faint and cold, compared with this.

ISAAC WATTS, 1674-1748.

HYMN 239.

HESPERUS. L. M.   HENRY BAKER, 1835—

A · MEN.

1.

O GOD, I thank thee for each sight
    Of beauty that thy hand doth give, —
For sunny skies and air and light :
    O God, I thank thee that I live.

2.

That life I consecrate to thee :
    And ever, as the day is born,
On wings of joy my soul would flee,
    And thank thee for another morn, —

3.

Another day in which to cast
    Some silent deed of love abroad,
That, greatening as it journeys past,
    May do some earnest work for God,

4.

Another day to do, to dare,
    To tax anew my growing strength,
To arm my soul with faith and prayer,
    And so reach heaven and thee at length.

CAROLINE ATHERTON MASON, 1823-1890.

Hymn 240.

MORNING HYMN. L. M.   FRANÇOIS HIPPOLITE BARTHÉLÉMON, 1741—1808.

A · MEN.

1.

A WAKE, my soul, and with the sun
  Thy daily stage of duty run,
Shake off dull sloth, and joyful rise
To pay thy morning sacrifice !

2.

Wake and lift up thyself, my heart,
And with the angels bear thy part,
Who all night long unwearied sing
High praise to the eternal King !

3.

Lord, I my vows to thee renew :
Disperse my sins as morning dew,
Guard my first springs of thought and will,
And with thyself my spirit fill.

4.

Direct, control, suggest this day
All I design, or do, or say, —
That all my powers, with all their might,
In thy sole glory may unite.

THOMAS KEN, 1637-1711.

Hymn 241.

NAYLOR. L. M.   JOHN NAYLOR, 1838—

A · MEN.

1.

O NCE more the daylight shines
    abroad ;
O brethren, let us praise the Lord,
Whose grace and mercy thus have kept
The nightly watch while we have slept.

2.

Eternal God, almighty Friend,
Whose deep compassions have no end,
Whose never-failing strength and might
Have kept us safely through the night,—

3.

Now send us from thy heavenly throne
Thy grace and help, through Christ thy
    Son,
That with thy strength our hearts may
    glow,
And fear nor man nor ghostly foe.

4.

We offer up ourselves to thee,
That heart, and word, and deed may be
In all things guided by thy mind,
And in thine eyes acceptance find.

MICHAEL WEISSE, circa 1480-1514.
TR. CATHERINE WINKWORTH, 1829-1878.

HYMN 242.

KEBLE. L. M.　　　　　　　　JOHN BACCHUS DYKES, 1823 — 1876.

A - MEN.

1.

Lord of all being, throned afar,
Thy glory flames from sun and star;
Centre and soul of every sphere,
Yet to each loving heart how near!

2.

Sun of our life, thy quickening ray
Sheds on our path the glow of day:
Star of our hope, thy softened light
Cheers the long watches of the night.

3.

Our midnight is thy smile withdrawn;
Our noontide is thy gracious dawn;
Our rainbow arch, thy mercy's sign:
All, save the clouds of sin, are thine.

4.

Lord of all life, below, above,
Whose light is truth, whose warmth is love:
Before thy ever-blazing throne
We ask no lustre of our own.

5.

Grant us thy truth to make us free,
And kindling hearts that burn for thee,
Till all thy living altars claim
One holy light, one heavenly flame.

OLIVER WENDELL HOLMES, 1809-1894.

Hymn 243.

MELCOMBE. L. M.   SAMUEL WEBBE, 1740—1816.

A - MEN.

1.

O TIMELY happy, timely wise,
  Hearts that with rising morn arise,
Eyes that the beam celestial view
Which evermore makes all things new!

2.

New every morning is the love
Our wakening and uprising prove, —
Through sleep and darkness safely brought,
Restored to life, and power, and thought.

3.

New mercies, each returning day,
Hover around us while we pray, —
New perils past, new sins forgiven,
New thoughts of God, new hopes of heaven.

4.

If on our daily course our mind
Be set to hallow all we find,
New treasures still, of countless price,
God will provide for sacrifice.

5.

The trivial round, the common task,
Would furnish all we ought to ask, —
Room to deny ourselves, a road
To bring us daily nearer God.

6.

Only, O Lord, in thy dear love
Fit us for perfect rest above,
And help us. this and every day,
To live more nearly as we pray.

JOHN KEBLE, 1702-1866.

HYMN 244.

ELVET. C. M.   JOHN BACCHUS DYKES, 1823—1876.

A · MEN.

1.

E ARLY, my God, without delay,
    I haste to seek thy face ;
My thirsty spirit faints away
    Without thy cheering grace :

2.

So pilgrims on the scorching sand,
    Beneath a burning sky,
Long for a cooling stream at hand,
    And they must drink or die.

3.

Thus, till my last expiring day,
    I 'll bless my God and King ;
Thus will I lift my hands to pray,
    And tune my lips to sing.

ISAAC WATTS, 1674-1748

HYMN 245.

ST. PETER. C. M.   ALEXANDER ROBERT REINAGLE, 1799 — 1877.

A-MEN.

1.

O GOD, whose daylight leadeth down
   Into the sunless way,
Who, with restoring sleep, dost crown
   The labor of the day,

2.

What I have done, Lord, make it clean
   With thy forgiveness dear,
That so to-day what might have been
   To-morrow may appear.

3.

And, when my thought is all astray,
   Yet think thou on in me,
That with the new-born innocent day
   My soul rise fresh and free.

4.

Nor let me wander all in vain
   Through dreams that mock and flee,
But even in visions of the brain
   Go wandering towards thee.

GEORGE MACDONALD, 1824-

HYMN 246.

TWILIGHT. 11. 11. 11. 5.   JOSEPH BARNBY, 1838—1896.

A · MEN.

246.

1.

NOW God be with us, for the night is closing;
   The light and darkness are of his disposing,
And 'neath his shadow here to rest we yield us,
      For he will shield us.

2.

Let pious thoughts be ours when sleep o'ertakes us,
Our earliest thoughts be thine when morning wakes us,
All day serve thee, — in all that we are doing
      Thy praise pursuing.

3.

We have no refuge. none on earth to aid us,
Save thee, O Father, who thine own hast made us;
But thy dear presence will not leave them lonely
      Who seek thee only.

4.

Father, thy name be praised, thy kingdom given,
Thy will be done on earth as 't is in heaven,
Keep us in life, forgive our sins, deliver
      Us now and ever!

PETRUS HERBERT, -1571.
TR. CATHERINE WINKWORTH, 1829-1878.

HYMN 247.

EVENTIDE. 10. 10. 10. 10.

WILLIAM HENRY MONK, 1823 — 1889.

A · MEN.

247.

1.

ABIDE with me! fast falls the eventide,
The darkness deepens: Lord, with me abide!
When other helpers fail, and comforts flee,
Help of the helpless, O, abide with me!

2.

Swift to its close ebbs out life's little day;
Earth's joys grow dim, its glories pass away;
Change and decay in all around I see:
O thou who changest not, abide with me!

3.

I need thy presence every passing hour:
What but thy grace can foil the tempter's power?
Who like thyself my guide and stay can be?
Through cloud and sunshine, O, abide with me!

4.

I fear no foe, with thee at hand to bless;
Ills have no weight, and tears no bitterness:
Where is death's sting? where, grave, thy victory?
I triumph still if thou abide with me.

5.

Hold thou thy cross before my closing eyes,
Shine through the gloom, and point me to the skies.
Heaven's morning breaks, and earth's vain shadows flee:
In life and death, O Lord, abide with me!

HENRY FRANCIS LYTE, 1793-1847

HYMN 248.

HURSLEY. L. M.   PETER RITTER, 1760—1846.

A · MEN.

1.

'TIS gone, that bright and orbèd blaze,
Fast fading from our wistful gaze ;
Yon mantling cloud has hid from sight
The last faint pulse of quivering light.

2.

Sun of my soul, thou Saviour dear,
It is not night if thou be near :
O, may no earth-born cloud arise
To hide thee from thy servant's eyes.

3.

When the soft dews of kindly sleep
My wearied eyelids gently steep,
Be my last thought, how sweet to rest
Forever on my Saviour's breast.

4.

Abide with me from morn till eve,
For without thee I cannot live ;
Abide with me when night is nigh,
For without thee I dare not die.

5.

Come near and bless us when we wake,
Ere through the world our way we take,
Till in the ocean of thy love
We lose ourselves in heaven above.

JOHN KEBLE, 1792-1866.

HYMN 249.

CRUCIFIXION. 8.7.8.7.   JOHN STAINER, 1840—

A-MEN.

1.

W HEN the light of day is waning,
    When the night is dark and drear,
God of love, in stillness reigning,
    Teach me to believe thee near.

2.

When my heart is faint and drooping,
    When my faith is dead and cold,
Kindly to my weakness stooping,
    Draw me upwards as of old, —

3.

Nearer to the peace unbroken,
    Nearer to the changeless calm,
All my wish a prayer unspoken,
    All my life a silent psalm.

4.

Teach me to abide in patience
    All the little storms of time,
Making every day's temptations
    Steps for faltering feet to climb.

5.

Let me find thee in my sorrow,
    Nor forget thee in my joy,
And from thee my sunshine borrow,
    And by thee my gloom destroy.

6.

God of day, the dark dispelling,
    Guide, Redeemer, Father, Friend,
God of love, in stillness dwelling,
    Lead me to my journey's end !

EDMUND MARTIN GELDART. 1844-1885.

HYMN 250.

ALL HALLOWS. 8. 6. 8. 6. 8. 6. ARTHUR HENRY BROWN, 1830 — .

A - MEN.

250.

1.

O SHADOW in a sultry land,
   We gather to thy breast,
Whose love, enfolding like the night,
   Brings quietude and rest, —
Glimpse of the fairer life to be,
   In foretaste here possessed.

2.

From aimless wanderings we come,
   From drifting to and fro,
The wave of being mingles deep
   Amid its ebb and flow:
The grander sweep of tides serene
   Our spirits yearn to know.

3.

That which the garish day had lost
   The twilight vigil brings,
While softlier the vesper bell
   Its silver cadence rings, —
The sense of an immortal trust,
   The brush of angel wings.

4.

Drop down behind the solemn hills,
   O day with golden skies,
Serene, above its fading glow,
   Night, starry-crowned, arise!
So beautiful may heaven be
   When life's last sunbeam dies.

CHARLOTTE MELLEN PACKARD, 1830.

HYMN 251.

ST. LEONARD. C. M. D.   HENRY HILES, 1826—   .

A - MEN.

251.

1.

THE shadows of the evening hours
   Fall from the darkening sky;
Upon the fragrance of the flowers
   The dews of evening lie.
Before thy throne, O Lord of heaven,
   We kneel at close of day:
Look on thy children from on high,
   And hear us while we pray.

2.

Slowly the rays of daylight fade;
   So fade within our heart
The hopes in earthly love and joy
   That one by one depart.
Slowly the bright stars, one by one,
   Within the heavens shine;
Give us, O Lord, fresh hopes in heaven,
   And trust in things divine.

3.

Let peace, O Lord, — thy peace, O God, —
   Upon our souls descend,
From midnight fears and perils thou
   Our trembling hearts defend,
Give us a respite from our toil,
   Calm and subdue our woes.
Through the long day we suffer, Lord, —
   O, give us now repose.

ADELAIDE ANNE PROCTER, 1825-1864.

HYMN 252.

GERMANY. L. M.   LUDWIG VAN BEETHOVEN, 1770—1827.

A - MEN.

252.

1.

AGAIN, as evening's shadow falls,
We gather in these hallowed walls,
And vesper hymn and vesper prayer
Rise mingling on the holy air.

2.

May struggling hearts that seek release
Here find the rest of God's own peace,
And, strengthened here by hymn and prayer,
Lay down the burden and the care.

3.

O God, our Light, to thee we bow;
Within all shadows standest thou.
Give deeper calm than night can bring,
Give sweeter songs than lips can sing.

4.

Life's tumult we must meet again,
We cannot at the shrine remain;
But in the spirit's secret cell
May hymn and prayer forever dwell.

SAMUEL LONGFELLOW, 1819-1892.

Hymn 253.

FORGIVENESS. 7. 7. 7. 7.   George Mursell Garrett, 1834 —

A - MEN.

1.

SLOWLY, by thy hand unfurled,
   Down around the weary world
Falls the darkness.   O, how still
Is the working of thy will !

2.

Mighty Maker, ever nigh,
Work in me as silently,
Veil the day's distracting sights,
Show me heaven's eternal lights ;

3.

Living worlds to view be brought
In the boundless realms of thought,
High and infinite desires,
Flaming like those upper fires ;

4.

Holy truth, eternal right,
Let them break upon my sight,
Let them shine, serene and still,
And with light my being fill.

WILLIAM HENRY FURNESS, 1802-1896.

HYMN 254.

WEBER. 7. 7 7.7.   CARL MARIA VON WEBER, 1786 — 1826.

A - MEN.

1.

SOFTLY now the light of day
    Fades upon my sight away ;
Free from care, from labor free,
Lord, I would commune with thee.

2.

Thou, whose all-pervading eye
    Nought escapes, without, within,
Pardon each infirmity,
Open fault, and secret sin.

3.

Soon for me the light of day
Shall forever pass away ;
Then, from sin and sorrow free,
Take me, Lord, to dwell with thee.

GEORGE WASHINGTON DOANE, 1799–1859.

HYMN 255.

PENITENTIA. 10. 10. 10. 10.   EDWARD DEARLE, 1806—1891.

A · MEN.

255.

1.

O LORD, who by thy presence hast made light
  The heat and burden of the toilsome day,
Be with me also in the silent night,
  Be with me when the daylight fades away.

2.

As thou hast given me strength upon the way,
  So deign at evening to become my guest;
As thou hast shared the labors of the day,
  So also deign to share and bless my rest.

3.

Fraught with rich blessing, breathing sweet repose,
  The calm of evening settles on my breast;
If thou be with me when my labors close,
  No more is needed to complete my rest.

4.

Come, then. O Lord, and deign to be my guest,
  After the day's confusion. toil, and din:
O, come to bring me peace, and joy, and rest,
  To give salvation, and to pardon sin!

5.

Bind up the wounds. assuage the aching smart
  Left in my bosom from the day just past.,
And let me, on a Father's loving heart,
  Forget my griefs, and find sweet rest at last.

CARL JOHANN PHILIPP SPITTA, 1801-1859
Tr. RICHARD MASSIE, 1800-1887.

HYMN 256.

BENEDICTION. 10. 10. 10. 10. EDWARD JOHN HOPKINS, 1818— .

1ST STANZA.

Sav·iour, a · gain to thy dear name we raise With one ac-

cord our part·ing hymn of praise; We stand to bless thee

ere our wor·ship cease, Then, low·ly kneel·ing, wait thy word of peace.

2D Stanza.

Grant us thy peace up - on our home-ward way. With thee be-gan, with thee shall end the day; Guard thou the lips, from sin, the hearts from shame, That in this house have called up - on thy name.

256. — CONTINUED.

3D STANZA.

Grant us thy peace, through this ap·proach·ing night, Turn thou for us its dark·ness in·to light. From harm and dan·ger keep thy chil·dren free; For dark and light are both a·like to thee.

256. — CONCLUDED.

4TH STANZA.

Grant us thy peace through-out our earth-ly life, Our balm in

sor - row, and our stay in strife. Then, when thy voice shall

bid our conflict cease, Call us, O Lord, to thine e - ter-nal peace. A - MEN

JOHN ELLERTON, 1826–1893.

HYMN 257.

ASPIRATION. C. M. D.   JOSEPH BARNBY, 1838—1896.

A - MEN.

257.

1.

O LOVE divine, of all that is
    The sweetest still and best,
Fain would I come and rest to-night
    Upon thy tender breast.
I pray thee turn me not away,
    For, sinful though I be,
Thou knowest everything I need,
    And all my need of thee.

2.

And yet the spirit in my heart
    Says, wherefore should I pray
That thou shouldst seek me with thy love,
    Since thou dost seek alway,
And dost not even wait until
    I urge my steps to thee,
But in the darkness of my life
    Art coming still to me?

3.

I do not pray because I would;
    I pray because I must:
There is no meaning in my prayer
    But thankfulness and trust;
And thou wilt hear the thought I mean,
    And not the words I say,
Wilt hear the thanks among the words
    That only seem to pray.

4.

I would not have thee otherwise
    Than what thou still must be;
Yea, thou art God, and what thou art
    Is ever best for me.
And so, for all my sighs, my heart
    Shall sing itself to rest,
O Love divine, most far and near,
    Upon thy tender breast.

JOHN WHITE CHADWICK, 1840-

Hymn 258.

TEMPLE. 8.4.8.4.8.8.8.4.   Edward John Hopkins, 1818—

A · MEN.

258.

1.

GOD that madest earth and heaven,
　　Darkness and light,
Who the day for toil hast given,
　　For rest the night, —
May thine angel guards defend us,
Slumber sweet thy mercy send us,
Holy dreams and hopes attend us,
　　This livelong night.

2.

Guard us waking, guard us sleeping,
　　And when we die
May we in thy mighty keeping
　　All peaceful lie.
When the last dread trump shall wake us,
Do not thou, our Lord, forsake us,
But to reign in glory take us
　　With thee on high!

REGINALD HEBER, 1783-1826.
RICHARD WHATELY, 1787-1863.

HYMN 259.

ST. BEES. 7.7.7.7.   JOHN BACCHUS DYKES, 1823 — 1876.

A · MEN.

1.

NOW the wings of day are furled
    And the earth has gone to rest:
Take me, Shepherd of the world,
    Home to sleep upon thy breast.

2.

All the night from dream to dream,
    Keep my spirit pure and bright,
Fill the darkness with the stream
    Of thine everlasting light.

3.

If I waken, calm and fair
    Be the thoughts that in me rise,
And thy presence in the air
    Make my heart a paradise ;

4.

But if trouble in my heart,
    Or fierce pain me restless keep,
Then to me thy peace impart,
    Give me, thy belovèd, sleep.

5.

So, when morning with his wing
    Wakens me to work and play,
I may rise with joy and sing :
    " God has turned my night to day."

STOPFORD AUGUSTUS BROOKE, 1832-

HYMN 260.

MERRIAL. 6 5. 6. 5
JOSEPH BARNBY, 1838 — 1896.

A · MEN

1.

NOW the day is over,
  Night is drawing nigh;
Shadows of the evening
  Steal across the sky.

2.

Jesus, give the weary
  Calm and sweet repose;
With thy tenderest blessing
  May our eyelids close.

3.

Comfort every sufferer
  Watching late in pain.
Those who plan some evil
  From their sin restrain.

4.

Through the long night watches
  May thine angels spread
Their white wings above me,
  Watching round my bed.

5.

When the morning wakens,
  Then may I arise
Pure, and fresh, and sinless
  In thy holy eyes.

SABINE BARING-GOULD, 1834-

HYMN 261.

EISENACH. L. M.   JOHANN HERMANN SCHEIN, 1586—1630.

A - MEN.

1.

O THOU true life of all that live,
    Who dost, unmoved, all motion sway,
Who dost the morn and evening give,
    And through its changes guide the day,—

2.

Thy light upon our evening pour,
    So may our souls no sunset see,
But death to us an open door
    To an eternal morning be !

St Ambrose, 340-397.
Tr Edward Caswall, 1814-1878.

HYMN 262.

ABENDS. L. M.   HERBERT STANLEY OAKELEY, 1830—

A · MEN.

1.

THUS far the Lord has led me on,
   Thus far his power prolongs my days ;
And every evening shall make known
   Some fresh memorial of his grace.

2.

Much of my time has run to waste,
   And I, perhaps, am near my home ;
But he forgives my follies past,
   He gives me strength for days to come.

3.

I lay my body down to sleep,
   Peace is the pillow for my head,
While well-appointed angels keep
   Their watchful stations round my bed.

4.

Faith in his name forbids my fear :
   O, may thy presence ne'er depart,
And in the morning make me hear
   The love and kindness of thy heart.

ISAAC WATTS, 1674-1748.

HYMN 263.

LUX BENIGNA. 10. 4. 10. 4. 10. 10.   JOHN BACCHUS DYKES, 1823 — 1876.

A · MEN.

263.

1.

LEAD, kindly Light, amid the encircling gloom,
    Lead thou me on!
The night is dark, and I am far from home, —
    Lead thou me on!
Keep thou my feet! I do not ask to see
The distant scene — one step enough for me.

2.

I was not ever thus, nor prayed that thou
    Shouldst lead me on;
I loved to choose and see my path; but now
    Lead thou me on!
I loved the garish day, and, spite of fears,
Pride ruled my will: remember not past years!

3.

So long thy power hath blest me, sure it still
    Will lead me on,
O'er moor and fen, o'er crag and torrent, till
    The night is gone,
And with the morn those angel faces smile
Which I have loved long since, and lost awhile.

JOHN HENRY NEWMAN, 1801-1890

Hymn 264.

TALLIS'S CANON. L. M.

THOMAS TALLIS, 1520 — 1585.

A · MEN.

1.

A LL praise to thee, my God, this night,
   For all the blessings of the light !
Keep me, O, keep me, King of kings,
Beneath thy own almighty wings !

2.

Forgive me, Lord, for thy dear Son,
The ill that I this day have done,
That with the world, myself, and thee,
I, ere I sleep, at peace may be.

3.

When in the night I sleepless lie,
My soul with heavenly thoughts supply,
Let no ill dreams disturb my rest,
No powers of darkness me molest.

4.

O, may my soul on thee repose,
And with sweet sleep mine eyelids close,
Sleep that may me more vigorous make
To serve my God when I awake.

THOMAS KEN, 1637–1711.

Hymn 265.

DUKE STREET. L. M.

JOHN HATTON, —1793

A·MEN.

1.

GREAT God, we sing that mighty hand
By which supported still we stand :
The opening year thy mercy shows ;
That mercy crowns it till it close.

2.

By day, by night, at home, abroad,
Still are we guarded by our God,
By his incessant bounty fed,
By his unerring counsel led.

3.

With grateful hearts the past we own ;
The future, all to us unknown,
We to thy guardian care commit,
And, peaceful, leave before thy feet.

4.

In scenes exalted or depressed,
Thou art our joy, and thou our rest ;
Thy goodness all our hopes shall raise,
Adored through all our changing days.

PHILIP DODDRIDGE, 1702-1751.

HYMN 266.

NEUMARK. 9. 8. 9. 8. 8. 8.

GEORG NEUMARK, 1621 — 1681.

A · MEN.

266.

1.

HELP us, O Lord! behold, we enter
    Upon another year to-day;
In thee our hopes and thoughts now centre;
    Renew our courage for the way.
New life, new strength, new happiness,
We ask of thee. O, hear and bless!

2.

May every plan and undertaking
    This year be all begun with thee;
When I am sleeping or am waking,
    Still let me know thou art with me;
Abroad, do thou my footsteps guide,
At home, be ever at my side!

3.

And grant, Lord, when the year is over,
    That it for me in peace may close;
In all things care for me, and cover
    My head in time of fear and woes:
So may I, when my years are gone,
Appear with joy before thy throne.

JOHANN RIST, 1607-1667.
Tr. CATHERINE WINKWORTH, 1829-1878.

HYMN 267.

BRISTOL. C. M.   EDWARD HODGES, 1796—1867.

A - MEN.

1.

THE glory of the spring how sweet !
  The new-born life how glad !
What joy the happy earth to greet
  In new, bright raiment clad !

2.

Divine Renewer, thee I bless ;
  I greet thy going forth ;
I love thee in the loveliness
  Of thy renewèd earth.

3.

But, O, these wonders of thy grace,
  These nobler works of thine,
These marvels sweeter far to trace,
  These new-births more divine, —

4.

Creator Spirit, work in me
  These wonders sweet of thine !
Divine Renewer, graciously
  Renew this heart of mine !

THOMAS HORNBLOWER GILL, 1819- .

HYMN 268.

NUREMBERG. 7.7.7.7. JOHANN RUDOLPH AHLE, 1625—1673.

A-MEN.

1.

PRAISE to God, immortal praise,
   For the love that crowns our days !
Bounteous source of every joy,
Let thy praise our tongues employ !

2.

All that Spring with bounteous hand
Scatters o'er the smiling land ;
All that liberal Autumn pours
From her rich o'erflowing stores, —

3.

These to thee, my God, we owe,
Source whence all our blessings flow ;
And for these my soul shall raise
Grateful vows and solemn praise.

4.

Should thine altered hand restrain
The early and the latter rain,
Blast each opening bud of joy
And the rising year destroy, —

5.

Yet to thee my soul should raise
Grateful vows and solemn praise,
And, when every blessing's flown,
Love thee for thyself alone.

ANNA LAETITIA BARBAULD, 1743-1825.

HYMN 269.

NUN DANKET. 6. 7. 6. 7. 6. 6. 6. 6.　　　　JOHANN CRÜGER, 1598 — 1662.

A - MEN.

269.

1.

NOW thank we all our God,
    With heart and hands and voices,
Who wondrous things hath done,
  In whom his world rejoices,
    Who from our mother's arms
      Hath blessed us on our way
    With countless gifts of love,
    And still is ours to-day.

2.

O, may this bounteous God
  Through all our life be near us,
With ever joyful hearts
  And blessèd peace to cheer us,
    And keep us in his grace,
      And guide us when perplexed,
    And free us from all ills
    In this world and the next.

MARTIN RINKART, 1586-1649.
Tr. CATHERINE WINKWORTH, 1829-1878.

HYMN 270.

CAMDEN L M.   JOHN BAPTISTE CALKIN, 1827 —

A · MEN.

1.

SILENT, like men in solemn haste,
   Girded wayfarers of the waste,
We press along the narrow road
That leads to life, to bliss, to God.

2.

No idling now, no wasteful sleep,
From Christian toil our limbs to keep,
No shrinking from the desperate fight,
No thought of yielding or of flight,

3.

No love of present gain or ease,
No seeking man nor self to please :
With the brave heart and steady eye,
We onward march to victory.

4.

What though with weariness oppressed ?
'T is but a little, and we rest, —
Finished the toil, the rest begun :
The battle fought, the triumph won.

HORATIUS BONAR, 1808-1889.

Hymn 271.

SCHUMANN. S. M. ROBERT SCHUMANN, 1810 — 1856.

A - MEN.

1.

" FOREVER with the Lord ! "
   Amen : so let it be ;
Life from the dead is in that word,
   'T is immortality.

2.

Here in the body pent,
   Absent from him I roam,
Yet nightly pitch my moving tent
A day's march nearer home.

3.

My Father's house on high,
   Home of my soul, how near
At times to faith's foreseeing eye
   Thy golden gates appear !

4.

I hear at morn and even,
   At noon and midnight hour,
The choral harmonies of heaven
   Earth's Babel-tongues o'erpower.

5.

Then, then I feel that he,
   Remembered or forgot,
The Lord, is never far from me,
   Though I perceive him not.

JAMES MONTGOMERY, 1771-1854.

HYMN 272.

EWING. 7.6.7.6.7 6.7.6.

ALEXANDER EWING, 1830—1895.

A - MEN.

272.

1.

JERUSALEM the golden,
  With milk and honey blest,
Beneath thy contemplation
  Sink heart and voice oppressed.
I know not, O, I know not,
  What social joys are there,
What radiancy of glory,
  What light beyond compare!

2.

They stand, those halls of Zion,
  Conjubilant with song,
And bright with many an angel
  And all the martyr throng.
And they who, with their Leader,
  Have conquered in the fight,
Forever and forever
  Are clad in robes of white.

3.

Jerusalem the glorious,
  The glory of the elect,
O dear and future vision
  That eager hearts expect.
New mansion of new people,
  Whom God's own love and light
Promote, increase, make holy,
  Identify, unite!

BERNARD OF MORLAIX, *circa* 1125.
Tr. JOHN MASON NEALE, 1818-1866.

Hymn 273.

ALFORD. 7. 6. 8. 6. 7. 6. 8. 6.   John Bacchus Dykes, 1823 — 1876.

A - MEN.

273.

TEN thousand times ten thousand,
  In sparkling raiment bright,
The armies of the ransomed saints
  Throng up the steeps of light.
'T is finished, all is finished,
  Their fight with death and sin;
Fling open wide the golden gates,
  And let the victors in!

2.

What rush of alleluias
  Fills all the earth and sky!
What ringing of a thousand harps
  Bespeaks the triumph nigh!
O day, for which creation
  And all its tribes were made!
O joy, for all its former woes
  A thousand-fold repaid!

3.

O, then what raptured greetings
  On Canaan's happy shore,
What knitting severed friendships up,
  Where partings are no more!
Then eyes with joy shall sparkle
  That brimmed with tears of late,
Orphans no longer fatherless,
  Nor widows desolate.

HENRY ALFORD, 1810–1871.

HYMN 274.

First Tune.

PILGRIMS. 11. 10. 11. 10. 9. 11.

HENRY SMART, 1813—1879.

A-MEN.

274.

1.

HARK, hark, my soul! angelic songs are swelling
  O'er earth's green fields and ocean's wave-beat shore:
How sweet the truth those blessèd strains are telling
  Of that new life when sin shall be no more!
    Angels of Jesus, angels of light,
    Singing to welcome the pilgrims of the night!

2.

Far, far away, like bells at evening pealing,
  The voice of Jesus sounds o'er land and sea,
And laden souls by thousands meekly stealing,
  Kind Shepherd, turn their weary steps to thee.
    Angels of Jesus, angels of light,
    Singing to welcome the pilgrims of the night!

3.

Onward we go, for still we hear them singing,
  "Come, weary souls, for Jesus bids you come;"
And through the dark, its echoes sweetly ringing,
  The music of the gospel leads us home.
    Angels of Jesus, angels of light,
    Singing to welcome the pilgrims of the night!

4.

Angels! sing on, your faithful watches keeping;
  Sing us sweet fragments of the songs above.
While we toil on, and soothe ourselves with weeping,
  Till life's long night shall break in endless love.
    Angels of Jesus, angels of light,
    Singing to welcome the pilgrims of the night!

FREDERICK WILLIAM FABER, 1814-1863

HYMN 274.

Second Tune.

CARMEN COELI. 11. 10. 11. 10. 9. 11.

JOSEPH BARNBY, 1838 — 1896.

A-MEN.

274.

1.

HARK, hark, my soul! angelic songs are swelling
    O'er earth's green fields and ocean's wave-beat shore:
How sweet the truth those blessèd strains are telling
    Of that new life when sin shall be no more!
        Angels of Jesus, angels of light,
        Singing to welcome the pilgrims of the night!

2.

Far, far away, like bells at evening pealing,
    The voice of Jesus sounds o'er land and sea,
And laden souls by thousands meekly stealing,
    Kind Shepherd, turn their weary steps to thee.
        Angels of Jesus, angels of light,
        Singing to welcome the pilgrims of the night!

3.

Onward we go, for still we hear them singing,
    "Come, weary souls, for Jesus bids you come;"
And through the dark, its echoes sweetly ringing,
    The music of the gospel leads us home.
        Angels of Jesus, angels of light,
        Singing to welcome the pilgrims of the night!

4.

Angels! sing on, your faithful watches keeping;
    Sing us sweet fragments of the songs above,
While we toil on, and soothe ourselves with weeping,
    Till life's long night shall break in endless love.
        Angels of Jesus, angels of light,
        Singing to welcome the pilgrims of the night!

FREDERICK WILLIAM FABER, 1814-1863.

HYMN 275.

SARUM. 10. 10. 10. 4.   JOSEPH BARNBY, 1838—1896.

A . MEN.

275.

1.

FOR all the saints, who from their labors rest,
Who thee by faith before the world confessed,
Thy name, O Jesus, be forever blessed.

Alleluia !

2.

Thou wast their rock, their fortress, and their might;
Thou, Lord, their captain in the well-fought fight;
Thou, in the darkness drear, their one true light.

Alleluia !

3.

O, may thy soldiers, faithful, true, and bold,
Fight as the saints, who nobly fought of old,
And win with them the victor's crown of gold.

Alleluia !

4.

O blest communion, fellowship divine !
We feebly struggle, they in glory shine ;
Yet all are one in thee, for all are thine.

Alleluia !

WILLIAM WALSHAM HOW, 1823-

HYMN 276.

ANGELUS. L. M.　　　　　　　　　　　　　　　GEORG JOSEPHI, *circa* 1657.

A - MEN.

276.

1.

LIKE shadows gliding o'er the plain,
　　Or clouds that roll successive on,
Man's busy generations pass;
　　And while we gaze their forms are gone.

2.

"He lived, — he died;" behold the sum,
　　The abstract, of the historian's page!
Alike in God's all-seeing eye
　　The infant's day, the patriarch's age.

3.

O Father, in whose mighty hand
　　The boundless years and ages lie,
Teach us thy boon of life to prize,
　　And use the moments as they fly, —

4.

To crowd the narrow span of life
　　With wise designs and virtuous deeds.
So shall we wake from death's dark night
　　To share the glory that succeeds.

JOHN TAYLOR, 1750–1826.

HYMN 277.

ELVET. C. M.   JOHN BACCHUS DYKES, 1823—1876.

A · MEN.

1.

EARTH, with its dark and dreadful ills,
  Recedes, and fades away ;
Lift up your heads, ye heavenly hills,
  Ye gates of death, give way !

2.

My soul is full of whispered song,
  My blindness is my sight,
The shadows that I feared so long
  Are all alive with light.

3.

The while my pulses faintly beat,
  My faith doth so abound
I feel grow firm beneath my feet
  The green immortal ground.

4.

That faith to me a courage gives
  Low as the grave to go :
I know that my Redeemer lives ;
  That I shall live, I know.

5.

The palace walls I almost see,
  Where dwells my Lord and King :
O grave, where is thy victory ?
  O death, where is thy sting ?

ALICE CARY, 1820-1871.

HYMN 278.

HORSLEY. C. M.

WILLIAM HORSLEY, 1774—1858.

A · MEN.

1.

THUS heaven is gathering, one by one,
  In its capacious breast
All that is pure and permanent,
  And beautiful and blest;

2.

The family is scattered yet,
  Though of one home and heart,—
Part militant in earthly gloom,
  In heavenly glory part.

3.

But who can speak the rapture when
  The circle is complete,
And all the children sundered now
  Around one Father meet? —

4.

One fold, one Shepherd, one employ,
  One everlasting home:
"Lo, I come quickly!" "Even so,
  Amen, Lord Jesus, come!"

EDWARD HENRY BICKERSTETH, 1825-

HYMN 279.

ST. ALPHEGE. 7. 6. 7. 6.   HENRY JOHN GAUNTLETT, 1805 — 1876.

A - MEN.

1.

BRIEF life is here our portion,
  Brief sorrow, short-lived care ;
The life that knows no ending,
  The tearless life, is there.

2.

And after fleshly scandal,
  And after this world's night,
And after storm and whirlwind,
  Is calm and joy and light.

3.

There grief is turned to pleasure,
  Such pleasure as, below,
No human voice can utter,
  No human heart can know :

4.

The peace of all the faithful,
  The calm of all the blest,
Inviolate, unvaried,
  Divinest, sweetest, best.

5.

That peace, — but who may claim it?
  The guileless in their way,
Who keep the ranks of battle,
  Who mean the thing they say.

6.

Strive, man, to win that glory,
  Toil, man, to gain that light,
Send hope before to grasp it,
  Till hope be lost in sight !

BERNARD OF MORLAIX, *circa* 1125.
Tr. JOHN MASON NEALE, 1818-1866.

HYMN 280.

ST. GILES. 7. 6. 7. 6. JOHN STAINER, 1840—

A · MEN.

1.

AROUND my path life's mysteries
  Their deepening shadows throw ;
And, as I gaze and ponder,
  They dark and darker grow.

2.

Yet still, amid the darkness,
  I feel the light is near,
And in the awful silence
  God's voice I seem to hear.

3.

And I hear a voice above me
  Which says, " Wait, trust, and pray ;
The night will soon be over,
  And light will come with day."

4.

Amen ! the light and darkness
  Are both alike to thee :
Then to thy waiting servant
  Alike they both shall be.

5.

To him I yield my spirit ;
  On him I lay my load :
Fear ends with death ; beyond it
  I nothing see but God.

SAMUEL GREG, 1804-1877.

HYMN 281.

MELITA. 8. 8. 8. 8. 8. 8.   JOHN BACCHUS DYKES, 1823 — 1876.

A - MEN.

281.

1.

GOD of the living, in whose eyes
  Unveiled thy whole creation lies,
All souls are thine; we must not say
That those are dead who pass away:
From this our world of flesh set free,
We know them living unto thee.

2.

Released from earthly toil and strife,
With thee is hidden still their life;
Thine are their thoughts, their works, their powers,
All thine, and yet most truly ours:
For well we know, where'er they be,
Our dead are living unto thee.

3.

Not spilt like water on the ground,
Not wrapped in dreamless sleep profound,
Not wandering in unknown despair
Beyond thy voice, thine arm, thy care,
Not left to lie like fallen tree:
Not dead, but living unto thee.

4.

O Breather into man of breath,
O Holder of the keys of death,
O Quickener of the life within,
Save us from death, the death of sin,
That body, soul, and spirit be
Forever living unto thee!

John Ellerton, 1826–1893.

HYMN 282.

ST. MARTIN'S. C. M.   WILLIAM TANSUR, 1700 — 1783.

A - MEN.

282.

1.

G IVE ear, ye children, to my law
    Devout attention lend,
Let the instructions of my mouth
    Deep in your hearts descend.

2.

My tongue, by inspiration taught,
    Shall parables unfold:
Dark oracles, but understood,
    And owned for truths of old,

3.

Which we from sacred registers
    Of ancient times have known,
And our forefathers' pious care
    To us has handed down.

4.

Let children learn the mighty deeds
    Which God performed of old,
Which, in our younger years, we saw,
    And which our fathers told.

5.

Our lips shall tell them to our sons,
    And they again to theirs, —
That generations yet unborn
    May teach them to their heirs.

NAHUM TATE, 1652-1715.
NICHOLAS BRADY, 1659-1726.
ISAAC WATTS, 1674-1748.
JEREMY BELKNAP, 1744-1798.

HYMN 283.

HARVARD HYMN. 8. 8. 8. 7. 8. 8. 8. 7.   JOHN KNOWLES PAINE, 1839 —

1. De · us om · ni · um cre · a · tor, Re · rum mun · di   mo · de · ra · tor,
2. Pa · tres nos · tri huc per · la · ti, Tu o mo · ni · tu,   per · gra · ti,
3. Qua de spe fac te pre · ca · mur In e · ven · tu   ne fal · la · mur
4. Sic dum ci · vi · tas man · e · bit, Cla · rum lu · men   hic lu · ce · bit,

Cres · cat cu · ius es fun · da · tor, Nos · tra Un · i · ver · si · tas,
De · di · ca · runt ve · ri · ta · ti Par · vum tum con · le · gi · um,
Sed ma · io · ra dum co · na · mur Fa · ve · as la · bo · ri · bus,
Lu · ce an · gu · los re · ple · bit, Fu · ge · rit ob · scu · ri · tas,

283.

In·te·gri sint cu·ra·to·res, E·ru·di·ti pro·fes·so·res,
Id·que tu·o post fa·vo·re Auc·tum sem·per et a·mo·re
Si·mul gra·ti·as ha·be·mus Quod tam di·u iam flo·re·mus
Er·ror ter·ri·tus la·te·bit, Vir·tus vi·vi·da va·le·bit,

Lar·gi·an·tur do·na·to·res Be·ne par·tas co·pi·as.
Bo·nam spem os·ten·tat fo·re Tem·plum qua·si re·gi·um.
Nec au·di·re re·mit·te·mus Ve·ri·ta·tis mo·ni·tus.
Et in·sig·ni·or flo·re·bit Nos·tra U·ni·ver·si·tas. A·MEN.

JAMES BRADSTREET GREENOUGH, 1833~

HYMN 284.

ERFURT. L. M.

MARTIN LUTHER, 1483—1546.

A · MEN.

284.

1.

O GOD! beneath thy guiding hand
   Our exiled fathers crossed the sea;
And, when they trod the wintry strand,
   With prayer and psalm they worshipped thee.

2.

Thou heard'st, well pleased, the song, the prayer:
   Thy blessing came; and still its power
Shall onward through all ages bear
   The memory of that holy hour.

3.

Laws, freedom, truth, and faith in God
   Came with those exiles o'er the waves;
And where their pilgrim feet have trod,
   The God they trusted guards their graves.

4.

And here thy name, O God of love,
   Their children's children shall adore,
Till these eternal hills remove,
   And spring adorns the earth no more.

LEONARD BACON, 1802-1881.

Hymn 285.

EISENACH. L. M.　　　　　　　JOHANN HERMANN SCHEIN, 1586—1630.

A-MEN.

1.

O LORD of hosts, almighty King,
　Behold the sacrifice we bring !
To every arm thy strength impart,
Thy spirit shed through every heart.

2.

Wake in our breasts the living fires,
The holy faith, that warmed our sires !
Thy hand hath made our nation free ;
To die for her is serving thee.

3.

Be thou a pillared flame to show
The midnight snare, the silent foe,
And, when the battle thunders loud,
Still guide us in its moving cloud !

OLIVER WENDELL HOLMES, 1809-1894.

Hymn 286.

FARRANT. C. M.　　　　　　　　　　　　RICHARD FARRANT, 1530 — 1580.

A - MEN.

1.

O LORD of life and death, we come
　In sorrow to thy throne,
Yet not bewildered, blind, and dumb,
　Before some power unknown.

2.

The scourge is in our Father's hand,
　The plague comes forth from thee :
O, give us hearts to understand,
　And faith thy ways to see !

3.

Forgive the foul neglect that brought
　Thy chastening to our door, —
The homes uncleansed, the souls untaught,
　The unregarded poor ;

4.

The slothful ease, the greed of gain,
　The wasted years, forgive ;
Purge out our sins by needful pain,
　Then turn, and bid us live !

5.

So shall the lives for which we plead
　Be spared to praise thee still,
And we, from fear and danger freed,
　Be strong to do thy will.

JOHN ELLERTON, 1826-1893.

HYMN 287.

AMERICA.   6. 6. 4. 6. 6. 6. 4.   HENRY CAREY, 1685 — 1743.

A - MEN.

287.

1.

MY country, 't is of thee,
　　Sweet land of liberty,
　Of thee I sing:
Land where my fathers died,
Land of the pilgrims' pride,
From every mountain side
　Let freedom ring!

2.

My native country, thee, —
Land of the noble, free, —
　Thy name I love;
I love thy rocks and rills,
Thy woods and templed hills;
My heart with rapture thrills
　Like that above.

3.

Our fathers' God, to thee,
Author of liberty, —
　To thee we sing:
Long may our land be bright
With freedom's holy light!
Protect us by thy might,
　Great God, our King!

SAMUEL FRANCIS SMITH, 1808-1895.

HYMN 288.

OLD HUNDREDTH. L. M.

LOUIS BOURGEOIS.
GENEVAN PSALTER, 1551.

A - MEN.

1.

FROM all that dwell below the skies,
    Let the Creator's praise arise !
Let the Redeemer's name be sung
Through every land, by every tongue !

2.

Eternal are thy mercies, Lord ;
Eternal truth attends thy word :
Thy praise shall sound from shore to shore
Till suns shall rise and set no more.

ISAAC WATTS, 1674-1748

AMENS. 289

DRESDEN FORM.   JOHANN GOTTLIEB NAUMANN, 1741 — 1801.

No. 1. — *For Keys of C and G.*   No. 2. — *For Keys of D and A.*

A - men, A - - - - - men.   A - men, A - - - - - men.

No. 3. — *For Keys of F and B flat.*   No. 4. — *For Keys of B flat and E flat.*

A - men, A - - - - - men.   A - men, A - - - - - men.

ACKNOWLEDGMENTS.

GRATEFUL acknowledgment is made, for permission to use their original hymns, to Rev. Seth C. Beach, Rev. John W. Chadwick, Rev. Octavius B. Frothingham, Rev. Washington Gladden, Professor James B. Greenough, Col. Thomas W. Higginson, Rev. Frederick L. Hosmer, Miss Charlotte M. Packard, Miss Eliza Scudder, and Rev. Samuel F. Smith: and, for permission to use copyrighted hymns, to the Misses Very for two hymns by Jones Very; to Messrs. Houghton, Mifflin & Co. for the hymns of Samuel Longfellow, Samuel Johnson, Oliver Wendell Holmes, John Greenleaf Whittier, Alice Cary, Harriet Beecher Stowe, Caroline A. Mason, William H. Burleigh, William H. Furness, and a hymn from *Hymns of the Spirit;* to Messrs. D. Appleton & Co. for a hymn by William Cullen Bryant; to Messrs. G. P. Putnam's Sons for a sonnet by Theodore Parker; to Messrs. Roberts Brothers for two hymns by Nathaniel Langdon Frothingham; and to Messrs. E. P. Dutton & Co. for the hymn by Phillips Brooks.

Grateful acknowledgment is made, for permission to use their original tunes, to Professor Horatio W. Parker for " Parker; " to Professor John K. Paine for " Harvard Hymn; " to Rev. John S. B. Hodges for " Matins; " to Dr. Walter B. Gilbert for " Gilberts " and " Maidstone; " to the " Editors of the Tucker Hymnal " for permission to use the tunes " Rest," " Grace Church," " St. Ambrose," " Sears," and " All Saints; " to the Oliver Ditson Co. for the tune " Bethany; " and to Rev. Charles L. Hutchins for valuable advice and assistance in the adaptation of tunes. In the preparation of the biographical indexes free use has been made of Julian's *Dictionary of Hymnology*, of Love's *Scottish Church Music*, and of the notes to the *Church Hymnal by permission of the General Synod of the Church of Ireland*, the *Church of England Psalmody*, and the *Chorale Book for England*. To Mr. James Warrington, of Philadelphia, especial thanks are due for his kindness in putting his valuable library of books on Psalmody at the service of the University, and for revising the Index of Composers.

BIOGRAPHICAL INDEX.

AUTHORS AND TRANSLATORS.

Adams, Sarah Flower [1805-1848], daughter of Benjamin Flower, editor: born at Harlow, Essex: contributed to *Hymns and Anthems*, London, 1841, collected by the Rev. W. J. Fox, for use in his chapel, London, 13 hymns. These she reprinted in *The Flock at the Fountain*, London, 1845, and from that book has been here taken unchanged,

Nearer, my God, to thee 85

Addison, Joseph [1672-1719], son of the Rev. Lancelot Addison, sometime dean of Lichfield: born at Milston, Wiltshire: Amesbury, Salisbury, Lichfield, and Charterhouse Schools; then Queen's then Magdalen College, Oxford, B. A., 1691, M. A., 1693, fellow of Magdalen College, 1697-1711: published in the *Spectator* on several Saturdays of 1712, 5 hymns. From the issue of August 9, printed there in 13 stanzas of 4 lines, have been here taken stanzas 1, 5, 8, 10, beginning,

When all thy mercies, O my God 6

From the issue of August 23, suggested by Psalm xix. [compare also the passage beginning "Look how the floor of heaven," Act v., Scene i., *Merchant of Venice*], and printed there in 3 stanzas of 8 lines, has been here taken unchanged,

The spacious firmament on high 51

From the issue of July 26, suggested by Psalm xxiii., and printed there in 4 stanzas of 6 lines, has been here taken, omitting stanza 4,

The Lord my pasture shall prepare 151

Albinus, Johann Georg [1624-1679], son of Pastor Zacharius Albinus, Unter-Nessa, Saxony: born at Unter-Nessa: University of Leipzig: printed in 1655 his hymn "Straf mich nicht in deinem Zorn." It was repeated in Luppius's *Andächtig Singender Christen Mund*, Wesel, 1692, and again in the *Geistlicher Lieder Schatz*, Berlin, 1863, in 7 stanzas of 8 lines. From the translation of Miss Winkworth, *q. v.*, of stanzas 1, 3, 5, 6, 7, in 8 lines each, are here given stanzas 1 and 2.

Not in anger, mighty God 187

Alexander, James Waddell [1804-1859], son of the Rev. Archibald Alexander, D. D., of Hopewell, Virginia: born at Hopewell: Princeton, A. B., 1820, professor of rhetoric and Latin language and literature, 1833-1844, and of ecclesiastical history and Church government, Princeton Seminary, 1849-1851; S. T. D., Lafayette College, 1843, Harvard, 1854: minister of the Fifth Avenue Presbyterian Church, New York, 1851-1859. His translation in 10 stanzas of 8 lines of "O Haupt voll Blut und Wunden," by Paulus Gerhardt, *q. v.*, itself a translation of "Salve caput cruentatum," by St. Bernard, *q. v.*, was published in *The Breaking Crucible and Other Translations*, New York, 1861, and again in Schaff's *Christ in Song*, New York, 1869. From the *Christ in Song* has been here taken a cento beginning,

O sacred head, now wounded 115

Biographical Index

Alexander, William Lindsay [1808–1884], son of William Alexander, Leith: born near Leith: Universities of Edinburgh, St. Andrews, and Halle; D. D., St. Andrews, 1846; LL. D., Edinburgh, 1884; professor of theology and Church history in the Theological Hall of the Congregational Churches of Scotland: member of Old Testament Revision Company, 1870: published *A Selection of Hymns*, Edinburgh, 1849, for the use of the Augustine Church, of which he was minister. From the seven hymns which he contributed to that book have been here taken stanzas 1, 3, 6, 7 of the 7 stanzas of 4 lines, beginning,

Alford, Henry [1810–1871], son of the Rev. Henry Alford, rector of Ashton Sandford, Buckinghamshire: born at London: Trinity College, Cambridge, B. A., with honors, 1832, M. A., 1835, S. T. B., 1850, Hulsean lecturer, 1841–1842: dean of Canterbury, 1857–1871: editor of the Greek Testament: published in his *Year of Praise*, London, 1867, in 3 stanzas of 8 lines, the hymn the first line of which is given below. It was reprinted in his *Life*, London, 1874, with an additional stanza sung at his funeral, and, omitting this additional stanza, is here given unchanged.

Ambrosius (St. Ambrose) [340–397], son of Ambrosius, prefect of the Gauls: born in Gaul: educated at Rome: bishop of Milan : " Father of Church Song." The hymn "Jam lucis orto sidere," given in Newman's *Hymni Ecclesiæ*, 1838 and 1865, in 6 stanzas of 4 lines, which is certainly ancient, and possibly as old as the 5th century, has often been assigned to St. Ambrose, but the evidence is not satisfactory. Stanzas 1, 2, 4 of the translation in 6 stanzas of 4 lines made by John Henry Newman, *q. v.*, from the Paris Breviary text and published in his *Verses*, 1868, are here given.

The hymn "Splendor paternae gloriae " is probably by St. Ambrose. It is assigned to

him by the Benedictine editors of his works. It is given in *Daniel* 1., No. 17, in 8 stanzas of 4 lines. From the translation of Edward Caswall, *q. v.*, in 9 stanzas of 4 lines, published in *Lyra Catholica*, 1849, and *Hymns*, 1873, have been here taken stanzas 2, 4, 7.

The hymn " Rerum Deus tenax vigor " has been assigned to St. Ambrose by Biraghi, but this authorship is not established. It is given in *Daniel* 1., No. 42, in 2 stanzas of 4 lines. From the translation of Edward Caswall, *q. v.*, in 2 stanzas and a doxology, published in *Lyra Catholica*, 1849, and in *Hymns*, 1873, the 2 stanzas have been here taken.

Auber, Harriet [1773–1862], daughter of James Auber: born at London: published in her *Spirit of the Psalms*, London, 1829, for Whitsunday, in 7 stanzas of 4 lines, stanzas 1, 4, 5, 6, 7 here used,

Bacon, Leonard [1802–1881], son of David Bacon, missionary to the Indians: born at Detroit: Yale, A. B., 1820, A. M., 1823, professor of theology, 1866–1871, lecturer on Church history, 1871–1881 ; Andover, 1824; D.D., Hamilton, 1842; LL. D., Harvard, 1870: minister of First Church, New Haven, 1825–1871: with others, compiled *Psalms and Hymns for Christian Use and Worship*, published by the General Association of Connecticut, 1845. To this he contributed an abbreviated and altered version of his hymn "The Sabbath morn is as bright and calm," made for the bi-centenary of New Haven, 1838. This revised version is here given, omitting the 3d stanza.

Baker, Sir Henry Williams, Bart. [1821–1877], son of Admiral Sir Henry Loraine Baker: born at London: Trinity College, Cambridge, B. A., 1844, M. A., 1850: editor of *Hymns Ancient and Modern*, to which he con-

# of Authors and Translators.

tributed 33 hymns. In the 1868 *Appendix* to that book was first published his version of Psalm xxiv. The 3d stanza, "Perverse and foolish oft I strayed," was repeated by the dying lips of the author. This version is here given unchanged.

Ball, William [1784-1869], English writer and adapter: in 1846 translated the German book of words of *St. Paul*. Into this oratorio Mendelssohn had incorporated the 1st stanza of a translation into German of the "Gloria in Excelsis," made by Nicolaus Decius, *q. v.*, together with the melody which Decius had written for his translation. Mr. Ball's version of this stanza is here given unchanged.

Barbauld, Anna Laetitia [1743-1825], daughter of the Rev. John Aikin, D. D.: born at Kibworth-Harcourt, Leicestershire: published in *Poems Revised*, 1792, with the text "Come unto me," the hymn the first line of which is given below. It was reprinted in her *Works With a Memoir*, 1826, in 5 stanzas of 4 lines, stanzas 1, 2, 3, 5 here used.

In Dr. Enfield's *Hymns for Public Worship*, 1772, she published, reprinted as above, in 9 stanzas of 4 lines, stanzas 1, 4, 5, 8, 9 here used,

Baring-Gould, Sabine [1834-   ], son of Edward Baring-Gould: born at Exeter: Clare College, Cambridge, B. A., 1857, M. A., 1860: rector of Lew Trenchard, Devon: published in the *Church Times*, Oct. 15, 1864, in 6 stanzas of 8 lines and a chorus, stanzas 1, 3, 6 and chorus here used,

and wrote, 1865, for the children of St. John's Mission Church, Horbury Bridge, Yorkshire, where he was then curate, and published in the same paper, Feb. 16, 1867, in 8 stanzas of 4 lines, stanzas 2, 4, 8 here omitted,

Barton, Bernard [1784-1849], of Quaker parentage: born at Carlisle: educated at a Quaker school at Ipswich: friend of Southey and Lamb: published in his *Devotional Verses*, 1826, with the title "Walking in the light," and text 1 John i. 7, in 6 stanzas of 4 lines, stanzas 2 and 5 here omitted,

Bathurst, William Hiley [1796-1877], son of the Rt. Hon. Charles Bragge [afterwards Bathurst]: born at Clevedale, near Bristol: Winchester; then Christ Church, Oxford, B. A., 1818, M. A., 1822: published in *Psalms and Hymns for Public and Private Use*, 1831, with the title "The Power of Faith," and reference to Luke xviii. 5, in 6 stanzas of 4 lines, stanzas 4 and 5 here omitted,

and with the title "For an increase of Grace," in 5 stanzas of 4 lines, stanza 2 here omitted,

Baxter, Richard [1615-1691], son of Richard Baxter, yeoman: born at Rowton, Shropshire: educated at Wroxeter School: holy orders, 1638; curate of Kidderminster, 1640; chaplain to one of Cromwell's regiments about 1645; chaplain to Charles II., 1660; refused bishopric of Hereford; became a nonconformist minister after the Act of Uniformity: published in *POETICAL FRAGMENTS: Heart Imployment with God and Itself; The Concordant Discord of a Broken-healed Heart; London, at the Door of Eternity. Richard Baxter*, 1681, a poem of 16 stanzas of 8 lines, with the title "A Psalm of Praise to the tune of 148th Psalm." From this have been here taken stanzas 1, 8, 13, 15.

From another poem in the same book, in 8 stanzas of 8 lines, with the title "The Covenant and Confidence of Faith. To the Common Tunes," have been here taken stanzas 4 and 7.

Biographical Index

Beach, Seth Curtis [1837-   ], son of Luther Markham Beach: born at Marion, New York: A. B., Union College, 1863; Harvard Divinity School, 1866: minister of the Independent Congregational Society, Bangor, Maine: wrote for Visitation Day, Harvard Divinity School, 1866, and first published in *The Hymn and Tune Book* of the American Unitarian Association, Boston, 1868, in 4 stanzas of 4 lines, here given unchanged,

Belknap, Jeremy [1744-1798], son of Joseph Belknap, merchant: born at Boston: Harvard, A. B., 1762, S. T. D., 1792, overseer, 1792: founder of the Massachusetts Historical Society; author of a *History of New Hampshire*, 1784-92: published in his *Sacred Poetry, consisting of Psalms and Hymns adapted to Public Worship*, Boston, 1795, his version of Psalm lxxviii. This is made up of the first 3 stanzas in 4 lines of Tate and Brady's translation — the first line of the first stanza altered by Dr. Belknap from "Hear, O my people, to my law," to "Give ear, my people, to my law," — and stanzas 1, 3, 4 of Dr. Watts' translation in 4 stanzas of 4 lines. This version has been sung at the Commencement dinner at Harvard certainly since 1830, and may have been sung earlier. The practice before that date is described by the Rev. Dr. John Pierce, in his record of Harvard Commencement exercises, which he attended from 1813 to 1848, published in the Proceedings of the Massachusetts Historical Society for 1890. He there says "at the Commencement dinner it has been the invariable practice, since the foundation of the College, to sing some version of a portion of Psalm lxxviii. This version has varied with the taste of the times, from that of Sternhold and Hopkins, appended to the Geneva Bible, so called; next, to that of the New England version of 1639, by Weld, Eliot, and Mather, the 26th edition of which was published in 1744; then, Tate and Brady's version; then, Dr. Watts';

and last, not least, Dr. Belknap's, 1795. Not only have versions varied, but the number of stanzas, so there is nothing in our usages to prevent the use of a still improved version, should such a one in process of time appear; retaining, however, for its basis Psalm lxxviii., as in our common translation of the Bible." The version of Dr. Belknap, above described, omitting the last stanza, is here given.

Bernard of Clairvaux [1091-1153], son of Tecelin, knight, vassal and friend of the Duke of Burgundy: born near Dijon: educated at Chatillon: abbot, doctor, saint: by some of the best authorities is thought to have written "Salve mundi salutare," included in his *Opera Omnia*, Paris, 1609, and there entitled "A rhythmical prayer to any one of the members of Christ." It is given in *Daniel*, I., No. 207; II., p. 359; and IV., pp. 224-231. It is divided into seven parts:

I.	Salve mundi salutare.	To the feet.	
II.	Salve Jesu, Rex sanctorum.	"	" knees.
III.	Salve Jesu, pastor bone.	"	" hands.
IV.	Salve Jesu, summe bonus.	"	" side.
V.	Salve salus mea, Deus.	"	" breast.
VI.	Summi Regis cor aveto.	"	" heart.
VII.	Salve caput cruentatum.	"	" face.

The last of these, Paulus Gerhardt, *q. v.*, translated into German, in 10 stanzas of 8 lines, as "O Haupt voll Blut und Wunden," from which Dr. J. W. Alexander, *q. v.*, made his translation, beginning,

Bernard of Morlaix [*circa* 1125], monk of Cluny: of English parentage: about 1145 wrote "De Contemptu Mundi," a poem of about 3000 lines. From the beginning of this John Mason Neale, *q. v.*, translated and published in *Mediæval Hymns*, 1851, 96 lines, and in the *Rhythm of Bernard de Morlaix on the Celestial Country*, 1858, 218 lines. These were reprinted in *Mediæval Hymns*, 2d edition,

# of Authors and Translators.

1863, whence has been here taken a cento beginning,

and a cento beginning,

Bickersteth, Edward Henry [1825-   ], son of the Rev. Edward Bickersteth: born at Islington: Trinity College, Cambridge, chancellor's medalist, 1844, 1845 and 1846, B. A., with honors, 1847, M. A., 1850, Seatonian prize, 1854: dean of Gloucester 1855; bishop of Exeter, same year: wrote in 1860, and published in *Two Brothers*, 1871, and again, in *From Year to Year*, 1883, for the first Sunday after Christmas, with text Isaiah lx. 8, in 4 stanzas of 8 lines, stanza 4 here omitted,

and published in *From Year to Year*, for the sixteenth Sunday after Trinity, with text Ephesians iii. 14-15, in 1 stanza of 6 lines and 2 stanzas of 8 lines, the last stanza only here used and divided into 4 stanzas of 4 lines,

Bode, John Ernest [1816-1874], son of William Bode of the General Post Office: Eton and Charter House, 1830-1834; Christ Church, Oxford, B. A., 1837, M. A., 1840, tutor of his college, 1841-1847, Bampton lecturer 1855: rector of Castle Camps, Cambridgeshire, 1860: contributed to the 1869 *Appendix* to the S. P. C. K. *Psalms and Hymns*, in 6 stanzas of 8 lines, repeated in *Church Hymns*, 1871, with the omission of stanza 4, and with a text Luke ix. 57, the hymn the first line of which follows. From *Church Hymns* are here given stanzas 1, 3, 4.

Boethius, Anicius Manlius Severinus [475-525], son of Flavius Manlius Boethius: philosopher, statesman, man of letters; consul 510: wrote, while imprisoned in Pavia by Theodoric, *De Consolatione Philosophiae*. From

Book III., Metrum IX., Dr. Johnson, *q. v.*, quoted 6 lines as a motto for No. 7 of the *Rambler*, and below the quotation gave a translation in 2 stanzas of 4 lines, which is here given unchanged.

Bonar, Horatius [1808-1889], son of James Bonar, solicitor: born at Edinburgh: High School and University of Edinburgh; D. D., University of Aberdeen, 1853: minister of Chalmer's Memorial Church, Edinburgh: published in the second series of *Hymns of Faith and Hope*, 1861, with the title "Christ in All," in 10 stanzas of 4 lines, stanzas 1, 5, 7, 8 here used,

and in 5 stanzas of 4 lines, stanza 4 here omitted,

and in the first series of *Hymns of Faith and Hope*, 1857, in 7 stanzas of 4 lines, stanza 4 here omitted,

and in 1843, in a small book, and the same year in *Songs of the Wilderness*, and again in the first series of *Hymns of Faith and Hope*, 1857, with the title "The Useful Life," and a quotation

Ψυχή μου, ψυχή μου,
'Ανάστα· τί καθεύδεις;

from an old Greek hymn, in 8 stanzas of 4 lines, stanzas 1, 2, 3, 8 here used,

and in the second series of *Hymns of Faith and Hope*, 1861, with the title "Let us go forth," and text Heb. xiii. 13, in 9 stanzas of 6 lines, portions of stanzas 1, 3, 6, 7, 8 here used,

Bowring, Sir John [1792-1872], son of Charles Bowring, of Larkbeare, Devonshire: born at Exeter: friend and literary executor of Jeremy Bentham; editor of the *Westminster Review*,

Biographical Index

1825; governor of Hong Kong, 1854; statesman, linguist, economist: LL. D., Groningen, 1828: published in his *Hymns*, 1825, in 5 stanzas of 4 lines, stanza 1 repeated for 5, the repetition here omitted,

God is love; his mercy brightens 24

and in *Matins and Vespers*, 1824, in 4 stanzas of 4 lines, all here used,

The offerings to thy throne which rise . . . 37

and in 5 stanzas of 4 lines, stanza 4 here omitted,

Father and Friend, thy light, thy love 52

and in *Hymns*, 1825, in 3 stanzas of 8 lines, all here used,

Watchman ! tell us of the night 89

and in *Matins and Vespers*, 1824, in 4 stanzas of 4 lines, stanza 4 here omitted,

How sweetly flowed the gospel's sound 98

and in the *Hymns*, 1825, in 5 stanzas of 4 lines, stanza 5 here omitted,

In the cross of Christ I glory 119

Brady, Nicholas [1659-1726], son of Major Nicholas Brady: born at Brandon, Ireland: Westminster; then Christ Church, Oxford, 1678-1682; Trinity College, Dublin, B. A., 1685, M. A., 1686, B. D. and D. D., 1699: chaplain to William III.; rector of Richmond, Surrey, 1696-1726; incumbent of Stratford-on-Avon, 1702-1705: published with Nahum Tate, *q. v.*, in 1696, *A New Version of the Psalms of David.* From their version of Psalm lxxviii., in 30 stanzas of 8 lines, unequally divided into three parts, have been here taken the first 12 lines, as altered by Jeremy Belknap, *q. v.*, for the first 3 stanzas of the Commencement hymn.

Give ear, ye children, to my law 282

Brooke, Stopford Augustus [1832-   ], son of the Rev. Richard S. Brooke of Kingston, Ireland: born at Letterkenny, Ireland: Trinity College, Dublin, B. A., 1856, M. A., 1862; the Downes and the vice-chancellor's prizes for English verse: chaplain to the Eng-

lish embassy, Berlin, 1863-1865; chaplain in ordinary to the Queen, 1872; minister of Bedford Chapel, London, 1876: on seceding from Church of England in 1881 published, for the use of his congregation, *Christian Hymns.* From the revised edition of this, 1893, have been here taken unchanged the 6 stanzas of 6 lines beginning,

Oft as we run the weary way 153

and the 5 stanzas of 4 lines beginning,

Now the wings of day are furled 259

Brooks, Phillips [1835-1893], son of William Gray Brooks: born at Boston: Boston Latin School, 1851, Harvard, A. B., 1855, A. M., 1858, S. T. D., 1877, overseer, 1870-1882, and again 1883-1889; preacher to the University, 1886-1891; S. T. D., Union, 1870. Oxford, 1885, Columbia, 1887; Theological School, Alexandria, Virginia, 1859: rector of Church of the Advent, then of Holy Trinity, Philadelphia, 1859-1869; rector of Trinity Church, Boston, 1869-1891; bishop of Massachusetts, 1891-1893. He spent the Christmas of 1866 at Bethlehem, and on his return wrote for the Christmas festival, 1868, of the Sunday-school of the Church of the Holy Trinity, Philadelphia, in 4 stanzas of 8 lines, all here used,

O little town of Bethlehem 93

Bryant, William Cullen [1794-1878], son of Dr. Peter Bryant: born at Cummington, Massachusetts: Williams College: reformer, journalist, poet: wrote for Sewall's *Collection of Psalms and Hymns*, New York, 1820, the hymn the first line of which follows. It was afterwards revised, and republished in his *Poetical Works*, New York, 1883, in 4 stanzas of 4 lines, and of that form are here given stanzas 1, 3, 4.

O God, whose dread and dazzling brow . . . 166

Buckoll, Henry James [1803-1871], son of the Rev. James Buckoll, rector of Siddington, Gloucestershire: born at Siddington: Rugby; then Queen's College, Oxford, B. A., 1826, M. A., 1829: assistant master with Dr. Arnold

# of Authors and Translators.

at Rugby, 1826: holy orders, 1827: editor of *Psalms and Hymns for the Use of Rugby School Chapel*, the first English Public School Hymn-Book: published in Dr. Arnold's *Christian Life*, London, 1841, in 11 stanzas of 6 lines, a translation of Von Canitz's, *q. v.*, "Seele du musst munter werden," omitting stanzas 2, 4, 8. Stanzas 1, 4, 5, 11 of this translation are here given.

Bulfinch, Stephen Greenleaf [1809-1870], son of Charles Bulfinch, architect, designer of the National Capitol: born at Boston: Columbian College, Washington, A. B., 1827, S. T. D., 1864; Harvard Divinity School, 1830: published in *Contemplations of the Saviour*, Boston, 1832, and repeated in *Lays of the Gospel*, Boston, 1845, in 5 stanzas of 4 lines, stanzas 1, 4, 5 here used.

Burleigh, William Henry [1812-1871], son of Rinaldo Burleigh, teacher: born at Woodstock, Connecticut: reformer, journalist; harbor master, then port-warden of New York, 1853-1870: probably gave to Prof. Charles D. Cleveland in manuscript for publication in his *Lyra Sacra Americana*, New York, 1868, the hymn the first line of which follows. It was reprinted in *Poems*, New York, 1871, in 4 stanzas of 4 lines, and is here given unchanged.

Canitz, Friedrich Rudolph Ludwig von [1654-1699], son of Ludwig von Canitz, privy counsellor, Berlin: born at Berlin: Universities of Leyden and Leipzig: magistrate, diplomate, privy counsellor. His hymns were edited by Dr. J. Lange, and published anonymously as *Nebenstunden unterschiedener Gedichte*, Berlin, 1700. Of these, "Seele du musst munter werden," in 14 stanzas of 6 lines, was partially translated by H. J. Buckoll, *q. v.*, and of this translation stanzas 1, 4, 5, 11 are here given.

Cary, Alice [1820-1871], daughter of Robert

Cary: born near Cincinnati: poet: published in *Ballads, Lyrics, and Hymns*, New York, 1866, with the title "The heaven that's here," in 7 stanzas of 4 lines, stanzas 5 and 6 here omitted,

and with the title "Dying Hymn," in 5 stanzas of 4 lines, here given unchanged,

Caswall, Edward [1814-1878], son of the Rev. Robert Clarke Caswall, vicar of Yately, Hampshire: born at Yately: Marlborough; then Brasenose College, Oxford, B. A., with honors, 1836, M. A., 1838; holy orders, 1838: incumbent of Stratford-sub-Castle, 1840-1847: entered Roman Catholic communion, 1847, joining Dr. Newman at Edgbaston, 1850: published in his *Masque of Mary*, London, 1858, 51 original hymns and 53 translations. From this book have been here taken, of his translation, in 5 stanzas of 4 lines, of "O Deus ego amo te," often attributed to Ignatius Loyola [see Latin Hymns], stanzas 1, 2, 4, 5, beginning,

and from his *Lyra Catholica*, 1849, containing nearly 200 translations from the Roman Breviary Missal, etc., have been here taken stanzas 1, 5, 6 of his translation, in 6 stanzas of 4 lines, of "O Deus ego amo te," a hymn composed possibly by St. Francis Xavier [see Latin Hymns], beginning,

and of his translation, in 9 stanzas of 4 lines, of the whole of "Splendor paternae gloriae," by St. Ambrose, *q. v.*, stanzas 2, 4, 7, beginning,

and stanzas 1, 2, 3, 4 of his translation, in 4 stanzas and a doxology, of "Lux ecce surgit aurea," the second part of "Nox et tenebrae, et nubila," a hymn by Prudentius, *q. v.*, beginning,

Biographical Index

and all but the doxology of his translation, in 2 stanzas and a doxology of 4 lines each, of "Rerum Deus tenax vigor," often assigned to St. Ambrose, *q. v.*, beginning,

O thou true Life of all that live **261**

Chadwick, John White [1840-   ], son of John White Chadwick: born at Marblehead, Massachusetts: Bridgewater State Normal school; Phillips Academy, Exeter; Harvard Divinity School, 1864, A. M., Harvard, 1888: since 1864 minister of the Second Unitarian Congregational Society, Brooklyn, New York: wrote for the 25th anniversary of his ordination, Dec. 25, 1889, in 5 stanzas of 4 lines, and contributed to this book, stanzas 1, 3, 4, 5 here used,

O thou whose perfect goodness crowns **35**

He wrote for the graduating exercises of his class in Harvard Divinity School, 1864, and, afterwards published unchanged in *A Book of Poems*, Boston, 1876, in 4 stanzas of 6 lines, stanzas 1 and 3 here used,

Eternal Ruler of the ceaseless round **165**

He wrote in 1865, published in *The Inquirer*, New York, and again in *A Book of Poems*, with the title "A Song of Trust," in 14 stanzas of 4 lines, the hymn the first line of which follows. The revised arrangement given in this book, in 4 stanzas of 8 lines, was made by Mr. Chadwick.

O Love divine, of all that is **257**

Charles, Elizabeth [1828-1896], daughter of John Rundle, M. P.: born at Tavistock, Devonshire: translated and published in her *Voice of Christian Life in Song*. 1858. stanzas 1, 2, 3 of "Förfäras ej, du lilla hop." the Swedish version of "Verzage nicht, du Häuflein klein," in 5 stanzas of 6 lines, a portion of which was possibly composed by Gustavus Adolphus, *q. v.* Mrs. Charles's translation is here given unchanged.

Be not dismayed, thou little flock **193**

Clarke, James Freeman [1810-1888], son of Samuel Clarke: born at Hanover, New Hamp-

shire: Boston Latin School; then Harvard, A. B., 1829, Divinity School, 1833, S. T. D., 1863, professor of natural religion and Christian doctrine, 1867-1871, overseer, 1863-1888, lecturer in the Divinity School, 1876-1877: minister of the Church of the Disciples, Boston, 1841-1850, and 1853-1888; wrote while in Kentucky, 1833, and published in No. III. of the *Dial*, January, 1841, in 10 stanzas of 4 lines, "Infinite Spirit, who art round us ever." Stanzas 3, 4, 10 of this he rewrote for his *Disciples Hymn Book*, Boston, 1856 edition, and they are here given as there printed.

Father, to us thy children, humbly kneeling . . **62**

Collet, Samuel [*circa* 1763]. The following communication from Dr. James Martineau gives all that has yet been discovered as regards Mr. Collet, to whom. in his *Hymns of Praise and Prayer*, Dr. Martineau assigned the hymn the first line of which follows. "The hymn, about which Dr. Peabody inquired, first appeared anonymously in *A Form of Prayer and a New Collection of Psalms for the Use of a Congregation of Protestant Dissenters in Liverpool*, 1763. This congregation was not either of the two Presbyterian Societies meeting respectively in Ben's Garden and in Kaye street, but was composed of some seceders from the former, with some liberal Church of England people who preferred a liturgical service. It met in an octagonal building in Temple Court; but after a few years was broken up, the majority returning to Ben's Garden, and taking with them their pastor, Dr. Clayton, to the pulpit there. From that *Form of Prayer*, lent me by an aged Liverpool friend, I took the hymn and the date, but not the author's name, which it does not give. As it remains 'anon.' in Kippis, in Dr. Enfield's and later Norwich collections, and in the subsequent Liverpool and other books consulted in my work, I have asked myself ' Whence have I got it,' and I am convinced, on close self-scrutiny, that I learned it from the old friend (Mr. Jos. Fletcher) who lent me the book, and who was an unfailing authority for all matters of congregational, and especially of hymnological, tradition. On learning the fact, I made an entry of the full name in notes which I still retain." Dr. Martineau writes further that in his belief Mr. Collet was the author of *A Practical Paraphrase on the Epistles of St. Paul to the Romans and to the Galatians, and on the Epistle to the Hebrews*, 1744, 8vo. In a volume of this *Paraphrase*, now in Dr. Williams's library, London, where the author's name is given on the title-page simply as Samuel Collet, at the end, after the first five announcements of other publications, it reads : "These five by Samuel Collet, Gent." Dr. Martineau infers therefrom that Mr. Collet was a layman. Dr. Martineau suggests further that Mr. Collet may have been the son of the Rev. Joseph Collet, sometime of Coat, in the county of Oxford, who died in 1741. Here is given, as printed in the *Form of Prayer* above mentioned,

Conder, Josiah [1789-1855], son of Thomas Conder, engraver and bookseller : born at London : bookseller, publisher, journalist, author : published in his *Star in the East with other Poems*, 1824, and repeated with slight changes in *Hymns of Praise, Prayer, and Devout Meditation*, 1856, from whence stanzas 1, 4, 5 are here taken, his hymn in 5 stanzas of 6 lines, entitled "A Thought on the Sea Shore," and beginning,

In the *Choir and the Oratory*, 1837, as one of six hymns "On the Lord's Prayer" to the words "Give us this day our daily bread," appeared the hymn the first line of which is given below. It was repeated in *Hymns, etc.*, as above, in 6 stanzas of 4 lines, stanzas 1, 2, 3, 4 here used.

Cotterill, Jane [1790-1825], daughter of the Rev. John Boak and mother of Henry Cotter-

ill, bishop of Edinburgh : contributed anonymously to the *Appendix* to the 6th edition of Cotterill's *Selection of Psalms and Hymns for Public and Private Use* (1st edition, 1810, 6th edition, 1815), and afterwards republished in Montgomery's *Christian Psalmist*, 1825, over her name and with the title "For Submission to the Divine Will," in 6 stanzas of 4 lines, stanzas 1, 2, 3, 6 here used,

Cowper, William [1731-1800], son of the Rev. John Cowper, chaplain to George II. : born in his father's rectory at Great Berkhampstead, Hertfordshire : educated at Westminster : called to the Bar, 1754 : published in J. Newton's *Twenty-six Letters on Religious Subjects ; to which are added Hymns, &c., by Omicron*, London, 1774, and again in *Olney Hymns*, 1779, Book III., No. 15, with the title "Light shining out of Darkness," in 6 stanzas of 4 lines, stanzas 1, 2, 4, 6 here used,

and in *Olney Hymns*, Book I., No. 65, with the title "The Future Peace and Glory of the Church," in 3 stanzas of 8 lines, stanzas 1 and 3 here used,

and in the 2d edition of R. Conyers's *Psalms and Hymns*, 1772, and again in *Olney Hymns*, Book I., No. 3, with the title "Walking with God," in 6 stanzas of 4 lines, stanzas 1, 3, 4, 5, 6 here used,

and in *Olney Hymns*, Book III., No. 48, with the title "Joy and Peace in believing," in 4 stanzas of 8 lines, all here used,

Decius, Nicolaus [-1541], in 1519 was head of the cloister of Steterburg, Bavaria. Influenced by the opinions of Luther, he left Steterburg in 1522, and in 1535 was pastor of the Church of St. Nicholas, Stettin, Pomerania. He is said to have been a popular preacher and a good musician. He translated into

Biographical Index

German the "Gloria in Excelsis," the "Sanctus," and the "Agnus Dei." The "Gloria in Excelsis" first appeared in low German, beginning "Alleine Got jn der höge sy ëre," in the *Rostock Gesang-Buch*, 1525. Mendelssohn included a high German version of the first stanza in the book of words of his oratorio of *St. Paul*, and made use of the melody which Decius had arranged for his translation, probably from a Latin plain song. This stanza, translated into English by William Ball, *q. v.*, and set to the melody of Decius, is here given, beginning,

To God on high be thanks and praise 13

Doane, George Washington [1799-1859], son of Jonathan Doane, master-builder: born at Trenton: A. B., Union, 1818; S. T. D., Columbia, 1833, Trinity, 1833; LL. D., St. Johns, Annapolis, 1841; president of Burlington College, 1846-1859. He was assistant minister of Trinity Church, New York, and when Washington, now Trinity, College was founded in Hartford, 1824, was appointed professor of rhetoric and belles-lettres, serving till 1828. In 1828 he was assistant minister, and in 1830 rector, of Trinity Church, Boston. In 1832 he became bishop of New Jersey. In his *Songs by the Way*, 1824, reprinted by his son, 1875, he published in 4 stanzas of 4 lines, stanza 4 here omitted,

Softly now the light of day 254

Doddridge, Philip [1702-1751], son of Daniel Doddridge: born at London: educated at the Grammar School, Kingston-upon-Thames, at St. Albans, and at Kibworth; D. D., Aberdeen, 1736. He refused a university course, and was selected by a general meeting of nonconformist ministers, 1829, to conduct their newly established school at Market Harborough, where he taught, preaching meanwhile at Northampton, till 1751, when his lack of health made necessary a voyage to Lisbon, where he died. He wrote over 500 hymns. In *Hymns founded on Various Texts in the Holy Scripture.*

By the late Reverend Philip Doddridge, D. D. Published from the Author's Manuscript by Job Orton, Salop MDCCLV., was published, with the title "God's Care a Rhemedy for ours," and text 1 Peter v. 7, in 4 stanzas of 4 lines, here given unchanged,

How gentle God's commands 23

and with the title "Acting as seeing him who is invisible," and text Heb. xi. 27, in 5 stanzas of 4 lines, here given unchanged,

Eternal and immortal King 27

and with the title "CHRIST'S Message," and text Luke iv. 18, 19, in 7 stanzas of 4 lines, stanzas 1, 5, 7 here used,

Hark the glad sound, the Saviour comes . . . 90

and with the title "The active Christian," and text Luke xii. 35-38, in 5 stanzas of 4 lines, stanza 5 here omitted,

Ye servants of the Lord 199

and with the title "Pressing on in the Christian Race," and text Phil. iii. 12-14, in 5 stanzas of 4 lines, stanza 5 here omitted,

Awake, my soul, stretch every nerve 204

and with the title "Help obtained of GOD," and text Acts xxvi. 22, "For New Year's Day," in 5 stanzas of 4 lines, stanza 5 here omitted,

Great God, we sing that mighty hand 265

Dryden, John [1631-1700], son of Erasmus Dryden: born at Aldwinkle, Northampton-shire: Westminster School under Dr. Busby; Trinity College, Cambridge, B. A., 1654: poet laureate and historiographer royal, 1670-1688. It has been recently claimed that he was the translator of about 120 Latin hymns, published anonymously in the *Primer, or Office of the Blessed Virgin Mary, in English*, 1706. From his *Miscellanies*, 1693, have been taken 30 lines, arranged in 5 stanzas of 6 lines, of his translation in 7 irregular stanzas, 39 lines in all, of "Veni Creator Spiritus" [see Latin Hymns], beginning,

Creator Spirit, by whose aid 12

# of Authors and Translators.

Ellerton John [1826-1893], son of George Ellerton : born at London : King William's College, then Trinity College, Cambridge, B. A., 1849, M. A., 1854 : curate of Eastbourne, Sussex, 1850; curate at Brighton and lecturer at St. Peter's, Brighton, 1852; vicar of Crewe Green and chaplain to Lord Crewe, 1860; rector of Hinstock, 1872, of Barnes, 1876, of White Roding, 1886: was one of the editors of the S. P. C. K., *Church Hymns*, writing the notes. Matthew Arnold said "he was the greatest hymn-writer of his time." From his *Hymns Original and Translated*, 1888, have been here taken stanzas 1, 2, 3, 6 of the 6 stanzas in 4 lines which he wrote in 1868, and first published that year in *Hymns compiled for use in Chester Cathedral*, beginning,

and all but the first 4 lines of stanza 3 of the 3 stanzas of 8 lines, written in 1870 "for a mid-day service in a City Church," beginning,

and all of the 4 stanzas in 4 lines, written in 1870 "at request of a friend, for use at the close of service on Sunday afternoons when, as in Summer, strictly evening hymns would be unsuitable," beginning,

and all of the revised and abridged version in 4 stanzas of 4 lines which he made for the 1868 *Appendix to Hymns Ancient and Modern*, from the hymn in 5 stanzas of 4 lines which he wrote for a Festival of Parochial Choirs, Nantwich, 1866, beginning,

and all but stanza 4 of the 5 stanzas of 6 lines, enlarged from the 3 stanzas of 4 lines which he wrote and first published in his *Hymns for Schools and Bible Classes*, 1858, beginning,

and all of the 5 stanzas in 4 lines written for *Church Hymns*, 1871, beginning,

Elliott, Charlotte [1789-1871], daughter of Charles Elliott of Clapham and Brighton : born at Brighton : published in the *Invalid's Hymn Book*, 1834, and again in her brother's, Rev. H. V. Elliott's, *Psalms and Hymns*, 1835, and again in *Hours of Sorrow*, 1836, different versions of her hymn the first line of which follows. From the *Hours of Sorrow*, stanzas 1, 4, 6, 7, of the 7 stanzas in 4 lines, have been here taken.

Faber, Frederick William [1814-1863], son of the Rev. Thomas Henry Faber, secretary to the bishop of Durham : born at Calverley vicarage, Yorkshire : Shrewsbury and Harrow; then Balliol College, Oxford, B. A., 1836, M. A., 1839, Newdigate prize for English poetry same year, fellow of University College, 1836-1844; holy orders, 1837 : joined Church of Rome, 1845; D. D., by pope Pius IX., 1854: published in *Jesus and Mary*, 1849, and repeated in his *Hymns*, 1862, with the title "The Will of God," in 14 stanzas of 4 lines, stanzas 1, 11, 13, 14 here used,

and as above, with the title "The Right must win," in 19 stanzas of 4 lines, stanzas 15, 11, 12, 13, 19 here used in that order,

He published in *Oratory Hymns*, 1854, and again in *Hymns*, 1862, with the title "The Pilgrims of the Night," in 7 stanzas of 4 lines with a refrain, stanzas 1, 4, 3, 7 and refrain here used,

Frothingham, Nathaniel Langdon [1793-1870], son of Ebenezer Frothingham, merchant, of Boston : born at Boston : Boston Latin School; Harvard, A. B., 1811, A. M., in course, S. T. D., 1836, instructor in rhetoric and oratory, 1812-1815, overseer, 1819-1850 : minister of First Church, Boston, 1815-1850: wrote for the ordination of William P. Lunt as minister of the Second Unitarian Congrega-

Biographical Index

tional Society, New York, 1828, and afterwards published in his *Metrical Pieces*, 1855 and 1870, in 5 stanzas of 4 lines, stanzas 1, 2, 3, 5 here used,

O God, whose presence glows in all 15

and wrote for the ordination of Henry W. Bellows at All Souls' Church, New York, 1839, and published as above, in 5 stanzas of 4 lines, stanza 5 here omitted,

O Lord of life and truth and grace 126

Frothingham, Octavius Brooks [1822–1895], son of the Rev. Nathaniel Langdon Frothingham, noted above : born at Boston : Boston Latin School ; Harvard, A. B., 1843, A. M., in course, Divinity School, 1846 : wrote for the graduating exercises of his class in the Divinity School, 1846, in 6 stanzas of 4 lines, stanzas 1, 2, 5, 6 here used,

Thou Lord of hosts, whose guiding hand . . . 19

Furness, William Henry [1802–1896], son of William Furness: born at Boston: Boston Latin School ; Harvard, A. B., 1820, A. M., in course, Divinity School, 1823, S. T. D., 1847 : 1825–1896, minister of First Congregational Unitarian Church, Philadelphia : wrote August, 1892, with the title " The Life Divine," in 6 stanzas of 4 lines, and first published in this book, stanzas 1, 2, 3, 6 here used,

That God is love, unchanging love 56

He wrote, in 1823, for the children of his Sunday-school, and published in *Christian Hymns for Public and Private Worship, Compiled by a Committee of the Cheshire Pastoral Association*, Boston, 1845, and then in his *Verses, Translation from the German, and Hymns*, Boston, 1892, with the title " Jesus, our Leader," in 5 stanzas of 4 lines, all here used,

Feeble, helpless, how shall I 113

In his *Manual of Domestic Worship*, 1840, and in his *Verses*, as above, with the title " The Soul," in 4 stanzas of 4 lines, he published the hymn the first line of which follows. The last two lines of stanza 4 were changed and an additional stanza added by an unknown hand, possibly that of Samuel Longfellow. The change and addition have been accepted and revised for this book by Dr. Furness, and the hymn, so changed and revised, is here printed.

What is this that stirs within 170

He wrote in 1823, and published in his *Manual*, and in his *Verses*, as above, with the title " Penitential," in 8 stanzas of 4 lines, stanzas 4, 6, 7, 8 here used,

Unworthy to be called thy son 176

and with the title " Morning," in 6 stanzas of 4 lines, stanza 5 here omitted,

In the morning I will raise 237

and with the title " Evening," in 7 stanzas of 4 lines, stanzas 1, 2, 4, 5 here used,

Slowly, by thy hand unfurled 253

Gaskell, William [1805–1884], son of William Gaskell, sail-canvas maker : born at Latchford, Cheshire : M. A., University of Glasgow, 1825 ; then Manchester New College, York ; secretary of Manchester New College, 1840–1846, then professor of English history and literature, 1846–1853 : minister of Cross Street Chapel, Manchester, 1828–1884 : contributed to Beard's *Collection of Hymns for Public and Private Worship*, London and Manchester, 1837, 79 hymns. From this collection have been here taken stanzas 1, 2, 3, 5 of the 5 stanzas of 4 lines beginning,

Father, we humbly would repose 137

and all of the 5 stanzas of 4 lines beginning,

Mighty God, the first, the last 173

and all of the 3 stanzas of 4 lines beginning,

Press on ! press on ! ye sons of light 206

Geldart, Edmund Martin [1844–1885], son of Thomas Geldart, sometime of Thorp, near Norwich : born at Norwich : Merchant Taylors' School then Manchester Grammar School ; then Balliol College, Oxford, B. A., 1867, M. A., 1873 : curate of All Souls, Manchester, then of St. George's, Everton,

# of Authors and Translators.

Liverpool; then, leaving the Church of England, minister of Hope Street Chapel, Liverpool, and of the Free Church, Croyden, 1873–1885: wrote "in an hour of depression," while residing at Athens, and afterwards published in his volume of sermons, entitled *Echoes of Truth*, London, 1886, in 7 stanzas of 4 lines, stanza 6 here omitted,

Gerhardt, Paulus [1607–1676], son of Christian Gerhardt, burgomaster of Gräfenhaynichen near Wittenberg: born at Gräfenhaynichen: educated at University of Wittenberg: Lutheran pastor: "the most gifted and popular hymn-writer of his Church, except Luther." In Crüger's *Praxis*, Frankfurt, edition of 1656, is given, in 10 stanzas of 8 lines, Gerhardt's translation, beginning "O Haupt voll Blut und Wunden," of the "Salve caput cruentatum" of St. Bernard, *q. v.* From this version by Gerhardt was made the translation into English by Dr. J. W. Alexander, *q. v.*, here given, beginning,

As above was also published an original hymn in 12 stanzas of 8 lines, beginning "Befiehl du deine Wege," an acrostic on Luther's version of Psalm xxxvii. 5, "Befiehl dem Herrn deine Wege und hoffe auf ihn, er wird's wohl machen." This has been called "the most comforting of all the hymns that resounded on Paulus Gerhardt's golden lyre, sweeter to many souls than honey and the honeycomb." Stanzas 1, 2, 3, 4, 6, 7, 8, 12 were translated by John Wesley, *q. v.*, and published in *Hymns and Sacred Poems*, 1739, and again in *The Poetical Works of Charles and John Wesley*, 1868–1872, in 16 stanzas of 4 lines, from which have been here taken stanzas 9, 10, 12, 13.

Gill, Thomas Hornblower [1819–   ], born at Bristol Road, Birmingham: educated at King Edward's Grammar School, Birmingham:

wrote for, and published in George Dawson's *Psalms and Hymns*, 1846, in 7 stanzas of 4 lines, and afterwards rewrote and published in the *Golden Chain of Praise*, 1869, with a quotation from Milton, and under the title "The glory of the latter days," in 8 stanzas of 4 lines, the hymn beginning as below. Mr. Gill says: "I approve of both forms, but the earlier text has more freshness and freedom." From this earlier text have been here taken stanzas 1, 2, 3, 5.

At Malvern on Whitsunday, 1863, "a day of singular spiritual enjoyment and outward loveliness," was written and afterwards published in the *Golden Chain*, with the title "A Breathing after the Holy Spirit," in 7 stanzas of 4 lines, stanzas 1 and 5 here omitted,

In 1853, born of the words of Augustine, "Secretissime et Praesentissime," was written and the same year published in George Dawson's *Psalms and Hymns*, and then in the *Golden Chain*, in 9 stanzas of 4 lines, stanzas 4, 5, 8, 9 here used,

In 1856 was composed and afterwards published in the *Golden Chain*, with the title "The Walk with God," and the motto "Order my footsteps to thy law," in 9 stanzas of 4 lines, stanzas 1, 5, 7, 8, 9 here used,

In 1847 "was composed with great ardour and stir of soul," and first published in the *Golden Chain*, with the title "Spiritual ups and downs," and the text "The flesh lusteth against the spirit, and the spirit against the flesh," in 7 stanzas of 4 lines, stanzas 1, 2, 3, 5, 7 here used,

In 1869, inspired by the words of St. Augustine, "Immutabilis mutans omnia," was written and contributed to *Songs of the Spirit*, New

Biographical Index

York, 1871, in 6 stanzas of 6 lines, stanzas 1, 4, 5 here used,

Lord God, by whom all change is wrought . . 227

In 1867, at Whitsuntide, was composed and afterwards first printed in the *Golden Chain*, with the title "The Divine Renewer," and the texts "Thou renewest the face of the earth," "Be renewed in the spirit of your minds," in 9 stanzas of 4 lines, stanzas 1, 3, 4, 7 here used,

The glory of the Spring how sweet 267

Gladden, Washington [1836-   ], son of Solomon Gladden, teacher: born at Pittsgrove, Pennsylvania: A. B., Williams, 1859; D. D., Roanoke College, 1884; LL. D., Wisconsin University, 1881: published in March, 1879, in the *Sunday Afternoon*, of which he was then editor, in 3 stanzas of 8 lines, stanzas 1 and 3 here used,

O Master, let me walk with thee 111

Grant, Sir Robert [1785-1838], son of Charles Grant, M. P., and a director in the East India Company: born at Bengal: Magdalene College, Cambridge, B. A., 1801, third wrangler and second chancellor medalist, M. A., 1804: M. P., 1826; privy councillor, 1831; governor of Bombay, 1834. His version of Psalm civ. has been called a resetting of that of W. Kethe, printed in the *Anglo-Genevan Psalter* of 1561, but the likeness is so slight that it deserves to be considered an original production. It was given in Bickersteth's *Church Psalmody*, 1833, and in a posthumous edition of his *Sacred Poems*, 1839, in 6 stanzas of 4 lines. Stanzas 3 and 6 are here omitted.

O worship the King all glorious above 7

Greenough, James Bradstreet [1833-   ]. son of James Greenough, merchant, of Boston: born at Portland, Maine: Boston Latin School; Harvard, A. B., 1856, tutor, 1865-1873, assistant professor of Latin, 1873-1883, professor of Latin, 1883: wrote in 1894, and contributed to this book, in 4 stanzas of 8 lines, here given unchanged,

Deus omnium creator 283

Greg, Samuel [1804-1877], son of Samuel Greg, manufacturer of cotton goods: born at Manchester: school at Nottingham, then Dr. Lant Carpenter, at Bristol, in the same class as Dr. James Martineau; then University of Edinburgh: wrote, in 1868, "in the midst of affliction," the hymn the first line of which follows. It was published in *A Layman's Legacy In Prose and Verse, compiled and edited by his wife and daughter*, London, 1877, in 11 stanzas of 4 lines, stanzas 2, 3, 7, 8, 10 here used.

Around my path life's mysteries 280

Gustavus Adolphus [Gustavus II.] [1594-1632], son of Charles IX.: born at Stockholm: king of Sweden, 1611; champion of Protestantism in the Thirty Year's War: is said to have told his chaplain, Dr. Jacob Fabricius, "the thoughts that were in his heart," and these thoughts his chaplain moulded into the hymn of 3 stanzas of 6 lines "Verzage nicht, du Häuflein klein." It is also maintained that the hymn was written by Pastor Johann Michael Altenburg. The evidence is so conflicting that it has been thought best to adopt the traditional assignment to Gustavus Adolphus. It was certainly made use of by him as a battle-song for his soldiers, and was sung by his army on the morning of the battle of Lützen, where Gustavus was killed. The translation of Mrs. Elizabeth Charles, *q. v.*, of all 3 stanzas, given in *The Voice of Christian Life in Song*, 1858, is here unchanged.

Be not dismayed, thou little flock 193

Hatch, Edwin [1835-1889], son of Samuel Hatch of Derby: born at Derby: King Edward's School, Birmingham; then Pembroke College, Oxford, B. A., with honors, 1857, M. A., 1867; vice principal of St. Mary Hall, 1867-1885; master of the Schools, 1868-1869, and 1873-1875; Bampton lecturer, 1880; Grinfield lecturer on the Septuagint, 1880-1884; classical professor, Trinity College, Toronto; fellow of McGill University, Montreal, 1859–1866; Hibbert lecturer, 1880; LL. D., Edinburgh, 1883: published in *Towards Fields of Light*, 1890, in 3 stanzas of 4 lines, all here used,

O Master of my soul 205

Havergal, Frances Ridley [1836–1879], daughter of the Rev. William Henry Havergal: born at Astley, Worcestershire: the author of many devotional works in prose and verse: wrote in 1874, and published in *Loyal Responses*, 1878, in 12 stanzas of 2 lines, stanzas 3, 4, 11, 12 here omitted,

Take my life, and let it be 77

Heber, Reginald [1783–1826], son of the Rev. Reginald Heber, co-rector of Malpas, Cheshire: born at Malpas: Brazenose College, Oxford, chancellor's prize for Latin poem "The Commencement of the New Century," in his first year, and the Newdigate prize for English poetry for his poem "Palestine," 1803, B. A., 1804, M. A., 1808, D. D., 1823; fellow of All Souls', 1804; Bampton lecturer, 1815; vicar of Hodnet, Shropshire, 1807–1822; preacher at Lincoln's Inn, 1822; bishop of Calcutta, with the whole of India for his diocese, 1823–1826: one of the original staff on the *Quarterly Review*. In his posthumous *Hymns*, 1827, was published for St. Stephen's Day, in 8 stanzas of 4 lines, stanzas 1, 2, 3, 4, 7, 8 here used,

The Son of God goes forth to war 105

and for Septuagesima Sunday, based on the parable of the laborers in the vineyard, in 6 stanzas of 4 lines, stanzas 1, 3, 6 here used,

The God of glory walks his round 195

and for Evening, in 1 stanza of 8 lines, used here unchanged [for stanza 2, see Richard Whately],

God that madest earth and heaven 258

Hedge, Frederic Henry [1805–1890], son of Levi Hedge, LL. D., professor at Harvard of logic and metaphysics, 1810–1827, and of philosophy, 1827–1832: born at Cambridge: studied in Germany; Harvard, A. B., 1825, A. M., in course, Divinity School, 1828, S. T. D., 1852, LL.D., 1886, professor of ecclesiastical history, 1857–1876, of German, 1872–1881: wrote for the ordination of David H. Barlow, in Lynn, 1829, in 10 stanzas of 4 lines, and afterwards abridged and altered for his *Hymns for the Church of Christ*, Boston, 1853, in 5 stanzas of 4 lines, stanzas 1, 2, 4, 5 here used,

Sovereign and transforming Grace 36

In the same collection he included his translation in full of the "Ein' feste Burg ist unser Gott" of Luther, *q. v.*, which he had previously contributed to the 2d edition of Dr. Furness's *Gems of German Verse*, 1852, here given unchanged, beginning,

A mighty fortress is our God 148

To the same collection he contributed in 4 stanzas of 4 lines, here given unchanged,

Beneath thine hammer, Lord, I lie 177

Hensley, Lewis [1827–   ], son of Lewis Hensley, M. R. C. S.: born at London: Trinity College, Cambridge, B. A., senior wrangler and first Smith's prize man, 1846, M. A., 1849; fellow and assistant tutor, Trinity College, 1846–1852; holy orders, 1851; curate of Upton-with-Chalvey, Bucks; then vicar of Ippolyts-with-Great-Wymondly, then of Hitchin, both in Hertfordshire; rural dean, 1867; canon of St. Albans, 1881: published in *Hymns for the Minor Sundays from Advent to Whitsuntide*, 1867, for the fourth Sunday in Advent, in 6 stanzas of 4 lines, stanza 5 here omitted,

Thy kingdom come, O God 131

Herbert, George [1593–1632], son of Richard Herbert of Montgomery Castle, Montgomeryshire: born in Montgomery Castle: Westminster; then Trinity College, Cambridge, B. A., 1611, M. A., and major fellow of his College, 1615, orator for the University, 1619: rector of Bemerton, 1630–1632: published in *The Temple*, 1633, in 6 stanzas of 4 lines, the

Biographical Index

hymn entitled "The Elixir," the first line of which follows. In 1738 John Wesley, *q. v.*, published in his *Collection of Psalms and Hymns* an altered version of all the stanzas of this hymn, and of this version stanzas 1, 2, 4, 5 are here given.

Herbert, Petrus [-1571], native of, or resident at Fulnek, Moravia: ordained priest of the Bohemian Brethren's Unity, 1562; member of Select Council, 1567; afterward consenior of the Unity: one of the principal compilers of the enlarged edition of the Brethren's German Hymn Book, 1566, to which he contributed about 90 hymns. Among these, in 5 stanzas of 7 lines, was the hymn beginning "Die Nacht ist kommen drin wir ruhen sollen." This was republished by Bunsen in his "*Versuch eines allgemeinen evangelischen Gesang- und Gebetbuches*," 1833, with an additional stanza by an unknown hand, given as stanza 5, the original 5 becoming 6. The whole of this version Miss Winkworth, *q. v.*, translated in the original metre and published in her *Chorale Book for England*, 1863, which translation, omitting stanzas 2 and 4, is here given,

Higginson, Thomas Wentworth [1823-], son of Stephen Higginson: born at Cambridge: Harvard, A. B., 1841, A. M., 1869, Divinity School, 1847: minister of Churches in Newburyport and Worcester, 1847–1858; colonel of the first colored regiment raised in the Civil War; editor of the *Harvard Memorial Biographies*, 1866: wrote for Longfellow and Johnson's *Book of Hymns*, Boston, 1846, with the title "The Hope of Man," in 5 stanzas of 4 lines, all here used,

and, with the title "Prayer for Guidance," in 4 stanzas of 4 lines, all here used,

Holmes, Oliver Wendell [1809–1894], son of the Rev. Abiel Holmes, D. D.: born at Cambridge: Phillips Academy, Andover; Harvard, A. B., 1829, M. D., 1836, LL. D., 1880, A. M., 1889, Parkman professor of anatomy and physiology, 1847–1882, then professor emeritus, dean of Medical School, 1847–1853, overseer, 1876–1882; LL. D., Edinburgh, 1886; Litt. D., Cambridge, 1886; D. C. L., Oxford, 1886; professor of anatomy and physiology, Dartmouth, 1838–1847: wrote for the anniversary of the Boston Young Men's Christian Union, 1893, in 6 stanzas of 4 lines, the hymn the first line of which follows. It was printed on a card for use at that meeting and for distribution. It is here given unchanged,

He published in *The Professor at the Breakfast Table*, in the *Atlantic Monthly*, November, 1859, with the title "Hymn of Trust," in 4 stanzas of 4 lines, here given unchanged,

and as above, in the following month, with the title "A Sunday Hymn," in 5 stanzas of 4 lines, here given unchanged,

He wrote for "A Grand Jubilee Concert," given in Music Hall, Boston, by call of Longfellow, Emerson, Quincy, Parkman, and others, to celebrate the issue of the Proclamation of Emancipation, the hymn the first line of which follows. It was sung to music composed for it by Mr. Otto Dresel. The hymn as sung was in 4 stanzas of 4 lines, but next day he gave to the newspapers for publication 2 additional stanzas of 4 lines. He afterwards revised the hymn, and it was printed with stanza 5 omitted, in his *Poetical Works*, Boston, 1892, from which have been here taken stanzas 1, 2, 3.

# of Authors and Translators.

Biographical Index

in the inmost parts, Ps.," in 9 stanzas of 4 lines, the first line of which follows. It has been said that it was suggested by a sermon of Maurice, published in his *Doctrine of Sacrifice*, entitled "The word of God conquering by sacrifice." As here given, stanzas 3, 4, 7, 8 are omitted.

O God of truth, whose living word 202

Hymns of the Spirit. In the collection of hymns thus entitled, Boston, 1864, edited by the Rev. Samuel Longfellow, *q. v.*, and the Rev. Samuel Johnson, *q. v.*, was printed as here given, and it has not been further traced,

Give forth thine earnest cry 196

John of Damascus [–*circa* 780], saint in both the Eastern and Western Churches, is said, in an account of his life written in the 10th century, and probably legendary, to have been the son of Sergius, a Christian but an officer of the caliph; to have been born at Damascus, and educated by Cosmas, a monk redeemed from captivity; to have succeeded to the office of his father, but afterwards to have retired to the Monastery of St. Saba, near Jerusalem, and late in life to have been ordained a priest of the Church of Jerusalem. He was certainly author of important theological works, and is called by Neale the greatest of the poets of the Greek Church. From the first of the eight odes that make up the "Golden, or Queen of Canons," set for Easter in the Greek Church, beginning Ἀναστάσεως ἡμέρα, John Mason Neale, *q. v.*, translated and published in his *Hymns of the Eastern Church*, 1862, in 3 stanzas of 8 lines, here given unchanged,

'T is the day of resurrection 116

Johns, John [1801–1847], son of Ambrose Bowden Johns, painter: born at Plymouth, Devonshire: educated at Plymouth and Edinburgh: minister of old Presbyterian Chapel at Crediton, 1820–1836; minister to the poor in Liverpool, 1836, dying of a fever contracted through devotion to his work: contributed 35

hymns to Beard's *Collection of Hymns*, 1837. Of one of these, entitled " Prayer for the Kingdom of God," in 5 stanzas of 4 lines, has been here taken all but stanza 5.

Come, kingdom of our God 127

Johnson, Samuel [1709–1784], son of Michael Johnson, bookseller: born at Lichfield, Staffordshire: Pembroke College, Oxford, M. A., 1755, D. C. L., 1775; LL. D., Dublin, 1765: placed as a motto to Number 7 of the *Rambler*, dated Tuesday, April 10, 1750, 6 lines from Book III. Metrum IX. of the *De Consolatione Philosophiae*, of Boethius, *q. v.*, with a translation in 2 stanzas of 4 lines, which is here given unchanged, beginning,

O thou whose power o'er moving worlds presides 21

Johnson, Samuel [1822–1882], son of Dr. Samuel Johnson: born at Salem, Massachusetts: Salem Schools; then Harvard, A. B., 1842, Divinity School, 1846: minister of the Free Church of Lynn, 1853–1870. He was joint editor with the Rev. Samuel Longfellow, *q. v.*, of *A Book of Hymns for Public and Private Devotion*, Boston, 1846, the same with *A Supplement*, 1848, and *Hymns of the Spirit*, Boston, 1864. He wrote for the graduating exercises of his class in Harvard Divinity School, 1846, and afterwards published in the *Supplement* named above, with the title " The Reformer's Vow," in 6 stanzas of 4 lines, stanzas 3 and 6 here omitted,

God of the earnest heart 17

To *Hymns of the Spirit*, with the title " Inspiration," he contributed, in 9 stanzas of 4 lines, stanzas 3, 4, 5, 6 here omitted,

Life of ages, richly poured 73

and to the *Book of Hymns*, with the title " For Divine Strength," in 4 stanzas of 4 lines, all here used,

Father, in thy mysterious presence kneeling . . 78

and to *Hymns of the Spirit*, with the title " City of God," in 5 stanzas of 4 lines, all here used,

City of God, how broad and far 123

# of Authors and Translators.

Keble, John [1792-1866], son of the Rev. John Keble, vicar of Coln St. Aldwyn, Gloucestershire: born in his father's house at Fairfield: educated at home; then Corpus Christi College, Oxford, where he won a scholarship in 1806, B. A., double first class in 1810 [a distinction gained before only by Sir Robert Peel], M. A., 1813; fellow of Oriel, 1812-1835; University prizes for both Latin and English essays; 1812; examining master in the Schools, 1814-1816; ordained priest in 1816; tutor at Oriel, 1822; professor of poetry, Oxford, 1831-1842; after minor charges, vicar of Hursley, 1835-1866: wrote in 1819, and published in the *Christian Year*, 1827, for Septuagesima Sunday, with the text "The invisible things of him, from the creation of the world, are clearly seen, being understood by the things that are made," Rom. i. 20, in 12 stanzas of 4 lines, stanzas 1, 2, 3, 11, 12 here used,

and published in the *Christian Year* for Whitsunday, with the text "And suddenly there came a sound from heaven as of a rushing mighty wind, and it filled all the house where they were sitting. And there appeared unto them cloven tongues like as of fire, and it sat upon each of them. And they were all filled with the Holy Ghost." Acts ii. 2-4, in 11 stanzas of 4 lines, stanzas 1, 7, 9, 11 here used,

and wrote in 1822, and published in the *Christian Year*, for "Morning," with the text "His compassions fail not. They are new every morning," Lament. iii. 22, 23, in 16 stanzas of 4 lines, stanzas 5, 6, 7, 8, 14, 16 here used,

and wrote in 1820, and published in the *Christian Year* for "Evening," with the text "Abide with us; for it is towards evening, and the day is far spent," Luke xxiv. 29, in 14 stanzas of 4 lines, stanzas 1, 3, 7, 8, 14 here used,

Ken, Thomas [1637-1711], son of Thomas Ken, attorney, of London : born at Berkhampstead, Hertfordshire: Winchester; then New College, Oxford, B. A., 1661, M. A., 1664-1665, B. D., 1678, D. D., 1679; holy orders same year; fellow of Winchester, 1666: rector of Wodhay, and prebendary of Winchester, 1669; chaplain to Princess Mary at the Hague, 1676; bishop of Bath and Wells, 1685; one of the seven bishops imprisoned in the tower, 1688; deprived of his see for refusing to take the oaths under William and Mary, 1691 : " approached," says Macaulay, " as near as human infirmity permits to the ideal perfection of Christian virtue." He published in 1674 *A Manual of Prayers for the Use of the Scholars of Winchester College*, in which he says " Be sure to sing the Morning and Evening Hymn in your chamber devoutly ; " but these hymns are not known to have been printed at that date. In the *Harmonia Sacra, or Divine Hymns and Dialogues . . . Composed by the Best Masters. London, Henry Playford, 1693*, was published " AN EVENING HYMN. The words by Bishop Ken. Set by Mr. Jeremiah Clarke," and, to an edition of the *Manual*, printed in 1695, were added versions of the Morning, the Evening, and the Midnight hymns. In 1709, an edition of the *Manual* was printed with a revised version of the 3 hymns. From that revised version of the Morning hymn, in 14 stanzas of 4 lines, including the doxology beginning " Praise God, from whom all blessings flow" which is common to the 3 hymns, have been here taken stanzas 1, 5, 12, 13, beginning,

and from that of the Evening hymn, in 12 stanzas of 4 lines, have been here taken stanzas 1, 2, 5, 4, in that order, beginning,

Biographical Index

Kethe, William [*circa* 1562], is said to have been of Scotch parentage : to have been in exile in Frankfurt in 1555; at Geneva, in 1557; sent on a mission to his fellow exiles in Basle, Strassburg, etc., in 1558; again in Geneva with their answer, in 1559; and to have been rector of Childe Okeford, Dorset, 1561. The version of Psalm c., the first line of which follows, was first published in the *Psalter* of John Daye, London, 1560-1561, without signature; then in the *Anglo-Genevan Psalter*, 1561, assigned to *Tho. Ster;* in Birtwell's *Psalter*, 1561, and in the *Scottish Psalter*, 1564, assigned to *W. Ke.;* in Daye's *Psalter*, 1587, assigned to *I. H.* The metre excludes Sternhold, and the testimony seems favorable to Kethe. As printed in Daye's *Psalter* is here given with the spelling modernized, but otherwise unchanged.

All people that on earth do dwell 11

Latin Hymns. VENI CREATOR SPIRITUS : Of all the hymns composed in the middle ages, with the exception of the *Te Deum*, this has been most used in modern times, but its author is unknown. It has been assigned to Charlemagne, to Saint Ambrose, to Gregory the Great, and to Rhabanus Maurus. The text is given in *Daniel* I., page 213 [but see Julian's *Dictionary of Hymnology*, 1892, page 1206]. The translation of John Dryden, *q. v.*, is here given, beginning,

Creator Spirit, by whose aid 12

O DEUS EGO AMO TE, NAM PRIOR TU AMASTI ME. This hymn has been assigned to Saint Ignatius Loyola but was probably written by a German Jesuit of the 17th Century. The text may be found in *Daniel* II., page 335. The translation of Edward Caswall, *q. v.*, is here given, beginning,

I love, I love thee, Lord most high 82

VENI, VENI, EMMANUEL. This hymn is based on 5 of the 7 greater antiphones, and was made by an unknown writer of about the 12th century. These antiphones are sentences sung in Advent, before and after the Magnificat, by the Roman Church, and were first translated for use of the English Church by John Henry Newman, and published in No. 75 of *Tracts for the Times*, 1846. In 1851, John Mason Neale, *q. v.*, first translated the hymn based on these antiphones, and published his translation in *Mediæval Hymns*, in 5 stanzas of 6 lines, of which stanzas 1, 4, 5 are here given.

Draw nigh, draw nigh, Emmanuel 92

O DEUS EGO AMO TE, NEC AMO TE UT SALVES ME. The original of this hymn is said to be a Spanish sonnet, assigned in Diepenbrock's *Geistlicher Blumenstrauss*, 1829, to Saint Francis Xavier. The Latin form is probably by Saint Francis, as it is given as early as 1668, in J. Scheffler's *Heilige Seelenlust*, as a translation of his work. The Latin text may be found in *Daniel* II., page 335. The translation of Edward Caswall, *q. v.*, is here given, beginning,

My God, I love thee : not because 164

Longfellow, Samuel [1819-1892], son of Hon. Stephen Longfellow : born at Portland, Maine : Harvard, A. B., 1839, Divinity School, 1846 : minister of churches in Fall River, Massachusetts, Brooklyn, New York, Germantown, Pennsylvania, 1848-1882 : wrote and printed, with the title "The light that lighteth every man," for the 2d Social Festival of the Free Religious Association, 1874, in 2 stanzas of 8 lines, the hymn the first line of which follows. He afterwards published it in *A Book of Hymns and Tunes for the Congregation and the Home*, Cambridge, 1876, with the title "Greeting," in 4 stanzas of 4 lines, and it is here given in that form unchanged. This, with all the other hymns of Mr. Longfellow herein given, was revised by him for this book.

O Life that maketh all things new 5

In *Hymns of the Spirit*, Boston, 1864, he published, with the title "God through all and in you all," in 5 stanzas of 4 lines, stanza 2 here omitted.

God of the earth, the sky, the sea 53

and with the title "John and Jesus," in 4 stanzas of 4 lines, all here used,

He wrote in 1860, and published in *Hymns of the Spirit*, with the title "The Church Universal," in 5 stanzas of 4 lines, all here used,

In the same book he published, with the title "Looking unto God," in 4 stanzas of 6 lines, all here used,

and with the title "Life's Mission," in 4 stanzas of 4 lines, all here used,

He wrote in Fall River, 1848, and published in the *Supplement to A Book of Hymns, Second Edition*, Boston, 1848, with the title "The New Commandment," in 3 stanzas of 4 lines, all here used,

He published in *Vespers*, New York, 1860, headed "Nox et tenebrae," in 2 stanzas of 8 lines, and reprinted in *Hymns of the Spirit*, 1864, with the title "Vesper Hymn," in 4 stanzas of 4 lines, here given in that form unchanged,

Löwenstern, Matthäus Appelles von [1594–1648], son of a saddler: born at Neustadt in Silesia: musical director and treasurer at Bernstadt, 1625; director of the school at Bernstadt, 1626; Rath and secretary, and also director of finance, 1631: published about 1644, in *The mottoes of His Royal Highness Carl Friedrich, Duke of Münsterberg, and of other noble persons, together with sundry hymns expressly collected herewith. Published by M. A. von L.*, 30 hymns. One of these, beginning "Christe, du Beistand deiner Kreuzgemeine," in 4 stanzas of 4 lines, was included by Bunsen in his *Versuch*, 1833, and used by Philip Pusey, *q. v.*, as a basis for his

hymn in 5 stanzas of 4 lines, stanzas 1, 3, 4, 5 here used, beginning,

Luise Henriette [1627–1667], daughter of Friedrich Heinrich, prince of Nassau-Orange and stadtholder of the United Netherlands; wife of elector Friedrich Wilhelm of Brandenburg; mother of Friedrich I. of Prussia: born at the Hague: contributed to the *D. M. Luther's und anderer vornehmen geistreichen und gelehrten Männer Geistliche Lieder und Psalmen*, Berlin, 1653, edited by Christopher Runge at her direction, as a Union Hymn Book for members of the Lutheran and Reformed Churches, 4 hymns, one of them in 10 stanzas of 6 lines, beginning "Jesus, meine Zuversicht." From a translation of this in the original metre by Miss Winkworth, *q. v.*, published in her *Chorale Book for England*, 1863, of all but stanzas 4, 5, 6, stanzas 1, 2, 3 have been here taken.

Luther, Martin [1483–1546], son of Hans Luther: born at Eisleben, Saxony: University of Erfurt, B. A., 1502, M. A., 1503: Augustinian monk, 1505; ordained priest, 1507: professor at University of Wittenberg, 1508, D. D., 1512: published his 95 theses, 1517; burnt the papal bull that condemned them, 1520; Diet of Worms, 1521: translated the Bible into German, 1521–1534: published in Klug's *Gesang-buch*, Wittenberg, 1529, with the title "Der xxxxvi. Psalm. Deus noster refugium et virtus," in 4 stanzas of 9 lines, his hymn beginning "Ein' feste Burg ist unser Gott." Authorities differ as to when it was written. The full translation of Dr. Frederic H. Hedge, *q. v.*, is here given unchanged.

Lynch, Thomas Toke [1818–1871], son of John Burke Lynch, M. D., of Great Dunmow, Essex: born at Great Dunmow: educated at a school in Islington, and at the Highbury In-

Biographical Index

dependent College : minister for many years of a congregation finally meeting in Mornington Church, Hampstead Road, London : published in *The Rivulet, a Contribution to Sacred Song,* London, 1855, in 6 stanzas of 6 lines, stanzas 1, 2, 5, 6 here used,

and in 6 stanzas of 4 lines, all here used,

Lyte, Henry Francis [1793-1847], son of Captain Thomas Lyte: born at Ednam, near Kelso, Roxburghshire: Royal School of Enniskillen; then Trinity College, Dublin, B. A., 1814, M. A., 1830, gaining the prize for English poetry three times; holy orders, 1815; perpetual curate, Lower Brixham, Devonshire, 1823-1847: published in his *Spirit of the Psalms,* 1834, his version of Psalm ciii., in 5 stanzas of 6 lines, all here used,

and of Psalm lxxxiv., in 4 stanzas of 8 lines, stanzas 1, 2, 3 here used,

In *Sacred Poetry,* Edinburgh, Oliphant and Sons, 3d edition, 1824, in 6 stanzas of 8 lines, signed "G," appeared the hymn the first line of which follows. It was given in the *Christian Psalmist,* 1825, and elsewhere was more than once reprinted, and then appeared with slight changes in Mr. Lyte's *Poems Chiefly Religious,* 1833, whence have been here taken stanzas 5 and 6.

In 1847, he gave to a relative, with music of his own composing, a copy of the hymn, in 8 stanzas of 4 lines, the first line of which follows. It was printed on a leaflet, 1847, in *Remains, &c.,* 1850, and in *Miscellaneous Poems,* 1868, in 8 stanzas of 4 lines. From this last have been here taken stanzas 1, 2, 6, 7, 8.

Macdonald, George [1824-], son of George Macdonald, corn merchant: born

at Huntly, near Aberdeen: University and Kings College, Aberdeen, A. M., 1845, LL. D., 1868; Highbury Independent College, London: after 1850, minister of several Congregational Churches; then a layman of the Church of England: published in the *Disciple and Other Poems,* 1860, revised and reprinted in *Works of Fancy and Imagination,* 1871, again revised and reprinted in *Poetical Works,* London, 1893, in 6 stanzas of 4 lines, stanzas 3 and 5 here omitted,

and published in *Works of Fancy and Imagination,* London, 1871, and reprinted unchanged in *Poetical Works,* London, 1893, in 4 stanzas of 4 lines, all here used,

Mant, Richard [1776-1848], son of the Rev. Richard Mant, master of the Southampton Grammar School: born at Southampton: Winchester; then Trinity College, Oxford, B. A., 1797, M. A., 1800, B. D. and D. D., 1815, chancellor's prize for English, same year, fellow of Oriel, 1798; holy orders, 1802; Bampton lecturer, 1812: bishop of Killaloe, 1820-1823, of Down and Connor, 1823, of Dromore, 1842-1848: published in *Ancient Hymns,* 1837, in 4 stanzas of 8 lines, a hymn beginning " Bright the vision that delighted." From this a cento, in 5 stanzas of 4 lines, has been here taken, beginning,

In his *Metrical Version of the Psalms,* 1824, he published, in 7 stanzas of 8 lines, stanzas 1, 2, 3 here used, his translation of Psalm cxlv., beginning,

Martineau, James [1805-], son of Thomas Martineau, manufacturer: born at Norwich, Norfolk: Norwich Grammar School and Dr. Lant Carpenter, Bristol; then Manchester New College, York; professor of mental and moral philosophy and political economy, Man-

# of Authors and Translators.

chester New College, 1840, then principal, 1869–1885; LL. D., Harvard, 1872; S. T. D., Leyden, 1875, and Edinburgh, 1884; D. C. L., Oxford, 1888: ministered to churches in Dublin, Liverpool, and London, 1828–1873: published in his *Hymns for the Christian Church and Home*, 1840, in 6 stanzas of 4 lines, stanza 4 here omitted,

Mason, Caroline Atherton [1823–1890], daughter of Dr. Calvin Briggs, of Marblehead, Massachusetts: born at Marblehead. In *The Lost Ring and Other Poems*, Boston, 1892, was published with the title "Perfect love casteth out fear," in 4 stanzas of 6 lines, all here used,

and with the title "Matin Hymn," in 6 stanzas of 4 lines, stanzas 3, 4, 5, 6 here used,

Massey, Gerald [1828–   ], son of a canal boatman: born at Tring, Herefordshire: educated at a penny school, and by reading at bookstalls, often going hungry to buy a book: friend of Maurice and Kingsley: said to have been the model for "Felix Holt": published in *A Tale of Eternity and other Poems*, 1870, with the title "His banner over me," in 3 stanzas of 6 lines, all here used,

Massie, Richard [1800–1887], son of the Rev. Richard Massie, of Coddington, Cheshire: born at Chester: privately educated. From his translation of the "Herr, des Tages Mühen und Beschwerden," of Carl J. P. Spitta, *q. v.*, published in his *Lyra Domestica*, 1860, in 4 stanzas of 8 lines, a cento has been here taken, beginning,

Matson, William Tidd, [1833–   ], son of John Matson: born at London: St. John's College, Cambridge, then Agricultural and Chemical College, Kennington: minister of Congregational Churches at Gosport, Highbury and Portsmouth: published in *The Inner Life*, 1866, as canto xl., in 5 stanzas of 4 lines, here given unchanged,

and as canto xxvi., in 5 stanzas of 4 lines, here given unchanged,

Merrick, James [1720–1769], son of John Merrick, M. D., of Reading, Berkshire: born at Reading: Reading Grammar School; then Trinity College, Oxford, B. A., 1739, M. A., 1742, fellow of Trinity, 1744: published in *Poems on Sacred Subjects*, 1763, with the title "The Ignorance of Man," in 8 stanzas of 4 lines, stanzas 5, 6, 7, 8 here used,

Milman, Henry Hart [1791–1868], son of Sir Francis Milman, court physician of George III.: born at London: Dr. Burney, at Greenwich; then Eton; then Brasenose College, Oxford, B. A., 1814, M. A., 1816, B. D. and D. D., 1849, Newdigate, Latin verse, Latin essay, and English essay prizes, fellow of Brasenose, 1814–1819; holy orders, 1816; professor of poetry, Oxford, 1821–1831; Bampton lecturer, 1827; rector of St. Margaret's and canon of Westminster, 1835–1849; dean of St. Paul's, 1849–1868: published in Bishop Heber's *Hymns*, 1827, in 6 stanzas of 4 lines, and in *Selection of Psalms and Hymns for the use of St. Margaret's, Westminster*, 1837, for the second Sunday in Lent, in 4 stanzas of 4 lines, and again in *Poetical Works*, in its original form, from which last are here used stanzas 1, 2, 3,

Milton, John [1608–1674], son of John Milton, scrivener: born at London: St. Paul's School; then Christ's College, Cambridge, B. A., 1628–29, M. A., 1632: Latin secretary to the Council of State, 1649–1659: when he was fifteen, translated Psalm cxxxvi., and in 1645 published this version in *Poems in English and Latin*, in 24 stanzas of 4 lines. From this have

Biographical Index

been here taken stanzas 1, 2, 15, 23, 1, in that order.

Let us, with a gladsome mind 16

In April, 1648, he published *Nine of the Psalms done into metre, wherein all, but what is in a different character, are the very words of the text, translated from the original*, containing his version of Psalms lxxx. to lxxxviii. From his translation in this of Psalm lxxxiv., in 12 stanzas of 4 lines, have been here taken stanzas 1, 2, 5, 7, beginning,

How lovely are thy dwellings fair 34

and from his translation of Psalms lxxxii., lxxxv., and lxxxvi., has been here taken a cento beginning,

Rise, God! judge thou the earth in might . . . 130

Monsell, John Samuel Bewley [1811–1875], son of Archdeacon Thomas Bewley Monsell: born at Londonderry: Trinity College, Dublin, B. A., 1832, LL. D., 1856; holy orders, 1832; chaplain to Bishop Mant; rector of St. Nicholas, Guilford: published in *Hymns of Love and Praise*, 1863, 2d edition, 1866, in 4 stanzas of 5 lines, stanzas 1, 2, 3 here used,

Fight the good fight 194

Montgomery, James [1771–1854], son of John Montgomery, Moravian minister: born at Irvine, Ayrshire: educated at Fulneck Seminary, Yorkshire: editor for 31 years of the *Sheffield Iris*; imprisoned by the government once for reprinting a song commemorating the fall of the Bastile, and again in 1796, for publishing an account of a riot at Sheffield; in 1833, pensioned by the government for his services to his countrymen: wrote, in 1824, for the anniversary of a Sheffield Sunday-school the hymn the first line of which follows. It was published, with slight changes, in the *Christian Psalmist*, 1825, and again in *Original Hymns*, 1853, in 6 stanzas of 4 lines, stanzas 1, 2, 3, 6 here used.

Stand up and bless the Lord 9

In 1823, he wrote for a meeting of a Missionary Society, published the same year in the *Evangelical Magazine*, revised for the *Christian Psalmist*, 1825, and again printed in his *Original Hymns*, 1853, in 6 stanzas of 4 lines, stanzas 1, 3, 4, 5 here used,

O Spirit of the living God 22

In 1819, he published in Cotterill's *Selection of Psalms and Hymns*, repeated in the *Christian Psalmist*, 1825, and in *Original Hymns*, 1853, with the title "Glory to God in the highest," in 6 stanzas of 4 lines, stanzas 1, 2, 3, 5 here used,

Songs of praise the angels sang 106

In 1822, he published in *Songs of Zion*, repeated in *Original Hymns*, 1853, his version of Psalm xci., in 5 stanzas of 8 lines, stanzas 1 and 5 here used.

Call Jehovah thy salvation 141

And as above, his version of Psalm xxiii., in 4 stanzas of 4 lines, all here used.

The Lord is my shepherd, no want shall I know 154

In 1818, at the request of the Rev. E. Bickersteth, and for his *Treatise on Prayer*, he wrote, and then printed on a broadside for use in a Sheffield Sunday-school, the hymn the first line of which follows. It was afterwards published, revised in Bickersteth's *Treatise on Prayer*, 1819, in the 8th edition of Cotterill's *Selection of Psalms and Hymns*, 1819, in the *Christian Psalmist*, 1825, and in *Original Hymns*, 1853. From this last version, in 8 stanzas of 4 lines, are here taken stanzas 1, 2, 3, 8.

Prayer is the soul's sincere desire 184

In 1822, in *Songs of Zion*, repeated in the various editions of his *Poetical Works*, he published his version of Psalm xlii., in 4 stanzas of 6 lines, stanzas 1 and 4 here used.

As the hart, with eager looks 185

In 1825, in the *Christian Psalmist*, repeated in *Original Hymns*, 1853, he published in 8 stanzas of 4 lines, stanzas 1, 2, 5, 6 here used,

One prayer I have — all prayers in one 186

In 1822, in *Songs of Zion*, repeated in the various editions of his *Poetical Works*, he pub-

# of Authors and Translators.

lished his version of Psalm xxvii., in 2 stanzas of 8 lines, here given unchanged.

In 1825, in the *Christian Psalmist*, repeated in *Original Hymns*, 1853, he published in 7 stanzas of 4 lines, stanzas 1, 2, 6 here used,

and as above, in 6 stanzas of 4 lines, stanzas 1, 2, 3, 4 here used,

In 1835, in the *Amethyst*, an annual, again in the *Poets' Portfolio*, the same year, then in *Poetical Works*, various editions, with the title "At Home in Heaven," and the text 1 Thess. iv. 17, appeared in 2 parts of 9 and 11 stanzas of 4 lines, stanzas 1, 2, 3, 8, 9 of the 1st part here used,

Moore, Henry [1732–1802], son of the Rev. Henry Moore, Presbyterian minister: born at Plymouth, Devonshire: educated at Doddridge's Academy, Northampton: minister at Modbury, and then at Liskeard, Devonshire. In the *Dunkinfield Collection*, 1822, appeared in 4 stanzas of 4 lines, the hymn the first line of which follows. The version printed in this book, which varies from that in *Dunkinfield*, has been copied from the original MS. in 7 stanzas of 4 lines, now [with that of 4 other hymns] in the possession of Sir Jerom Murch, through whose kindness the copy was made. Stanzas 5, 6, 7 of the original MS. have been here omitted.

In his *Lyrical and Miscellaneous Poems*, 1803, with the title "Wisdom and virtue sought from God," was published in 7 stanzas of 4 lines, stanzas 3, 4, 6, 7 here used,

Moore, Thomas [1779–1852], son of John Moore, grocer: born at Dublin: Trinity College, Dublin, B. A., 1799: registrar of the Admiralty Court, Bermuda, 1803: published in *Sacred Songs*, 1816, and again in the various editions of his *Collected Works*, in 2 stanzas of 8 lines, all here used,

and, as above, in 4 stanzas of 6 lines, stanzas 1, 2, 4 here used,

Neale, John Mason [1818–1866], son of the Rev. Cornelius Neale: born at London: Sherborne Grammar School; then Trinity College, Cambridge, B. A., 1840, M. A., 1845, members' prize, 1838; fellow and tutor, Downing College, 1840; Seatonian prize for a sacred poem, 1845 and for the ten succeeding years: translated from the text in *Daniel* II., page 336, a Latin hymn beginning " Veni, veni, Emmanuel," based on 5 of the 7 greater antiphones, written by an unknown author, probably of the 12th century [see Latin Hymns], and published his translation in *Mediæval Hymns*, 1851. This translation he altered for the *Hymnal Noted*, 1852, and reprinted this altered version in *Mediæval Hymns*, 3d edition, 1863, in 5 stanzas of 6 lines, stanzas 1, 4, 5 here given.

Of the eight odes which form the "Golden Canon" of St. John of Damascus, *q. v.*, the 1st, beginning Ἀναστάσεως ἡμέρα, he translated and published in *Hymns of the Eastern Church*, 1862, in 3 stanzas of 8 lines. It is here given unchanged.

From the "De Contemptu Mundi" of Bernard of Morlaix, *q. v.*, he translated 218 lines, and published them in *Mediæval Hymns*, 2d edition, 1863. From this translation has been here taken a cento beginning,

and a cento beginning,

Newman, John Henry [1801–1890], son of John Newman, banker: born at London:

Biographical Index

Ealing; then Trinity College, Oxford, B. A., with honors, 1820, M. A., 1823, B. D., 1836, fellow of Oriel, 1822–1845, tutor, 1826–1831; holy orders, 1824; vice-principal of St. Alban's Hall, 1825; incumbent of St. Mary's, Oxford, 1828; public examiner, 1827; one of the select University preachers, 1830: joined the Roman Church, 1845; rector of the Catholic University of Ireland, 1854–1858; cardinal, 1879: translated the Paris Breviary text of "Jam lucis orto sidere" (see Ambrosius), which is given in his *Hymni Ecclesiae*, 1838, in 6 stanzas of 4 lines, and published this translation in his *Verses on Religious Subjects*, 1853, and again in his *Verses on Various Occasions*, 1868, in 6 stanzas of 4 lines, stanzas 1, 2, 4 here used.

Now that the day-star glimmers bright **228**

He wrote while becalmed at sea between Corsica and Sardinia, June 16, 1833, and published in the *British Magazine*, March, 1834, with the motto "Faith-Heavenly Leadings," again in *Lyra Apostolica*, 1836, with the text "Unto the godly there ariseth up light in the darkness," and again in *Verses*, 1868, with the title "The Pillar of Cloud," in 3 stanzas of 6 lines, here given unchanged,

Lead, kindly Light, amid the encircling gloom . **263**

Newton, John [1725–1807], born at London: sailor, deserter, slave-trader, infidel, profligate; friend of Whitefield and Wesley: curate of Olney, Bucks; rector of St. Mary-Wolnoth, London: published in *Olney Hymns*, 1779, with the title "Zion, or the City of God," and the text Is. xxxiii. 20, 21, in 5 stanzas of 8 lines, stanzas 1 and 2 here used,

Glorious things of thee are spoken **125**

Norton, Andrews [1786–1853], son of Samuel Norton: born at Hingham, Massachusetts: Harvard, A. B., 1804, A. M., in course, librarian, 1813–1821, Dexter lecturer and professor of sacred literature, 1819–1830; A. M., Bowdoin, 1815: wrote in 1809, and published in September of that year in the *Monthly Anthology and Boston Review*, and revised and reprinted

in his *Verses*, 1853, in 4 stanzas of 4 lines, from which it is here taken unchanged,

My God, I thank thee! may no thought . . . **181**

Packard, Charlotte Mellen [1839–   ], daughter of the Rev. Charles Packard: born at Hamilton, Ohio: first published in the *Monthly Religious Magazine*, Boston, December, 1862, in 4 stanzas of 6 lines, given here unchanged,

O shadow in a sultry land **250**

Palgrave, Francis Turner [1824–   ], son of Sir Francis Palgrave the historian: born at Great-Yarmouth, 1824: Charterhouse, 1838; scholar of Balliol College, Oxford, 1842–1847, B. A., 1851, M. A., 1856, first class classical honors, 1847; fellow of Exeter College, 1847–1862; professor of poetry at Oxford, 1885; Ll. D., Edinburgh, 1878; secretary to the Right Hon. W. E. Gladstone: wrote about 1860, and gave in MS. to Lord Selborne, who included it in his *Book of Praise*, 1862, in 5 stanzas of 4 lines, the hymn the first line of which follows. It was repeated in Mr. Palgrave's *Hymns*, 1867, and revised and reprinted in *Amenophis and Other Poems*, 1892. From *Amenophis*, 1892, have been here taken stanzas 1, 2, 3, and from the *Hymns*, 1867, has been here taken stanza 4.

Lord God of morning and of night **43**

In the *Hymns*, 1867, was published in 5 stanzas of 6 lines, the hymn the first line of which follows. It was reprinted in *Amenophis*, 1892, with 2 additional stanzas, and a change in the order of the original stanzas. From the text of the *Hymns*, 1867, have been here taken stanzas 1, 2, 4, 5.

O thou not made with hands **132**

Palmer, Ray [1808–1887], son of Thomas Palmer, judge: born at Little Compton, Rhode Island: Phillips Academy, Andover; Yale, A. B., 1830, A. M., in course; D. D., Union, 1852: minister of various Congregational Churches, 1835–1865; corresponding secretary of the Congregational Union, 1865–

1878: in 1830, wrote, he says, "with very tender emotion, ending the last line with tears," the hymn the first line of which follows. It remained for three years in MS., then Lowell Mason, asking Mr. Palmer for a contribution to his new book, received and published it in *Spiritual Songs for Social Worship*, 1832, set to the tune " Olivet." It was there given in 4 stanzas of 7 lines, was reprinted in *Poetical Works*, New York, 1876, and is here given unchanged.

Parker, Theodore [1810–1860], son of John Parker: born at Lexington, Massachusetts: Harvard, A. M., 1840, Divinity School, 1836: minister of the First Parish, West Roxbury, Massachusetts, then of the Twenty-Eighth Congregational Society, meeting in Music Hall, Boston. In *A Book of Hymns*, Boston, 1846, appeared, in 3 stanzas of 4 lines, a slightly varied version of a sonnet written by Mr. Parker. This sonnet was published in his *Life*, Boston, 1874, by the Rev. O. B. Frothingham. From this latter, omitting the last two lines, has been here taken the hymn beginning,

Perronet, Edward [1726–1792], son of Vincent Perronet, vicar of Shoreham, Kent: born at Shoreham: friend and assistant of John and Charles Wesley: minister of a Congregational Church in Canterbury: published in the *Gospel Magazine*, for November, 1779, the first stanza of the hymn the first line of which is given below. In the issue for April, 1780, this stanza was repeated with 7 additional stanzas, each of 4 lines. In 1785 the hymn was included in Mr. Perronet's *Occasional Verses, Moral and Sacred*, with the title " On the resurrection." In 1787, in *A Selection of Hymns from the best authors*, by John Rippon, *q. v.*, a much altered version was given, and this is now the universally accepted form. Dr. Rippon changed stanzas 1, 4, 5, 7 of Mr. Perronet's hymn into 1, 2, 3, 4 of his version, and added three new stanzas. Of this altered

version, in 7 stanzas of 4 lines, stanzas 1, 6, 7 are here given.

Procter, Adelaide Anne [1825–1864], daughter of Bryan Waller Procter [Barry Cornwall]: born at London: published in *Legends and Lyrics*, edition of 1862, in 4 stanzas of 8 lines, stanza 2 here omitted,

Prudentius, Aurelius Clemens [348–*circa* 413], born in the north of Spain, of Spanish parents: lawyer, magistrate: retired in his fifty-seventh year into poverty and private life, and wrote for the service of the Christian Church a succession of sacred poems. " Lux ecce surgit aurea," (the second part of " Nox, et tenebrae, et nubila,") given in *Daniel* I., No. 105, in 4 stanzas of 2 lines, and 2 stanzas of 4 lines, was translated by Edward Caswall, *q. v.*, in 4 stanzas of 4 lines, and a doxology, and is here used without the doxology.

Pusey, Philip [1799–1855], son of Hon. Philip Pusey, and elder brother of Dr. Edward B. Pusey: born at Pusey, Berkshire: Eton; then Christ Church, Oxford, D. C. L., 1853: M. P., 1830–1832 and 1835–1852: contributed to A. R. Reinagle's *Psalm and Hymn Tunes*, Oxford, 1840, based on the " Christe, du Beistand deiner Kreuzgemeine " of M. A. von Löwenstern, *q. v.*, in 5 stanzas of 4 lines, stanza 2 here omitted,

Rands, William Brighty [1827–1882], son of William Rands, candle-maker: born at Chelsea, England : journalist, man of letters : published in *Good Words for the Young*, and again in his *Lilliput Lectures*, London, 1882, in 5 stanzas of 4 lines, all here used,

Reed, Andrew [1788–1862], son of Andrew Reed: born at London: Hackney College, London ; D. D., Yale, 1834: minister of Wyc-

Biographical Index

liffe Chapel, London; founder of "The London Orphan Asylum," "The Asylum for Fatherless Children," "The Asylum for Idiots," "The Infant Orphan Asylum," "The Hospital for Incurables": published, unsigned, in the *Evangelical Magazine*, June, 1829, with the title "Hymn to the Spirit," and republished in his *Hymn Book*, 1842, in 7 stanzas of 4 lines, stanzas 2 and 7 here omitted,

Spirit divine, attend our prayers 54

Rinkart, Martin [1586–1649], son of Georg Rinkart, cooper: born at Eilenburg, Saxony: Latin School, Eilenburg; St. Thomas's School, Leipzig; University of Leipzig, student of theology, 1602, M. A., 1616. In Crüger's *Praxis pietatis melica*, 1648, appeared, in 3 stanzas of 8 lines, the hymn beginning "Nun danket alle Gott." It is also given in Rinkart's *Jesu Hertz-Büchlein*, 1663, with a slightly varied text. Miss Winkworth, *q. v.*, published a full translation in her *Lyra Germanica*, 2d series, 1858, repeating it in her *Chorale Book for England*, 1863, from which stanzas 1 and 2 are here taken.

Now thank we all our God. 269

Rippon, John [1751–1836], born at Tiverton, Devonshire: educated for the ministry at the Baptist College, Bristol; Brown, A. M., 1784, S. T. D., 1792; minister of the Baptist Church, New Park Street, London, 1773–1836: published in *A Selection of Hymns from the best authors*, 1787, his version in 7 stanzas of 4 lines, stanzas 1, 6, 7 here used, of the hymn by E. Perronet, *q. v.*, beginning,

All hail the power of Jesus' name 87

Rist, Johann [1607–1667], son of Kaspar Rist, pastor at Ottensen, near Hamburg: born at Ottensen: Johanneum at Hamburg, then Gymnasium Illustre at Bremen; University of Rinteln and University of Rostock: pastor at Wedel near Hamburg, 1635–1667: wrote 680 hymns. In the *Drittes Zehn* of his *Himlische Lieder*, Lüneburg, 1642, in 16 stanzas of 6 lines,

was first published "Hilf, Herr Jesus, lass gelingen." In 1863, Miss Winkworth, *q. v.*, translated stanzas 1, 4, 8, 13, 15, 16, and published them in her *Chorale Book for England*. From her version have been here taken stanzas 1, 2, 6.

Help us, O Lord! behold, we enter 266

Scott, Sir Walter [1771–1832], son of Walter Scott: born at Edinburgh: Edinburgh High School; Edinburgh University: published in the 40th chapter of *Ivanhoe*, 1819, as a song for Rebecca, in 4 stanzas of 8 lines, stanzas 1 and 3 here used, the lines beginning,

When Israel, of the Lord beloved 142

Scudder, Eliza [1821–   ], daughter of Elisha Gage Scudder, merchant: born at Boston: wrote in 1852, and published in Dr. Edmund H. Sears's *Pictures of the Olden Time as shown in the Fortunes of a Family of Pilgrims*, Boston, 1867, in 6 stanzas of 4 lines, and reprinted unchanged in her *Hymns and Sonnets*, Boston, 1880, with the title "The Love of God," stanzas 4 and 5 here omitted,

Thou Grace divine, encircling all 25

and wrote in 1871, and printed in *Quiet Hours*, Boston, 1875, and again in her *Hymns and Sonnets*, with the title "Whom but Thee," in 5 stanzas of 4 lines, stanza 1 here omitted,

Thou Life within my life, than self more near . 61

and printed in *Hymns of the Spirit*, Boston, 1864, and again in her *Hymns and Sonnets*, with the title "The Quest," and the text "Whither shall I go from thy spirit? or where shall I flee from thy presence?" in 4 stanzas of 4 lines, all here used,

I cannot find thee. Still on restless pinion . . 149

and wrote in 1855, and printed in *Hymns of the Spirit*, Boston, 1864, and again in her *Hymns and Sonnets*, with the title "The New Heaven," in 10 stanzas of 4 lines, stanzas 7, 8, 9, 10 here used,

In thee my powers, my treasures, live 63

# of Authors and Translators.

Biographical Index

minister of the Free High Church, Edinburgh, 1876: published in *Thoughts and Fancies for Sunday Evenings*, 1887, in 6 stanzas of 4 lines, stanza 5 here omitted,

One thing I of the Lord desire **175**

Spitta, Carl Johann Philipp [1801-1859], son of Lebrecht Wilhelm Gottfried Spitta: born at Hanover: Gymnasium, Hanover, then University of Göttingen. D. D., 1855: published in his *Psalter und Harfe*, 1st series, 1833, in 4 stanzas of 8 lines, his hymn beginning "Herr, des Tages Mühen und Beschwerden." This, Richard Massie, *q. v.*, translated in full and published in his *Lyra Domestica*, 1860. Of this translation, stanza 1 and the last 4 lines of stanza 3 and of stanza 4 are here used.

O Lord, who by thy presence hast made light. . **255**

Stanley, Arthur Penrhyn [1815-1881], son of Edward Stanley, rector of Alderley, Cheshire, afterward bishop of Norwich: born at Alderley: Rugby, 1829; having won a Balliol scholarship, "the blue ribbon of undergraduates," Oxford, 1834, the Newdigate prize, Ireland scholarship (the highest test in Greek), and a first class in classical honors, all in 1837, B. A., 1838, prize for Latin essay, 1839, Ellerton prize for theological essay, 1840, fellow of University College, 1838-1851, M. A., 1840, college tutor, 1843-1851, select preacher for the University, 1845-1846, and 1872-1873, secretary of the Oxford University commissioners, 1850-1852, regius professor of ecclesiastical history, and canon of Christ Church, 1856-1864; LL.D., Cambridge, 1864, and St. Andrews, 1871; lord rector, St. Andrews, 1875; canon at Canterbury, 1851-1858; dean of Westminster, 1864-1881: published in *Macmillan's Magazine*, May, 1878, with the title "Our Future Hope," in 12 stanzas of 8 lines, divided into two equal parts, stanzas 4, 5, 6 of the 1st part here used,

Maker of the human heart **64**

and in the issue for December, 1872, with the title "Hymn for Advent," he published in 6 stanzas of 8 lines, stanzas 1, 2, 5, 6 here used,

The Lord is come. On Syrian soil **88**

and in the issue for April, 1870, in an article on "The Transfiguration," he published a hymn, in 6 stanzas of 8 lines, from which has been here taken a cento beginning,

Master! it is good to be **97**

Steele, Anne [1716-1778], daughter of William Steele, timber merchant, and Baptist minister, of Broughton, Hampshire: born at Broughton: published with 61 other hymns in Ash and Evans' *Collection of Hymns adapted to Public Worship*, Bristol, 1769, and again in her *Miscellaneous Poems* (added in 1780 as a third volume to her *Poems on subjects chiefly Devotional*, 1760), in 4 stanzas of 6 lines, stanzas 1 and 4 here used,

Great God, this sacred day of thine **39**

and in *Poems*, 1760, as above, with the title "Desiring Resignation and Thankfulness," in 10 stanzas of 4 lines, stanzas 1, 3, 8, 9, 10 here used,

When I survey life's varied scene **72**

and in *Poems*, 1760, as above, with the title "The Christian's Noblest Resolution," in 5 stanzas of 4 lines, stanzas 2, 4, 5 here used,

May I resolve with all my heart **200**

Sterling, John [1806-1844], son of Edward Sterling, editor of the *Times*, London: born at Kames Castle, Island of Bute: University of Glasgow; Trinity College and Trinity Hall, Cambridge, B. A., 1834, M. A., 1838: editor of the London *Athenaeum*: curate of Hurstmonceaux: published in *Poems*, 1839, in 11 stanzas of 4 lines, stanzas 7, 8, 9, 10, 11 here used,

O Source divine, and Life of all **28**

Sternhold, Thomas [-1549], said to have been born in Hampshire: and to have been educated at Oxford, and to have made his translation of the Psalms with John Hopkins, while living in Awre, Gloucestershire. He was Groom of the Robes to Henry VIII. and Edward VI. In *Psalmes of David in Englishe Metre, by Thomas Sterneholde and others: con-*

# of Authors and Translators.

fered with the Ebrue, & in certein places corrected (as the sense of Prophet required) and the Note ioyned withall. Veri mete to be vsed of all sortes of people priuatly for their godly solace and comfort: laiyng aparte all vngodlye Songes and Ballades which tende only to the nurishing of vice, and corrupting of youth: Newly set fourth and allowed, accordyng to the order appointed in the Quenes Maiesties Iniunctions, 1560, James V. If any be afflicted let him pray, and if any be mery let him singe Psalmes. [Colossians iii. 16, also quoted:] Imprinted at London, by Jhon Day, dwelling ouer Aldersgate. Cum gratia & priuilegio Regiae Maiestaties: commonly known as the Old Version, first appeared his translation of Psalm xviii., in 49 stanzas of 4 lines, stanzas 9, 10, 29, 30 here used, beginning,

Stowe, Harriet Beecher [1812–   ], daughter of the Rev. Lyman Beecher: born at Litchfield, Connecticut: published in the *Plymouth Collection*, New York, 1855, and reprinted in her *Religious Poems*, 1867, in 5 stanzas of 4 lines, stanza 5 here omitted,

and in 6 stanzas of 4 lines, stanzas 1, 3, 5, 6 here used,

Tate, Nahum [1652–1715], son of the Rev. Faithful Teate, D. D.: born at Dublin : Trinity College, Dublin, B. A., 1672: poet laureate, 1690–1715: published with Nicholas Brady, *q. v.*, in 1696, *A new Version of the Psalms of David*. From their version of Psalm lxxviii., in 30 stanzas of 8 lines, unequally divided into three parts, have been taken the first 12 lines, as altered by Jeremy Belknap, *q. v.*, for the first 3 stanzas of the Commencement hymn.

Taylor, John [1750–1826], son of Richard Taylor, Norwich, England: born at Norwich :

contributed to Dr. Enfield's *Selections of Hymns for Social Worship*, Norwich, 1795, the hymn the first line of which follows. It was given again in his posthumous *Hymns and Miscellaneous Poems, reprinted for Private Distribution*, 1863, in 3 stanzas of 8 lines, and is here given unchanged.

To R. Aspland's *Selection of Psalms and Hymns for Unitarian Worship*, Hackney, 1810, he contributed the hymn the first line of which follows. It was reprinted unchanged in *Hymns*, as above, in 5 stanzas of 4 lines, and is here given, omitting stanza 2.

Tersteegen, Gerhard [1697–1769], son of Heinrich Tersteegen, merchant of Meurs, Rhenish Prussia: born at Meurs: Latin School at Meurs: mystic, poet: published in his *Geistliches Blumen-Gärtlein*, 1729, in 8 stanzas of 10 lines, with the title " Remembrance of the glorious and delightful presence of God," the hymn beginning "Gott ist gegenwärtig." This, John Wesley, *q. v.*, translated and published in *Hymns and Sacred Poems*, 1739, in 6 stanzas of 6 lines, omitting stanzas 7 and 8 of the German. The translation was reprinted in the *Poetical Works of John and Charles Wesley*, 1868–1872, and of it are here given stanzas 1, 2, 4, beginning,

In the *Geistliches Blumen-Gärtlein*, 1729, in 10 stanzas of 7 lines, with the title "The longing of the soul quietly to maintain the secret drawings of the Love of God," he published the hymn beginning "Verborgne Gottesliebe du." This John Wesley, *q. v.*, translated and published in his *Psalms and Hymns*, 1838, in 8 stanzas of 6 lines, omitting stanzas 4 and 5 of the German. The translation was reprinted in the *Poetical Works*, as above, and of it are here given stanzas 1, 2, 3, 4, beginning,

Biographical Index

Trench, Richard Chenevix [1807-1886], son of Richard Trench : born at Dublin: Twyford and Harrow; then Trinity College, Cambridge, B.A., 1829, M.A., 1833, S. T. B., 1850; ordained priest, 1835; curate, in 1841, of the Rev. Samuel Wilberforce, at that time rector of Alverstock; vicar of Itchenstoke, Hants, 1845; Hulsean lecturer, 1845-1846; theological professor and examiner, King's College, London, 1847; dean of Westminster, 1856; archbishop of Dublin, 1864-1884: published in *Sabbation, Honor Neale, and Other Poems*, 1838, in 5 stanzas of 4 lines, and reprinted in his *Poems*, 1865, the hymn the first line of which follows. It is here given, omitting stanza 2.

Pour forth the oil, pour boldly forth **224**

Twells, Henry [1823-   ], son of Philip Meller Twells: born at Aston, near Birmingham : Birmingham Grammar School, there schoolfellow of Archbishop Benson, Bishop Westcott, and Bishop Lightfoot; then St. Peters College, Cambridge, B. A., 1848, M. A., 1851; holy orders, 1849; sub-vicar of Stratford-on-Avon, 1851-1854; master of St. Andrews House School, Mells, Somerset, 1854-1856; headmaster of Godolphin School, Hammersmith, 1855-1870; rector of Baldock, Herts, 1870; rector of Waltham-on-the-Wolds, 1871; select preacher at Cambridge, 1873-1874; honorary canon of Peterborough Cathedral, 1884: contributed to the 1868 *Appendix* to *Hymns, Ancient and Modern*, in 7 stanzas of 4 lines, the hymn the first line of which is given below. It was reprinted by the author in *Church Hymns*, 1871, with an addition of 4 lines, in 4 stanzas of 8 lines. From *Church Hymns*, the authorized text, have been taken stanza 1, the 1st 4 lines of stanza 2, the 2d 4 lines of stanza 3, and the 2d 4 lines of stanza 4.

At even, ere the sun was set **96**

Vaughan, Henry [1621-1695], born of a titled Welsh family, settled at Skethiog-on-Usk, in the parish of Llansaintfraed, Brecknockshire : was educated at Jesus College, Oxford. He published in *Silex scintillans, or Sacred Poems and Private Ejaculations. By Henry Vaughan, Silurist.* London, 1650, in 5 stanzas of 4 lines, his version of Psalm cxxi. This book was reprinted by the Rev. H. F. Lyte, as *The Sacred Poems and Private Ejaculations of Henry Vaughan, with a Memoir.* London, Pickering, 1847, from which has been here taken unchanged,

Up to those bright and gladsome hills **144**

Very, Jones [1813-1880], son of Jones Very, shipmaster : born at Salem, Massachusetts : Harvard, A. B., second in his class, 1836, tutor in Greek, 1836-1838 : published in his *Essays and Poems*, 1839, in the form of a sonnet, with the title "The Spirit Land," the hymn the first line of which follows. This was changed to a hymn of 4 stanzas of 4 lines, and first published, with the author's approval, in Longfellow and Johnson's *Book of Hymns*, 1846, from which it has been here taken unchanged.

Father, thy wonders do not singly stand **30**

He also published in *Essays and Poems*, with the title "Change," another sonnet, afterwards altered and republished as above, in 3 stanzas of 4 lines, all here used, beginning,

Father, there is no change to live with thee . . **231**

Ware, Henry [1794-1843], son of the Rev. Henry Ware, D. D., Hollis professor of divinity, Harvard, 1805-1845: born at Hingham, Massachusetts : Harvard, A. B., 1812, A. M., in course, S. T. D., 1834, professor of pulpit eloquence and the pastoral care, 1829-1842, overseer, 1820-1830: minister of the Second Church in Boston, 1817: wrote for the ordination of Jared Sparks, at Baltimore, 1819, in 4 stanzas of 4 lines, the hymn the first line of which follows. It was published in *Sewall's Collection of Psalms and Hymns*, New York, 1820, repeated in the first volume of his *Works*, Boston, 1846, and is here given unchanged.

Great God, the followers of thy Son **42**

# of Authors and Translators.

Biographical Index

of Authors and Translators.

In *Hymns and Sacred Poems*, 1742, as the second hymn on "Waiting for Christ the Prophet," reprinted as above, was first published in 6 stanzas of 8 lines, a hymn beginning "Christ my hidden life appear." Of this are here used stanzas 2, 6, 3, in that order.

In *Short Hymns on Select Passages of Holy Scripture*, 1762, reprinted as above, based on Lev. viii. 35, in 2 stanzas of 8 lines, the first 12 lines here used, was first published,

In *Hymns and Sacred Poems*, 1749, reprinted as above, in 5 stanzas of 8 lines, stanzas 2 and 3 here used, first appeared,

Wesley, John [1703-1791], son of the Rev. Samuel Wesley, rector of Epworth: born at Epworth: Charterhouse School, 1714-1720; Christ Church, Oxford, B. A., 1724, M. A., 1726-27; holy orders, 1725; fellow of Lincoln College, 1725; founder of the Methodist Church: published in his *Collection of Psalms and Hymns*, *Charles Town* (South Carolina), 1737, reprinted in *The Poetical Works of John and Charles Wesley*, London, 1868-1872, his altered version of "Sing to the Lord with joyful voice," by Isaac Watts, *q. v.* His alterations consist in the omission of stanzas 1 (which contains a reference to "The British Isles"), 4, 6, and the changing of the first two lines of stanza 2 from "Nations attend before his throne, With solemn fear, with sacred joy," to the form used in this book. Stanza 2 as altered by Wesley, and stanzas 3, 4, 5, 6 of Watts' original hymn, are here given.

In *Hymns and Sacred Poems*, 1739, reprinted as above, he published his translation of the "Gott ist gegenwärtig," of Gerhard Tersteegen, *q. v.*, in 6 stanzas of 6 lines, from which have been here taken stanzas 1, 2, 4, beginning,

In *A Collection of Psalms and Hymns*, reprinted as above, 1738, he published his translation of "Verborgne Gottesliebe du," by Gerhard Tersteegen, *q. v.*, in 8 stanzas of 6 lines, stanzas 1, 2, 3, 4 here used, beginning,

and his translation of "Seelenbräutigam, O du Gotteslamm," by N. L. von Zinzendorf, *q. v.*, in 6 stanzas of 4 lines, stanzas 1, 3, 6 here used, beginning,

and his version in full of the hymn of George Herbert, *q. v.* (altered to adapt it for singing), stanzas 1, 2, 4, 5 here used, beginning,

In his *Hymns and Sacred Poems*, 1739, reprinted as above, was first given his translation, in 16 stanzas of 4 lines, of "Befiehl du deine Wege," by Paulus Gerhardt, *q. v.*, from which a cento has been here taken, beginning,

Whately, Richard [1787-1863], son of the Rev. Joseph Whately, Nonsuch Park, Surrey: born at London: Oriel College, Oxford, double second class honors, 1808, M. A., 1812, B. D., and D. D., 1825, fellow of Oriel, 1811-1822, Bampton lecturer, 1822, principal of St. Alban's Hall, 1825-1831, professor of political economy, succeeding Senior, 1830: archbishop of Dublin, 1831-1863; bishop of Kildare, 1846-1863: freely translated an ancient antiphone, "Salva nos Domine, vigilantes," in 1 stanza of 8 lines, beginning "Guard us waking, guard us sleeping." This was published in T. Darling's *Hymns*, 1855, as stanza 2 of the hymn of Bishop Heber, *q. v.*, beginning as below, and was reprinted in the same form in the Archbishop's *Lectures on Prayer*, 1860, and is given here, as there, as stanza 2 of,

Whittier, John Greenleaf [1807-1892], son of John Whittier: born at Haverhill, Massachusetts: educated at Haverhill Academy;

Biographical Index

Harvard, A. M., 1860, LL. D., 1886; A. M., Haverford, 1860: journalist, editor, poet: wrote in 1859, and published in *The Tent on the Beach*, Boston, 1867, in 38 stanzas of 4 lines, the poem entitled "Our Master." It was repeated in his *Poetical Works*, Boston, 1888, with slight changes, whence stanzas 1, 2, 3, 9 have been here taken for the hymn beginning,

In 1827, October 5th, he published in the *Haverhill Gazette*, in 9 stanzas of 4 lines, a poem with the title "The Worship of Nature." From this were taken two hymns, one published in *Book of Hymns*, 1846, and the other in *Hymns for the Church of Christ*, 1853. The poem he afterwards greatly revised, and published in *The Tent on the Beach*, Boston, 1867, in 10 stanzas of 4 lines. It was reprinted, unchanged, in his *Poetical Works*, Boston, 1888, whence stanzas 1, 2, 5, 9, 10 have been here taken for the hymn beginning,

From "Our Master," written and published as above, have been taken stanzas 16, 18, 21, 22, 23 for the hymn beginning,

and stanzas 24, 25, 26, 34 for the hymn beginning,

He wrote in 1851, and published in *The Chapel of the Hermits and other Poems*, Boston, 1853, in 94 stanzas of 4 lines, and repeated, unchanged, in his *Poetical Works*, 1888, stanzas 11, 12, 18, 94 here used, the poem beginning,

He wrote in 1840, and published in *Lays of my Home*, 1843, with the title "To . . ., with a copy of Woolman's Journal," and reprinted in his *Poetical Works* as above, in 40 stanzas of 4 lines, stanzas 9, 13, 24, 26, 27 here used, the hymn the first line of which follows. It was addressed to Miss Harriet Winslow, afterwards Mrs. Samuel E. Sewall. His pub-

lishers say that the slight change in the order of the words made in these stanzas was authorized by Mr. Whittier.

He wrote in 1865, and published in *The Tent on the Beach*, 1867, in 22 stanzas of 4 lines, with the title "The Eternal Goodness," stanzas 11, 12, 13, 22 here used,

He wrote in 1859, and published in *Home Ballads, and Poems and Lyrics*, Boston, 1860, "My Psalm," in 17 stanzas of 4 lines. From this have been here taken stanzas 11, 12, 13, 14, 3, in that order, for the hymn beginning,

Williams, Helen Maria [1762-1827], daughter of Charles Williams, an officer in the English war department: born near Berwick-upon-Tweed: resident of Paris during the reign of terror: aunt and teacher of Athanase Coquerel: published in her *Poems*, 1786, in 6 stanzas of 4 lines, all here used,

Williams, William [1717-1791], born at Cefny-Coed, near Llandovery, Caermarthenshire: ordained deacon in the Church of England, but afterwards connected himself with the Calvinistic Methodists as an itinerant preacher. He wrote and published many hymns for his churches, doing for Wales what Watts had done for England. He published in his *Hallelujah*, Bristol, 1745, in 5 stanzas of 6 lines, his hymn beginning "Arglwydd, arwain trwy'r anialwch." Of this, stanzas 1, 3, 5 were put into English by Peter Williams, and published in his *Hymns on Various Subjects*, 1771. About 1772 William Williams adopted this translation of his 1st stanza, added to it a translation of his own of stanzas 3 and 4, wrote an additional stanza, and published the 4 stanzas as a leaflet, with the title *A Favorite Hymn, sung by Lady Huntington's young Collegians. Printed by the desire of many Christian*

# of Authors and Translators.

friends. Lord, give it thy blessing! About the same time it was included in *Lady Huntington's Collection*, 5th edition, Bath. From the text of the leaflet have been here taken stanzas 1, 2, 3.

Wilson, Lucy [1802–1863], published in her *Memoirs of John Frederic Oberlin*, London, 1829, in 4 stanzas of 5 lines, what she stated to be a translation of a hymn given out by Oberlin, in his Waldbach Church, June 11, 1820, and sung by his congregation in the presence of Dr. Steinkopff, secretary of the British and Foreign Bible Society, and of his wife. It has been said that the hymn had been written by Oberlin in German, that Dr. Steinkopff translated it into English, and Mrs. Wilson put it into verse. There is no evidence in the *Memoirs* that Oberlin wrote the hymn, nor has any German or French hymn been found that would seem to be the original of Mrs. Wilson's translation. It therefore has been assigned to Mrs. Wilson as a translation from an unknown author. It has been here taken from the *Memoirs* without change.

Winkworth, Catherine [1829–1878], daughter of Henry Winkworth, of Alderley Edge, Cheshire: born at London: published in her *Lyra Germanica*, 1st series, 1855, a translation of "Jesus, meine Zuversicht," by Luise Henriette, *q. v.* This she used for a new translation in the original metre of all but stanzas 4 and 6 of the German, which she published in her *Chorale Book for England*, 1863, in 7 stanzas of 6 lines, stanzas 1, 2, 3 here used.

In her *Chorale Book* as above, she published her translation of all but stanzas 2 and 4 of "Straf mich nicht in deinem Zorn," by Johann Georg Albinus, *q. v.* Of the 5 stanzas of 8 lines translated, stanzas 1 and 2 are here given.

In her *Lyra Germanica*, 2d series, 1858, reprinted in her *Chorale Book*, as above, was published her full translation of the "Es geht daher des Tages Schein" of Michael Weisse, *q. v.* Of the 7 stanzas of 4 lines of that translation are here used stanzas 1, 3, 4, 6.

In her *Chorale Book*, as above, she published her translation from the text in Bunsen's *Versuch*, 1833, of "Die Nacht ist kommen drin wir ruhen sollen," by Petrus Herbert, *q. v.* From this translation, in 6 stanzas of 4 lines, have been here taken stanzas 1, 3, 5, 6.

In her *Chorale Book*, as above, she published her translation of stanzas 1, 4, 8, 13, 15, 16 of "Hilf, Herr Jesus, lass gelingen," by Johann Rist, *q. v.* Of these 6 stanzas of 6 lines, have been here taken stanzas 1, 2, 6.

In her *Lyra Germanica*, 2d series, 1858, reprinted in her *Chorale Book*, she published her translation, in 3 stanzas of 8 lines, of "Nun danket alle Gott," by Martin Rinkart, *q. v.* Of this translation stanzas 1 and 2 have been here taken.

Wotton, Sir Henry [1568–1639], born in Kent: educated at Winchester; then New College, and afterwards Queen's College, Oxford, B. A., 1639: secretary to the earl of Essex; knighted by James I.; thrice sent as ambassador to Venice; provost of Eton, 1623–1639. His poems and other writings were published posthumously by Izaak Walton, 1651, entitled "Reliquiae Wottonianae." From this the Rev. Alexander Dyer revised and edited for the Percy Society, *Poems by Sir Henry Wotton*, London, 1843, from which have been here taken stanzas 1, 2, 4, 6 of the 6 stanzas of 4 lines beginning,

Biographical Index.

Zinzendorf, Nicolaus Ludwig von [1700–1760], son of Georg Ludwig von Zinzendorf: born at Dresden : educated at the Paedagogium, Halle, 1710–1716; University of Wittenberg, 1716–1719: licensed to preach by the University of Tübingen, 1734; consecrated bishop of the Moravian Brethren's Unity, 1737: wrote more than 2000 hymns. In 1725 he published in *Sammlung geistlicher und lieblicher Lieder*, Leipzig, in 11 stanzas of 6 lines, a hymn beginning "Seelenbräutigam, O du Gotteslamm," which he had written in 1721. In *Psalms and Hymns*, 1738, John Wesley, *q. v.*, published a free translation of the above, in 6 stanzas of 4 lines. Of this have been here taken stanzas 1, 3, 6.

BIOGRAPHICAL INDEX.

———•———

COMPOSERS.

Ahle, Johann Rudolph [1625-1673], born at Mühlhausen, Thuringia : Universities of Göttingen and Erfurt : organist and burgomaster at Mühlhausen : composed for the " Ja, er ist's, das Heil der Welt," of Burmeister, and published in his *Sonntagsandachten*, Sondershausen, 1664, and printed again set to the " Liebster Jesu wir sind hier," of Tobias Clausnitzer, in the *Altdorfer Gesangbuch*, 1671, a choral, from which has been adapted

Nuremberg **268**

Anonymous. To Samuel Webbe, sen., to Samuel Webbe, jun., and to Mozart, has been assigned the tune named below, but there is no evidence to justify such an assignment. It can be found, anonymous, in *A Church Hymn and Tune Book*, 1859, in Purday's *Psalm and Hymn Tunes*, 1860, in *Church and Home Metrical Psalter and Hymnal*, 1860, and in A violet's *Tunes and Chants*, 1862. In Vol. I. of the *Sacred Melodies* of William Gardiner, *q.v.*, set to the words " Come hither, all ye weary souls," may be found a melody from which it seems likely has been adapted

Belmont **5, 37**

As No. 37 of *Metrical Psalm and Hymn Tunes*, in Vol. III. of *The Parish Choir or Church Music Book*, London, 1851, published by the Society for Promoting Church Music, and probably adapted from a chanson by Thibaut, king of Navarre [1201-1253], may be found

Innocents **105**

In the *Church Choral-Book*, Boston, 1860, edited by B. F. Baker and J. W. Tufts, without the composer's name, may be found

Sebastian **173**

The tune named below is often attributed to Aaron Williams [1731-1776], but it does not appear in any of his collections. It is probably a tune of the latter end of the 17th century. It is in *A collection of Psalm Tunes for the use of Gosport in Hampshire*, [not later than] 1748, and is there called "Meer," but evidently had appeared earlier. It is also in a small collection of tunes *Printed by James A. Turner near the Town House. Boston*, 1752.

Mear **233**

Bach, Johann Sebastian [1685-1750], son of Johann Ambrosius Bach : born at Eisenach, in Saxe-Weimar : learned the rudiments of music from his brother Johann Christoph : chorister at the college of St. Michael, Lüneburg ; violinist in the band of the duke of Saxe-Weimar, 1703 ; organist of the church at Arnstadt in 1703 ; of the church of St. Blasius, Mühlhausen, in 1707 ; appointed court organ-

Biographical Index

of Composers.

As No. 20 in the first series of *Christmas Carols New and Old*, 1867, edited by the Rev. Henry R. Bramley and Sir John Stainer, he published

In 1868 he composed, and published in *Original Tunes*, Vol. I., 1869, to the words here used,

and

In the *Sarum Hymnal*, 1869, and again in *Original Tunes*, Vol. I., 1869, to the words here used, he published

Barthélémon, François Hippolite [1741-1808], officer in the Irish Brigade; then a distinguished violinist. In *The New Magazine of Knowledge*, 1791, and there called " The New Jerusalem," is the tune now known as

Beethoven, Ludwig van [1770-1827], son of Johann van Beethoven: born at Bonn: instructed by van den Eeden the court organist at Bonn; then by his successor Neefe; then studied under Haydn and Albrechtsberger at Vienna: assistant organist at Bonn, 1792; afterwards resident at Vienna. On page 126, Vol. II., of his *Sacred Melodies from Haydn, Mozart, and Beethoven, adapted to the best English Poets*, 1815, set to the words " As a shepherd gently leads," William Gardiner, *q. v.*, published the tune named below, headed " Subject from Beethoven." Although usually assigned to Beethoven, Sir George Grove and other authorities are of the opinion that it is not from any of his works.

From the choral part of the 9th Symphony has been adapted

Booth, Josiah [1852-   ], organist of Crouch End Congregational Church and joint editor of *Part II., Litanies and Chants with Music,*

and *Part III., Anthems*, of the *Congregational Church Hymnal*, London, 1887-1891, contributed to the *Congregational Church Hymnal*, London, 1887,

and

Bourgeois, Louis [*circa* 1500-   ], son of Guillaume Bourgeois: born at Paris. In 1539, when Calvin, expelled from Geneva, was at Strasburg, he compiled a small collection of psalms with tunes. This was the basis of the *Genevan Psalter*, which Calvin prepared on his return to Geneva in 1542. The tunes in the Strasburg book were mostly German, those in the Genevan book were partly taken from the Strasburg book and partly new. To the enlarged editions of 1543, 1551, and the complete edition of 1562, new tunes were added. In the earlier editions tunes were modified, transferred from one psalm to another, and new tunes substituted for old ones, but after 1562 no change was made. The *Genevan Psalter* contains melodies only. There is positive evidence that Louis Bourgeois was the musical editor, 1545-1557, and there is reason to believe that he edited the book from its beginning in 1542, and that the new tunes were composed by him. To Psalm cxxxiv., in the 1551 edition, was set the tune which is now known as " Old Hundredth." It was first published, set to Psalm c., in John Daye's *Psalter*, London, 1562.

To Psalm ci., in the *Genevan Psalter* of 1543, was set the original form of the tune now known as " St. Michael." In John Daye's *Psalter* of 1562, it was abridged to its present form, and set to Psalm cxxxiv.

Boyd, William [1846-   ], son of William Boyd, Montego Bay, Jamaica: St. Edmunds, Oxford, then Worcester College, B. A., M. A., 1882: curate of Charlecombe, Sussex, 1877-

Biographical Index

1882; of Stoke Bishop, Gloucestershire, 1882–1884; rector of Wiggenholt, Sussex, 1884–1893: wrote, in 1860, at the request of the Rev. S. Baring-Gould for a simple tune to be sung by the Yorkshire miners, among whom he was then working, as a setting to "Come, Holy Ghost, our minds inspire," the tune known as "Pentecost." It was first published in *Thirty-two Hymn Tunes composed by members of the University of Oxford*, 1868.

Pentecost 83, 194, 238

Brown, Arthur Henry [1830–], born at Brentwood, Essex: organist of the Church of St. Thomas the Martyr, Brentwood, 1842–1853; of the Church of St. Edward the Confessor, Romford, till 1858; then again organist of Brentwood and professor of music there: composed in 1862, and first published in the *Bristol Tune Book*, 1863,

All Hallows 67, 250

Burney, Charles [1726–1814], son of James Macburney: born at Shrewsbury: Oxford, Mus. Bac. and Mus. Doc., 1769; pupil of Dr. Arne: organist of St. Dionis Back Church, London, 1749; of King's Lynn Church, 1751; organist of Chelsea College, 1783–1814: in Thomas Williams's *Psalmodia Evangelica, a Collection of Psalm & Hymn Tunes in Three Parts for Public Worship*, *Vol. II.*, 1789, appeared anonymously, though since commonly assigned to Dr. Burney,

Truro 208

Calkin, John Baptiste [1827–], born at London: studied under his father: organist of St. Columba College, Ireland, 1846–1853; of Woburn Chapel, 1853–1857; of Camden Road Chapel, 1863–1868; of St. Thomas Church, Camden New Town, London, 1870–1884; professor in the Guildhall School of Music: published in *The Hymnary*, 1872, for hymn 521 (second tune),

Camden 206, 270

and in the *Christian Hymnal*, 1875,

Nox Praecessit 222

Cautional, New Gotha [1715]. A collection of sacred songs and chorals for use in the schools and churches of Gotha, edited by Johann Michael Schallo, *Part I., Feast-Day Songs*, 1646; *Part II., Christian Church and School Songs*, 1647; *Part III., Funeral Hymns*, 1648, was called *The Gotha Cautionals*. An edition issued in 1715, called the *New Gotha Cautional*, was edited by Christian Friedrich Witt, and in this, set to "Sollt es gleich bisweilen scheinen," first appeared

Stuttgart 120

Carey, Henry [1685–1743], reputed son of George Saville, marquis of Halifax: born at London: composed for the hymn by Addison to which it is here set, and published in *John Church's Psalmody*, 1723,

Careys 151

In 1740, at a dinner given to celebrate the taking of Portobello, it is said he sang as his own composition, and the assertion has not been disproved, the words of the English National Hymn, and the tune now used with the English, Prussian, Danish, and American National Hymns. In the *Harmonia Anglicana*, about 1742, appeared the earliest known form, and in Lyon's *Urania*, Philadelphia, 1761, is apparently the first appearance as a hymn tune, of

America 287

Choralbuch, Magdeburg [1540]. It is said that Luther in 1526 introduced the singing, in German, of the "Agnus Dei" set to the tune named below. It is to be found in the *Magdeburg Choralbuch*, 1540.

Oberlin 157

Choralbuch, Johann Samuel Müller's [1754]. In this book, set to the words "Was ist das mich betrübt," was published a choral, questionably attributed to Johann Georg Ebeling, and here called

Franconia 17

Biographical Index

Wittenberg: cantor of St. Nicholas Church, Berlin, 1622–1662: edited *Praxis Pietatis Melica*, 1644, the most important of all Lutheran hymn and tune books of the 17th century. It passed through 46 editions in Berlin, and 12 in Frankfurt. From a choral, set to "Nun begeh'n wir das Fest," to be found in the 1698 edition of the *Praxis*, and perhaps earlier, has been adapted

The choral set to the words "Jesus, meine Zuversicht," which were written by Luise Henriette, *q. v.*, appeared in *D. M. Luther's und anderer vornehmen geistreichen und gelehrten Männer Geistliche Lieder und Psalmen*, Berlin, 1653, to which Crüger contributed 37 melodies. It was given again in the *Praxis* of 1656, and is here modified from that form.

In the 3d edition of the *Praxis*, 1648, and used by Mendelssohn in his "Song of Praise," may be found

Cutler, Henry Stephen [1825–], son of Roland Cutler, merchant, Boston: born at Boston: Mus. Doc., Columbia, 1862; studied under George F. Root and A. W. Hayter, 1840–1843; then studied the piano and violin at Frankfort-on-the-Main, 1844–1845: organist and choir-master of Grace Church, Boston, 1852; of the Church of the Advent, Boston, 1854–1858; of Trinity Church, New York, 1858–1865: composed for *The Hymnal with Tunes Old and New*, New York, 1872, edited by Dr. J. Ireland Tucker,

Dearle, Edward [1806–1891], born at Cambridge: Cambridge, Mus. Bac., 1836, Mus. Doc., 1842: chorister at King's, Trinity, and St. John's Colleges, Cambridge; organist of St. Paul's, Deptford, 1827; of St. Peter and St. Paul Parish Church, Wisbeach, 1832–1833; of St. Mary Parish Church, Warwick, 1833–1835; of St. Mary Magdalen Parish Church, and

master of the Song School, Newark-on-Trent, 1835–1864: published in *Church Hymns*, 1874,

Decius, Nicolaus [–1541]. See Index of Authors: published in 1539, or earlier, set to "Allein Gott in der Höh' sei Ehr',"

Dykes, John Bacchus [1823–1876], grandson of the Rev. Thomas Dykes, incumbent of St. John's, Hull: born at Kingston-upon-Hull: scholar of St. Catherine's Hall, Cambridge, B.A., 1847, M.A., 1850; Mus. Doc., Durham, 1861; conductor of the University Musical Society; holy orders, 1847: curate of Malton, Yorkshire; then minor canon and precentor of Durham Cathedral, 1849; vicar of St. Oswald's, Durham, 1862: first published in *A Manual of Psalm and Hymn Tunes* edited by the Hon. and Rev. John Grey, 1857,

and in *Hymns Ancient and Modern*, 1861,

and in the English Presbyterian *Psalms and Hymns for Divine Worship*, London, 1867,

and in *A Hymnal for use in the English Churches with Accompanying Tunes*, 1866,

and in the *Appendix* to *Hymns Ancient and Modern*, 1868,

and in *Hymns Ancient and Modern*, 1875,

and

and

and

and composed for *The Children's Hymnal*, Hartford, 1874, edited by Dr. J. Ireland Tucker,

# of Composers.

In *Easy Music for Church Choirs*, London, 1853, there appeared a tune which is common in Roman Catholic books, and of which an arrangement made by Dr. Dykes appeared in the *Appendix* to *Hymns Ancient and Modern*, 1868, there called

First appeared in *Hymns Ancient and Modern*, 1861,

and in the *Congregational Hymn and Tune Book*, 1862, edited by the Rev. R. R. Chope,

and in *Hymns Ancient and Modern*, 1861,

For the Rev. R. Brown-Borthwick's *The Supplemental Hymn and Tune Book*, 1867, there called "Slingsby," was composed

In the *Congregational Hymn and Tune Book*, 1862, edited by the Rev. R. R. Chope, first appeared

and

In the *Parish Tune Book*, 2d edition, compiled by George F. Chambers, London, 1868, and then in the *Appendix* to *Hymns Ancient and Modern*, 1868, appeared, but without any distinguishing mark in either, showing the tune had probably been published earlier,

In *Hymns Ancient and Modern*, 1875, first appeared

Elliot, James William [1833-], born at Warwick: pupil of Sir George Macfarren: chorister at Leamington Parish Church, 1846-1848; organist of Leamington Episcopal Chapel, 1847-1852; of the Parish Church, Banbury, 1860-1862; of St. Mary, Boltons, Brompton, 1862-1864; of All Saints', St. John's Wood, 1864-1874; since then of St. Mark's Church, Hamilton Terrace: assistant

of Sir Arthur Sullivan in preparing *Church Hymns*, 1874, in which appeared his tune

Elvey, Sir George Job [1816-1893], born at Canterbury: educated at the Cathedral School there; Oxford, Mus. Bac., 1838, Mus. Doc., 1840: organist of St. George's Chapel, Windsor, 1835-1883: knighted, 1871. For *Sacred Music for the Home Circle*, edited by E. H. Thorne, 1859, he composed

and for *The Hymnal with Tunes Old and New*, New York, 1872, edited by Dr. J. Ireland Tucker,

Ewing, Alexander [1830-1895], son of Alexander Ewing, M. D.: born at Aberdeen: Marischal College, Aberdeen: officer in the English army: husband of the author of Jackanapes, Lob-lie-by-the-fire, etc.: composed, 1853, in triple time, for a portion of Dr. Neale's translation of *The Rhythm of St. Bernard of Morlaix*, and published on single slips, and then in common time in *Hymns Ancient and Modern*, 1861,

Eyre, Alfred James [1853-], born at London: organist of St. Peter's, Vauxhall, 1867-1872; again 1874-1881; of St. Ethelburga's, Bishopsgate, 1872-1874; of the Crystal Palace, 1880-1891: composed for *Hymns Ancient and Modern*, 1889,

Farrant, Richard [circa 1530-1580], gentleman of the Chapel Royal, 1564; afterwards master of the children of St. George's Chapel, Windsor, where he is said to have been also lay vicar and organist. In Page's *Harmonia Sacra*, 1800, is the first printed copy of the anthem "Lord, for Thy tender mercies sake," there, and usually, attributed to Farrant, though it is doubtful if he wrote it. Dr.

Biographical Index

Edward Hodges, *q. v.*, adapted from this anthem the tune here called

Farrant 66, 286

Freylinghausen, Johann Anastasius [1670–1739], born in Gandersheim: Universities of Jena and Halle: minister of St. Ulric's Church at Halle, and director of the Orphan Houses, 1727: edited in 1704 a collection of hymns for the use of the Orphan Houses, entitled *Geistreiches Gesangbuch*. In this, set to "Gott sei Dank durch alle Welt," appeared

Lübeck . . . . *q. v.* 135

Gardiner, William [1770–1853], born at Leicester: musical author and adapter; did much to introduce to the British public the works of the German composers. He published six volumes of *Sacred Melodies from Haydn, Mozart and Beethoven, adapted to the best English Poets*. In Vol. I., 1812, set to the words "My shepherd is the living Lord," he printed anonymously

Dedham 217

Garrett, George Mursell [1834–], born at Winchester: studied under Dr. Samuel Sebastian Wesley, whose assistant, as organist in the Cathedral and the College at Winchester, he became about 1851; organist of the Cathedral, Madras, 1854; organist and choirmaster of St. John's College, Cambridge, since 1856; Mus. Bac., 1857, Mus. Doc., 1867; organist to the University of Cambridge, 1873; University lecturer in harmony and counter-point, 1882; M. A. "propter merita" by special grace of the Senate: published in *The Hymnary*, 1872, for hymn 610.

Forgiveness 36, 253
and for hymn 619 (second tune),

Garrett 211

Gauntlett, Henry John [1805–1876], son of the Rev. Henry Gauntlett, vicar of Olney, Bucks: born at Wellington, Shropshire: organist of the Parish Church, Olney, 1814, and also choir-master, 1819–1825; organist and choir-master of St. Olave's, Southwark, 1827–

1847; degree of Mus. Doc. conferred on him by the archbishop of Canterbury, and appointed organist to the king of Hanover, 1842; choir-master (honorary) of St. John, Milton-next-Gravesend, 1844–1851; of All Saints, Kensington Park, 1861–1863; of St. Bartholomew-the-Less, Smithfield, 1872: wrote for *The Congregational Psalmist*, 1858, which he edited with Henry Allon, D.D.,

Newland 65

and for *The Church Hymn and Tune Book*, 1852, which he edited with the Rev. J. Blew, a collection of hymns and tunes, many of which had previously appeared on separate slips,

University College 73, 237
and

St. Fulbert 145, 221
and

St. Alphege 279

Gibbons, Orlando [1583–1625], born at Cambridge: Mus. Doc., Oxford, 1622: organist of the Chapel Royal, 1604; of Westminster Abbey, 1623: composed for George Wither's *Hymnes and Songs of the Church*, 1623, the tune called "Angels' Song." There are, in Wither's book, three settings of the same air, one of them being to the words "Thus angels sung and thus sing we." In the original it is in common time, but the syncopations really make it triple time, and at an early date it was so arranged, as may as 1762 in Thomas Moore's *Delightful Pocket Companion*, Glasgow.

Angels' Hymn 35, 168

Gilbert, Walter Bond [1829–], born at Exeter, Devonshire: Mus. Bac., Oxford, 1854; Mus. Doc., Trinity University, Toronto, Canada, 1886; and Oxford, 1888: organist of Topsham Parish Church, Devonshire, 1847; of Bideford, 1849; of Tunbridge, 1854; of Maidstone, 1859; of Lee, Kent, 1866; of Boston, Lincolnshire, 1868; since 1869 organist of Trinity Chapel, New York: fellow of the

# of Composers.

Biographical Index

Haydn, Franz Joseph [1732–1809], son of Mathias Haydn, wheelwright: born at Rohrau, in Lower Austria: Mus. Doc., Oxford, 1791; learned the rudiments of music from a relation, a schoolmaster, Johann Mathias Frankh: chorister at St. Stephen's, Vienna, 1740–1748; music-director to Prince Anton and Prince Nicolaus Esterhazy, 1761–1791. From the chorus "The heavens are telling," in his oratorio of the *Creation*, has been adapted

Creation **51**

For Hauschka's National Hymn "Gott erhalte Franz den Kaiser," he composed the music in January, 1797, and this was first publicly sung on the emperor's birthday in the following February. Dr. Miller in his *Sacred Music*, London, 1800, used this as a hymn tune, and it is here given, called

Austria **125**

Hayne, Leighton George [1836–1883], born at St. David's Hill, Exeter: Eton, then Queen's College, Oxford; Mus. Bac., 1856, Mus. Doc., 1860; holy orders, 1861: organist of Eton College, 1868; rector of Mistley and vicar of Bradfield, Essex, 1871. In the *Merton Tune Book*, 1863, which he edited, appeared

St. Cecilia **131, 179**

Hermann, Nicolaus [–1561], precentor and schoolmaster at Joachimsthal, in Bohemia, 1518– *circa* 1548. In 1560, in his collection of chorals, set to the words "Lobt Gott, ihr Christen all' zugleich," appeared the original form of

Hermann **80, 90**

Hiles, Henry [1826–   ], born at Shrewsbury: taught by his brother John; then organist at Bury, 1846; at Bishop-Wearmouth, 1847–1850; of St. Michael's, Wood Street, 1859; of the Blind Asylum, Manchester, 1860; of Bowdon Parish Church, 1861; of St. Paul's, Manchester, 1864–1867; Oxford, Mus. Bac., 1862, Mus. Doc., 1867; lecturer on harmony and composition at the Owens College, Victoria

University, 1880; professor of composition, Royal Manchester College of Music, 1893; editor of the *Quarterly Musical Review*: published in *Twelve Tunes to Original or Favorite Hymns*, London, 1868,

Sweden **52**
and
St. Leonard **251**

Hodges, Edward [1796–1867], born at Bristol: Mus. Doc., Cambridge, 1825: organist of Clifton Church and afterwards of the churches of St. James and St. Nicholas, Bristol; organist of St. John's, Trinity Parish, New York, 1840; of Trinity Church, New York, 1846. In the *New York Sacred Music Society's Collection*, New York, 1843, with the name "Hodges," and in the *National Lyre*, Boston, 1848, appeared

Bristol **169, 267**

Hodges, John Sebastian Bach [1830–   ], son of Edward Hodges, *q.v.*: born at Bristol: Columbia, A. B., 1850, A. M., 1853; D. D., Racine, 1867: rector of Grace Church, Newark, New Jersey, 1861–1870; of St. Paul's Parish, Baltimore, 1870–: published in his *Hymn Tunes*, New York, 1891,

Matins . . . . (1st Tune) **230**

Holden, Oliver [1765–1844], born at Shirley, Massachusetts: music-seller; editor of several tune books, and author of twenty-one tunes: composed for his *Union Harmony or Universal Collection of Sacred Music. Printed Typographically at Boston*, 1793,

Coronation **87**

Hopkins, Edward John [1818–   ], born at Westminster, London: Mus. Doc. by the archbishop of Canterbury, 1882: chorister at the Chapel Royal, 1826–1833; organist of Mitcham Parish Church, Surrey, 1834–1838; of St. Peter's, Islington, 1838–1841; of St. Luke's, Berwick Street, London, 1841–1843; of Temple Church, London, 1843–. In the

# of Composers.

Rev. R. R. Chope's *Congregational Hymn and Tune Book*, 1862, first appeared

In the 3d edition of the Rev. R. Brown-Borthwick's *The Supplemental Hymn and Tune Book*, 1868, arranged for unison singing, and in the *Appendix* to the *Bradford Tune Book*, harmonized by the composer, appeared, elsewhere called " Ellers,"

In *A Collection of Tunes and Chants for Public Worship, compiled by the Rev. Wm. Harrison, the arrangements by John Hopkins*, London, 1848, and in his *Temple Church Hymn Book*, bound in with his *Temple Church Choral Service*, 1867, with the date 1850, may be found

In his *Temple Church Hymn Book*, as above, without date, may be found

and with the date 1867,

Horsley, William [1774–1858], born at London: Mus. Bac., Oxford, 1800: assistant organist, 1798, organist, 1802, at the Asylum for Female Orphans; organist of Belgrave Chapel, Grosvenor Place, 1812; of Charterhouse, 1837: published in *Twenty-four Psalm Tunes and Eight Chants (never before printed)*, 1844.

Howard, Samuel [1710–1782], born at London: Mus. Doc., Cambridge, 1769: chorister at the Chapel Royal under Dr. Croft; organist of St. Clement Danes; of St. Bridget's, Fleet Street: contributed to William Riley's *Parochial Harmony*, 1762,

Irons, Herbert Stephen [1834–   ], born at Canterbury: chorister at Canterbury Cathedral, 1844–1849; precentor and master of the choristers, St. Columba College, Ireland, 1856–1857; organist and master of the choristers, Southwell Minster, Notts, 1857–1872;

assistant organist, Chester Cathedral, 1873–1875; since 1876, organist of St. Andrew's Church, Nottingham: first published in *Hymns Ancient and Modern*, 1861,

Isaac, Heinrich [*circa* 1500], born in Germany: chapel-master of the Church of San Giovanni, Florence, about 1488; entered the service of Emperor Maximilian I., as director of his choir, about 1510. For the words " Innsbruck, ich muss dich lassen," was first written the tune the name of which follows. It was afterwards set to the hymn " O Welt, ich muss dich lassen," in *Neu Catechismusgesangbuch*, Hamburg, 1598, and later to Paulus Gerhardt's " Nun ruhen alle Wälder." Bach employed it in his *Grosse Passions Musik*, No. 44, to the words " Wer hat dich so geschlagen," and Mendelssohn in his unfinished oratorio *Christus*.

Jones, William [1726–1800], born at Lowick, Northamptonshire. Charterhouse; then University College, Oxford, B. A., 1749: vicar of Bethersden, Kent, 1764; afterwards rector of Pluckley; of Paston, Northamptonshire; of Hollingbourne, Kent, 1798; perpetual curate of Nayland, Suffolk, about 1776: published at the end of *Ten Church Pieces for the Organ with Four Anthems*, 1789, set to Psalm xxiii.,

Josephi, Georg [*circa* 1657], musician at the chapel of the prince-bishop of Breslau in the middle of the 17th century. In Kocher's *Zionsharfe*, 1854–1855, set to the hymn " Du meiner Seelen gold'ne Zier," appeared the present form of " Angelus." It is an adaptation of a tune published in Johann Scheffler's *Heilige Seelenlust oder Geistliche Hirtenlieder*, Breslau, 1657.

Knapp, William [1698–1768], born at Wareham: for thirty-nine years parish clerk of

Biographical Index

St. James's Church, Poole. In *A Sett of New Psalm Tunes and Anthems in Four Parts; on Various Occasions*, 1738, set to Psalm xxxvi., first appeared

Knecht, Justin Heinrich [1752–1817], born at Biberach, in Suabia: music-director at Biberach, 1771; at Stuttgart, 1807–1808; again at Biberach, 1809–1817: composed in 1797, and set to the words "Ohne Rast und unverweilt," and published in his *Choralmelodien*, 1799,

Kocher, Conrad [1786–1872], born at Ditzingen, in Würtemberg: organist of the Stiftskirche, Stuttgart, 1827–1865: published in *Stimmen aus dem Reiche Gottes*, 1838, set to "Treuer Heiland! wir sind hier," the original of the tune named below. From this the present form was adapted by W. H. Monk, *q. v.*, and published in *Hymns Ancient and Modern*, 1861.

Lahee, Henry [1826–], born at Chelsea: studied under Sir John Goss and Sir William Sterndale Bennett: organist of Holy Trinity, Brompton, 1847–1874: first published, set to a Christmas hymn in the *Metrical Psalter*, 1855, which he edited, and reprinted later in *One Hundred Hymn Tunes*,

Langran, James [1835–], born at London: Mus. Bac., Oxford, 1884: organist of Holy Trinity, Tottenham, 1859–1870, and of the Parish Church, 1870–: wrote in 1861 or 1862, for "Abide with me," and printed on slips, and afterward published in *Psalms and Hymns adapted to the Services of the Church of England*, 1863, edited by John Foster, known also as "Even Song" and "St. Agnes,"

Luther, Martin [1483–1546]: see Index of Authors: published in the *Geistliche Lieder*, printed by Joseph Klug, Wittenberg, 1529, as a setting to his hymn, the music which here accompanies it.

In Lotther's *Magdeburg Gesangbuch*, 1540, set to the words "Vom Himmel hoch da komm' ich her," appeared

Lyra Davidica [1708]. In a collection of hymns entitled *Lyra Davidica or a Collection of Divine Songs and Hymns, partly new composed, partly translated from the High German and Latin Hymns, and set to easy and pleasant tunes*, London, 1708, set to a hymn translated from the Latin, "Jesus Christ is risen to-day" (but not to be confounded with the hymn written by Charles Wesley, and in this book set to this tune), appeared

Mainzer, Joseph [1801–1851], born at Trèves: educated in the Maîtrise of Trèves Cathedral: priest, 1826; afterwards abbé: published in *Mainzer's Choruses*, before 1845, set to Psalm cvii.,

Mason, Lowell [1792–1872], born at Medfield, Massachusetts: educated in the public schools; self-taught as to music; Mus. Doc., University of the City of New York, 1855: went to Savannah, where he compiled his first collection of music; removed to Boston in 1827 "to take general charge of the music in the churches there;" introduced musical instruction in the public schools; established the Boston Academy of Music, 1832: in 1830 published in *The Boston Händel and Haydn Society Collection of Church Music*,

In 1856 he adapted and printed on slips with 4 or 5 other tunes, and then published in *The Sabbath Hymn and Tune Book*, 1859,

# of Composers.

He wrote in 1830, and first published in 1831 in *Spiritual Songs*, edited by Hastings and Mason, there called " Conflict,"

Laban 99
He arranged, in 1824, from the first Gregorian tone, and published in the 3d edition of *The Boston Händel and Haydn Society Collection of Church Music*, 1825,

Hamburg 133
From the eighth Gregorian tone, for the same book, he arranged

Olmütz 197

Matthews, Timothy Richard [1826–   ], born at Colmworth rectory, near Bedford: B. A., Gonville and Caius College, Cambridge, 1853: curate, St. Mary's, Nottingham, 1853–1859; curate-in-charge, North Coates, Lincolnshire, 1859–1869; rector, North Coates, since 1869: composed about 1872, and first published in *Church Hymns*, 1874,

Ludborough 56, 82

Mendelssohn-Bartholdy, Jacob Ludwig Felix [1809–1847], son of Abraham Mendelssohn, and grandson of Moses Mendelssohn: born at Hamburg: studied with Madame Bigot at Paris, then with Ludwig Berger, Zelter, and Henning; afterwards with Moscheles; Ph. D., Leipzig, 1836. From Vol. I., No. I., of the "Lieder ohne Worte," Edward John Hopkins, *q. v.*, arranged and published in his *Temple Church Hymn Book*, bound in with his *Temple Church Choral Service*, 1867,

Angels' Song . . . . (2d Tune) 94

From choral No. 2 of his setting of Psalm xiii. to the English words by C. B. Broadley, for whom the work was composed in 1840, the following tune, known also as " Contemplation," has been adapted.

Trust 141

Miller, Edward [1731–1807], born at Norwich: Mus. Doc., Cambridge, 1786: organist of Doncaster, 1756–1807: published in his *The*

Psalms of David for the use of Parish Churches, 1790,

Rockingham 70, 109, 219

Missal, French. In a French missal of the 13th century, now in the National Library at Lisbon, may be found, it is said, the melody called

Veni Emmanuel 92

Monk, William Henry [1823–1889], born at London: Mus. Doc., Durham, 1882: organist and choir-master of Eaton Chapel, Pimlico, 1841–1843; of St. George's Chapel, Albemarle Street, 1843–1845; of Portman Chapel, Marylebone, 1845–1847; choir-master of King's College, London, 1847, organist in 1849, and professor of vocal music in 1874; organist of St. Matthias's Church, Stoke-Newington, 1852; musical editor of *Hymns Ancient and Modern*. In the 1861 edition of this first appeared

St. Matthias 63

First appeared in *The Hymnal, with Tunes Old and New*, New York, 1872, edited by Dr. J. Ireland Tucker,

St. Ambrose 100
and in *Hymns Ancient and Modern*, 1889,

Waltham 132
and in *Hymns Ancient and Modern*, 1861,

Eventide 247

Naumann, Johann Gottlieb [1741–1801], born at Blasewitz, near Dresden: educated at the Kreuzschule, Dresden; studied under Tartini at Padua, and Martini at Bologna, 1757–1765: music-director to the court of Saxony: wrote for use at the Hofkirche, Dresden, the

Amens 289

Naylor, John [1838–   ], born at Stanningley: Oxford, Mus. Bac., 1863, Mus. Doc., 1872: chorister at Leeds Parish Church, 1848; organist of Parish Church, Scarborough, 1856; of All Saints Church, Scarborough (of which the Rev. R. Brown-Borthwick was vicar), 1873; organist and choir-master of York

Biographical Index

of Composers.

his *Musae Sioniae*, 1609, set to the words " In Bethlehem ein Kindelein,"

Praetorius 155

Psalter, John Day's [1562]. In the *Whole Booke of Psalmes, collected into Englysh metre by T. Sternhold, I. Hopkins, and others: conferred with the Ebrue, with apt Notes to synge thē withal, Faithfully perused and alowed according to the ordre appointed in the Quenes maiesties Iniunctions. Imprinted at Lōdon by Iohn Day, dwelling ouer Aldersgate . . . An. 1562*, containing German, Genevan, new and native tunes, the melodies only being given, set to the Psalm cxxxii., appeared a tune from which has been adapted

St. Flavian 50, 176

Psalter, Thomas Este's [1592]. Thomas Este, a printer in London, published *The Whole Booke of Psalmes, with their wonted Tunes, as they are Song in Churches, composed into Foure Parts*, 1592. In this may be found (but see Christopher Tye)

Winchester Old 20, 129

Psalter, Genevan [1542-1562].

See Bourgeois, Louis.

Psalter, John Playford's [1671]. John Playford, born 1623; music publisher; clerk of the Temple Church, London: issued *Psalms and Hymns in Solemn Musick of Foure Parts*, 1671, in which may be found the version here used (but see Psalter, Scottish) of

London New 47, 121

Psalter, Scottish [1562]. In the 1615 edition of the Scottish Psalter entitled *The CL Psalmes of David in Prose and Meter With their whole usuall Notes and Tunes*, Edinburgh, printed by Andro Hart, may be found the oldest known version of (called also " French ")

Dundee 74, 201

and of

Dunfermline 130

In the 1635 edition, *Printed . . . by the Heires*

of *Andrew Hart*, may be found the earliest known form of

London New 47, 121

Reading, John [1677-1764], born at Winchester: organist of Dulwich College, 1700; junior vicar and poor clerk of Lincoln Cathedral, 1702; master of the choristers, 1703; afterwards organist of several London churches. " Adeste Fideles " appeared in Dr. Samuel Webbe's *Collection of Motetts or Antiphons*, 1792, but was in use before that date. It was called " Portuguese Hymn," from its use in the chapel of the Portuguese embassy, London. Vincent Novello, organist of that chapel, assigned this tune to John Reading, but lately a claim has been made that the tune was written by a Portuguese musician named Marcantoine Simao, who, going to Italy to produce his operas, was there nicknamed " Il Portogallo." He was chapelmaster to the king of Portugal, and went into exile with him to Brazil. In the ninth edition of *Brazil and the Brazilians*, Boston, on page v. of the preface, it is said that Portogallo composed this tune, but as no dates or references are given the traditional name has been adhered to. Simao had a brother who visited London and wrote considerable church music, and it is possible he composed the tune.

Adeste Fideles 154

Reinagle, Alexander Robert [1799-1877], born at Brighton: appointed organist of St. Peter's-in-the-East, Oxford, 1822 or 1823; resigned, 1853; published about 1826, in *Psalm Tunes for the Voice and Pianoforte*, set to Psalm cxviii.,

St. Peter 147, 245

In the Rev. R. Brown-Borthwick's *The Supplemental Hymn and Tune Book*, 1867, appeared

Ben Rhydding 48

Richardson, John [1816-1879], born at Preston: educated there at Fox Street Catholic School: member of St. Wilfrid's choir, then

Biographical Index

of that of St. Nicholas Catholic Chapel, Liverpool; organist of St. Mary's Catholic Church, Liverpool, 1835; then of St. Nicholas, as above, 1837; taught music at St. Edward's College, 1844-1857. In the *Merton Tune Book*, 1863, in *The Bristol Tune Book*, 1863, anonymous, and in Frederick Westlake's *The Popular Hymn and Tune Book*, 1869, assigned to Richardson, but probably arranged by him from a tune in *Tochter Zion*, Cologne, 1741, may be found

St. Bernard **84, 177**

Ritter, Peter [1760-1846], born at Mannheim: pupil of Abbé Vogler: chapel-master to the grand duke of Baden, 1811: wrote in 1792 the tune named below. It was apparently first adapted to English words in David Weyman's sequel to *Melodia Sacra*, published after 1814.

Hursley **248**

Rosenmüller, Johann [1615-1686], born in Saxony: assistant master in St. Thomas's School, Leipzig, and director of the choir; subsequently choir-master at Wolfenbüttel. In the *Praxis*, 1678, of Johann Crüger, *q. v.*, set to "Alle Menschen müssen sterben," appeared

Salzburg **38**

and in *Hundert Geistliche Arien*, Dresden, 1694, set to "Straf mich nicht in deinem Zorn,"

Nassau **187**

St. Alban's Tune Book. An adaptation of a 16th century melody, contributed to *The Monthly Packet*, in competition for a prize offered for a setting to Keble's "Sun of my Soul," subsequently issued in the *Appendix* to *The Hymnal Noted*, 1865-1866, commonly known as *St. Alban's Tune Book*, is here given, called

St. Alban **55, 225**

Schein, Johann Hermann [1586-1630], born at Grünhayn, near Zwickau, Saxony: chorister at the chapel of the elector of Saxony, 1599-1603; music-director at Weimar, 1613; precentor at St. Thomas's School, Leipzig, 1615: published in the 2d edition of his *Cantional* or *Gesangbuch Augsburgischer Confession*, Leip-

zig, 1645, set to "Mach's mit mir, Gott, nach deiner Güt',"

Eisenach **261, 285**

Schumann, Robert Alexander [1810-1856], born at Zwickau, Saxony: Ph. D., Jena, 1840; studied under Thibaut at Heidelberg, 1828-1830; at Leipzig under Friedrich Wieck and Heinrich Dorn: founder of the *Neue Zeitschrift für Musik*, and its editor, 1834-1844; professor of composition in Mendelssohn's newly founded Conservatoire at Leipzig, 1843; music-director at Düsseldorf, 1850-1853. From No. 4 of *Nachtstücke*, opus 23, has been adapted

Canonbury **183**

In *Cantica Laudis*, Boston, 1850, there called "White," appeared the tune named below. It is commonly assigned to Schumann, but Madame Schumann doubts if it has been taken from any of his works.

Schumann **271**

Smart, Sir George Thomas [1776-1867], son of George Smart, music-seller, London: born at London: chorister at the Chapel Royal; organist of St. James's Chapel, Hampstead Road, 1791; of the Chapel Royal, 1822; conducted the music at the coronations of William IV. and Queen Victoria; knighted, 1811: about 1800 published in *Divine Amusement, being a Selection of the most admired Psalms, Hymns, and Anthems used in St. James's Chapel*, London,

Wiltshire **180**

Smart, Henry [1813-1879], son of Henry Smart, musician, and nephew of Sir George Smart: born at London: organist of the Parish Church, Blackburn, Lancashire, 1831-1836; of St. Philip's, Regent Street, London, 1838-1839; of St. Luke's, Old Street, 1844-1864; of St. Pancras Church, 1865-1879: wrote for a non-conformist missionary meeting, 1836, and contributed to *Psalms and Hymns for Divine Worship*, London, 1867; and published in *The Hymnary*, 1872,

Lancashire **116, 143**

Carmel **165**

Biographical Index

of Composers.

www.ingramcontent.com/pod-product-compliance
Lightning Source LLC
Chambersburg PA
CBHW032022110726
47901CB00004B/1172